# MOON DELUXE

## STORIES

*Frederick Barthelme*

SIMON AND SCHUSTER
New York

MANUFACTURED IN THE UNITED STATES OF AMERICA
3   5   7   9   10   8   6   4   2

LIBRARY OF CONGRESS CATALOGING IN PUBLICATION DATA

BARTHELME, FREDERICK, DATE.
MOON DELUXE.

I. TITLE.
PS3552.A763M6   1983        813'.54        83-4735
ISBN 0-671-47268-2

*Of these stories, one originally appeared in* Esquire, *thirteen in* The New Yorker. *The author wishes to thank the National Endowment for the Arts and the University of Southern Mississippi for their support.*

For Catherine

# Contents

# Box Step

ANN IS PRETTY, divorced, a product model who didn't go far because of her skin, which is very fair and freckled. After lunch, she comes into my recently redecorated office—the company has done both of its floors in charcoal carpet, ribbed wallcovering, chipboard-gray upholstery, and gunmetal Levolors; the windows were already tinted. "I feel like I'm inside a felt hat," she says, waving a manila folder to indicate the room. "Your socks don't match, Henry." She points to my feet, which are balanced on the taupe Selectric II, then holds the folder out at arm's length. "The arrangements. You want to check me?"

The arrangements are for a regional sales meeting we've scheduled for the Broadwater Beach Hotel, in Biloxi; with the meeting still two weeks off, the preparations are complete. We picked Biloxi because of the beach, the Gulf, the rest of that; Ann did most of the work.

"What I really need is a new game."

She tosses the folder on my desk and stands by the window, smoothing her salmon-colored skirt with both hands. "What happened to the ant farm?"

"Died. The ants ate parts of each other. The parts they didn't eat they carried around—it wasn't fun."

She swings one of the gray Italian visitor's chairs around to face the window. "People don't have ant farms anymore anyway."

"I put it in the closet."

She nods, then puts her handbag on the corner of my desk and sits in the chair. "We should get a radio."

"I want you to come for drinks," I say, rolling my executive armchair to the window to inspect my socks. She meant they don't match each other.

"Is that a good idea?"

"I need help with these," I say, pointing to the socks.

"I'm flattered." Her skirt splits over her knees as she crosses her legs. She looks outside at a wet tree and at the startlingly bare office park. There's a seam in her hose across the open toe of one of her apricot pumps. "But you hate drinks, I'm vulnerable, and it's unseemly."

"Probably damage our working relationship." In the three months since Ann started working for me, she's been to my apartment once, to get a signature on some papers the week after my tonsillectomy; having her in the apartment made me nervous.

Karl Peters, a co-worker who wants to be a supervisor, sticks his head in my office door. "Hard at it?" he says, cracking his knuckles by pressing his fingers against the metal doorframe.

"Not me," Ann says. "I'm watching this rain and planning a giant party tonight at Henry's."

Peters hitches up his slacks, steps into the doorway, then turns sideways and leans against the frame. "You're serious? Hank's having people to his house?"

"No," Ann says, not looking away from the window. She doesn't like Karl; he knows it and can't leave her alone.

He wags a thumb at her back and gives me a knowing grin with lots of beige teeth. "I'd like to bring you know who, but I guess she's working." Then he slaps the wall and says, "I'll be there at eight, ready for anything."

When he's gone, I say, "Earth to Ann," and she twists her head backward over the chair to be sure we're alone.

"He's a spook," she says. "Why'd you invite him? Now you

have to invite somebody I like or I'm not coming. I'll go to the movies instead."

I swivel the chair through a complete circle. "Maybe Amos. You like Amos, don't you? I like Amos."

"He's wonderful, but I want somebody else, too. What about Gillian?"

Gillian's my older sister. Ann talks to her on the phone every week when she calls to see how I am. Gillian sells real estate out of a room in her house on Short Bay Street; she's single and the black sheep, and the only member of my family it is always a pleasure to see.

"O.K. What's Amos's number? You call Gillian." I pick up the receiver. "Karl won't come anyway. I promise."

"I play hostess? Are we sure about this?"

"We could go out."

"Maybe next week," Ann says.

I call Amos and invite him for after dinner. He says he'll talk to his wife and get back to me. "He's going to ask Felicia," I tell Ann.

"She'll probably hate me. Are you sure Karl won't come? I'm nervous."

"Me too, all the time. I don't know why."


I have a new dinosaur, a toy eight inches tall with an oddly human torso and perfectly proportioned legs. On its belly, in a small raised script, the word "Continental" curves over an embossed crown. The toy is a rubbery dirt-black with green trim, which looks sprayed on, and red eyes. At home with Ann and Gillian I turn it upside down, spilling wonton soup and rice out of its hollow inside onto my place mat. I ask the dinosaur if it wants a Gelusil, then wipe the toothy mouth with a napkin. The women laugh.

"He's a jerk," Gillian says.

"He had too much to eat," Ann says. She starts to clean up the mess I've made, but I elbow her away and clean it myself, wiping at the soup with a napkin, sweeping the rice into my palm from the edge of the polyurethaned white-pine tabletop.

"Henry I mean," my sister says.

Ann walks across the room and sits on the Victorian sofa. "He's a trifle nervous, the Hulk is, socially."

"That's not attractive," Gillian says. "Hulk."

"Can we get this cleaned up before the guests arrive?" I say, waving my fistful of rice at the dinner table.

"Do our best, Chief," Gillian says. She carries her plate to the kitchen.

Ann gets off the sofa and comes up to me with her palm out. "The rice, please." I give her the rice and the soupy napkin, then take the dinosaur into the bathroom to rinse its throat.

Amos and Felicia are early. I answer the door, follow them into the living room of my apartment, then do the introductions. Felicia's making fun of Amos. "He's wearing this Izod shirt, did you notice? He's very style-aware."

Gillian hugs Amos and frowns over his shoulder at Felicia. "I think he looks nice. The shirt's yellow."

"So this is Ann," Felicia says, shaking hands with Ann. "We hear a lot about you at our house." Felicia does an ugly little twist of her lips and then turns away, looking around the apartment.

"Hi," Ann says.

Amos picks Ann off the floor, twirls once, and puts her down on the sofa.

"Aren't you afraid you'll break her bones?" Felicia says.

"She's got bones like a horse," I say.

Felicia makes a face at me. "That's exactly what I mean, Henry."

Gillian says, "He doesn't mean the leg bones, Felicia, he means the other horse bones."

"Right," I say.

"Just beer for me," Amos says. He's in the corner of the room, looking at the zither, which is balanced on top of one of the natural-finish stereo speakers. He plucks a few strings, then looks at himself in a mirror mounted on the wall. "This reminds me of something," he says.

The doorbell rings. Ann pops up from the sofa and starts for the door. "Who's that? Is that Karl?"

"I hope so," Felicia says. She's leafing through an *Artscanada* from a stack of magazines on the coffee table. She turns to see Ann leave the room, then says, "What's so special about her?"

Amos sits on the sofa next to Gillian, who's brought a tray of Löwenbräu bottles and Pier 1 glasses. "My Felicia," he says, pointing to his wife.

Ann has a conversation at the door, but in the living room we can't quite hear what is being said. Amos hands a bottle of beer and a glass to Felicia and sits down again, taking a second bottle off the tray. He drinks from the bottle, then throws his arm over the back of the sofa and sighs. "This is nice," he says.

Felicia walks around the room filling her glass, ducking her head to suck the foam before it drips on her hand.

When Ann comes back from the door, she says, "Paper boy. I told him we take already."

"We?" Felicia says.

Gillian makes a little snorting sound. "Some of us are crazy for friendship."

Amos points around the room at the pictures and the few pieces of furniture. "You've changed it again, Hank. How come you're always changing it?"

"He doesn't want anybody to know what it looks like," Ann says. "I guess."

"This is new," Felicia says. She's standing in front of a framed Hockney print. "This one of those fifteen-dollar things he did a million of?"

"Wow," Gillian says, wiping her mouth with her wrist.

Amos slides forward on the peach-colored sofa and turns to look at Gillian. "So, what's new in real estate?"

"Henry got a new dinosaur," she says, nodding toward the toy, which is on its back legs, poised, on the dining table.

"Yeah," Amos says. "I saw it first thing when I came in. Is it yawning? Where'd you get it, Henry?"

I hold up the dinosaur. "T.G. & Y. Where else?"

Felicia wheels around and stares fiercely at me. "That's clever, Henry," she says, and she picks up her tan purse and stalks out, slamming the apartment door as she goes.

"Mistake?" I say.

"I'd better go after her," Amos says. He gets up from the couch and clicks his bottle back onto the tray. "It's nothing, Henry. I'll tell you about it tomorrow."

I walk him out; when I come back, Gillian is stretched on the sofa, unscrewing the cap of a new beer, and Ann is sitting at the table eating raisins out of a big red box.

"What's that about?" Gillian says. "They O.K.?"

"I guess. What did I say?"

"Said you bought this dinosaur," Ann says, picking up the toy. "That's all I heard." She gets up from the table, taking the dinosaur with her, and starts dancing, doing the box step, with the toy her partner. She hums and circles the room like a girl in a cowboy movie anticipating her first gala. When she's finished, she holds the dinosaur at arm's length, then pulls it to her and kisses it solidly on the jaw. "You're light on your feet," she says to the toy. "Or whatever these things are."


At nine the next morning Karl is sitting on the edge of Ann's desk, sipping coffee from a gray company mug. "Sorry I missed the party, Hank. I hear Felicia threw a fit."

"Don't look at me," Ann says.

I look at her. "Did we get the mail yet?"

She points at my open office door. "Karl was telling me that he went to a topless bar last night," she says. "All the women looked like me. He's going back tonight."

I look at Karl. He pushes off the desk, puts his mug on the blotter, and straightens his vest.

"And he thinks my underclothes don't fit."

"She's mad at me," Karl says, shrugging. "By the way, how's the meeting? Everything set?"

When I nod, he says, "Great," and walks off quickly. Ann follows me into my office. The mail is stacked in two piles on my desk. I start throwing away the junk while she adjusts the blinds to cut out the morning sun.

"Julio called last night," she says. Julio is her ex-husband, a photographer; he lives in Atlanta. "He wanted to know all about you."

"He should get together with Felicia. Where'd you put the baseball game?"

She bends across the desk and tries to open one of the drawers, but the desk is locked. "There," she says, tapping the drawer.

"So you told him what? About me I mean."

"I told him you weren't just a jerk." She pushes back off the desk, straightening the mail as she does so.

Amos comes in, carrying a small glass vase with two flowers in it. He presents the flowers to Ann.

She makes a joke out of the present, but it's obvious that she's touched. "Thank you," she says, leaning forward to kiss him on the cheek.

I unlock my desk and open the drawer Ann pointed to; the three-year-old electronic baseball game is in its box at the back of the drawer. "You want to play me, Amos?" I push the remaining mail to one side and point to the chair opposite mine. "Just one inning, what do you say?" I switch the game onto automatic for some practice, but even that's too hard for me. I miss several pitches.

Amos comes around behind my desk to look over my shoulder. "Sorry about last night," he says. "Connie—you remember our daughter Connie, don't you? Well, she's living with the manager of this T.G. & Y. over here on Snap Street—the one where you got the dinosaur, I think—and anyway, Felicia's upset. Connie's quit school again, and the guy's been married a couple of times—it's not a great deal."

A pitch goes right by my batter, making the third out, and I switch off the machine. "I'm sorry, Amos."

"Felicia has her abandoned with a kid already," he says. "I don't like it either, but—" He raises his hands and shakes them at the ceiling, goes back around the desk, and looks out the door at Ann, who is standing by her desk, facing away from us. "She won't be mad, will she? Ann I mean."

"Don't be silly. She likes you."

"I hope so," Amos says.

Ann's skirt is made out of a shiny red fabric that looks as if it could be used for spacesuits. She's wearing a transparent chiffon blouse and her usual three-inch heels—today they're opera pink. When Amos leaves, she catches me staring at her and makes a fish face.


At four o'clock I ask Ann to give me a ride home. "I was going shopping," she says, putting the papers on her desk into stacks, and putting objects—the tape dispenser, the stapler, the pencil holder—on top of the stacks. "I'll go to a movie, maybe." She tucks a rose straw handbag under her arm. In the parking lot I get into her new Ford sedan, banging my knees on the dashboard because she has the seat pulled so far forward.

The theater is small, one of four in a storefront that's part of a shopping center near the office—the shopping center where I got the dinosaur. By the time we get inside, the four-twenty show has started. Ann leads the way in the darkness, carrying popcorn and Coke. Halfway to the front she stops and steps aside. "Here," she whispers. I take the second seat in and she takes the aisle. The seats are dark plush—blue, or purple—and they rock. As the screen brightens after the credits, I see that there's no one else in the theatre. We hand the popcorn back and forth, staring at the screen.

After the movie we stop outside the theatre to look at the coming-attractions posters. It's just beginning to get dark, and the street lights are lime against the pale sky. The store signs have come on, blinking in oranges and blues and bright whites; along Snap Street the cars have amber and red running lights. The parking lot has fresh yellow lines on new blacktop, and off to the right clear bulbs dangle on black wires over Portofino's Fine Used Cars.

"Pretty," she says, looping her arm through mine and pulling us off the curb toward her car.

"Wait a minute," I say. "I'll be right back. I'll be just a minute." I trot along the edge of the parking lot in front of the stores; when somebody honks, I jump up onto the curb and go along the covered walkway in front of the big display windows, slapping at the square metal columns that support the overhang.

Amos's daughter is the only person in the T.G. & Y. She's tall and thin, with jagged-cut almost silver hair and punk-rock makeup. I say hello and tell her I don't know how I failed to recognize her yesterday.

"I recognized you," she says. "Did you want another dinosaur?"

"Sure." We walk down the aisle to the toy dinosaurs. Yesterday they were all jumbled together, but someone has straightened them, arranged them in flat-footed rows, so that the thirty or so rubber toys stare straight at us, scarlet eyes glaring, jaws wide, square white teeth silhouetted against dark throats.

"Which kind did you want today?"

I wonder why I've forgotten the names of the dinosaurs.

"Mr. Pfeister?"

"I think—one of these." I pick up a fleshy green dinosaur with a double line of large triangular fins running down its back. "You like this one?"

Connie giggles, then stops suddenly and stares at the toy in my hand. She seems nervous, and she doesn't know what to say; she wants me to leave. I stroke the toy's head as if it were a cat's. Finally Connie says, "Yeah. That's my favorite."

As we walk toward the cash register, I toss the toy from hand to hand, almost dropping it once because of the fins. Ann has pulled the car up along the curb in front of the T.G. & Y.

"You want a bag for him?" Connie asks.

"I don't think I need a bag, really." I strip the price tag off the dinosaur's foot and press the adhesive square onto the cuff of my shirt. "What's the tax on a dollar ninety-nine?"

"Twelve cents. It's two-eleven."

I give her two bills and drop two nickles and a penny into her cupped palm. When she starts to go behind the register, I grab her shoulder. She turns around, not sure what is coming next; I smell her perfume, which I think is the same one Ann wears. "I talked to Amos."

"I know," she says. She looks sad, resigned. "They talked to me. I don't know what to do about them."

I look outside at Ann, sitting in the Ford, her head turned toward the street, and I watch a short woman usher two small kids into the store. "Here's the answer: Do what you want and have an O.K. time. You can change it all later if you want to."

The woman with the kids has stopped just inside the door. She stares at us, pulls a can the size of a deodorant spray out of her purse, and advances, pointing the nozzle at my head. "You'd better ease up," she says. "You'd better just back off."

Connie is laughing—she can't stop laughing. A skull and crossbones is printed on the label of the can the woman is waving at my face. I let go of Connie's shoulder, but Connie doesn't move. "No, no," she says to the woman. "We're all right. Mr. Pfeister's a friend—really he is." Connie grins and wraps her arm around my back, pressing her cheek into my shoulder. "He works with my father," she explains to the woman.

"You're sure?" The woman is wary, reluctant to put away her weapon. "I can still blast him if you want me to."

Connie shakes her head.

"Well, it was hard to tell at first, the way he was holding you." The woman caps the spray can and drops it into the crinkle-finish plastic purse strung over her shoulder. "No offense, guy."

I shrug and show her the dinosaur. "Can't be too careful."

There's a click-click on the window glass; it's Ann, standing on the sidewalk, making a gesture that I take to mean "What's going on?" I wave at her and say, "Be out in a minute," and she does a puppetlike step and starts for the car.

"Is that your wife?" Connie asks, pointing outside.

The woman with the can moves off toward the back of the store to collect her kids, who are riding the cheap tricycles in circles around the inflatable swimming pools.

"Yes." I fluff the collar of Connie's blouse, then look at Ann. "Yes, it is."

Connie goes behind the counter and starts punching buttons on the register. When the cash drawer slides out, she catches it with her hip and slaps my two bills into the dollar compartment. "She seems very nice. When did you get married?"

"Recently. A couple of months ago. She was my secretary."

"No kidding?" Connie grins pleasantly, then reaches under

the counter and pulls out a white T.G. & Y. bag, which she
holds open alongside the register. "Do you mind?" she says.
"It's store policy. Nothing goes out without a bag."

Ann drives us to a restaurant on the edge of town. I tell her
about Connie and the manager, and about the woman with the
aerosol; she smiles and then laughs. The restaurant is an old
house that somebody has recently redone, extending it out in
back over a shallow ravine. It's called the Blue Crab, but it has
an automobile-size lobster hovering over the entrance. We get a
table by a window and, because Ann is hungry, order at once.
There are blue lights strung over the ravine.

She looks at the lights and at the flat, peanut-butter-colored
water below them. "This isn't so bad," she says.

"Thanks."

"I mean, it's at least possible." She shakes her head a couple
of times and fingers the clean black dish ashtray. "So—you want
me to teach you to smoke?"

"I forgot something," I say, sliding my chair away from the
table. I go out to the car and retrieve the T.G. & Y. bag from the
floor in the front seat; there's a little chain of perspiration on my
forehead when I get back to the table and make the presenta-
tion. The appetizers arrive. Ann loosens the staple at the top of
the bag with her fingernail, hands me the receipt, opens the bag,
and peers inside.

"I deserve this," she says.

She takes out the dinosaur, hops it onto the table, and stands
it up between our place settings. The toy rests on its hind feet
and tail; the fins on its back gleam; it looks as if it's singing. Ann
shakes hands with the dinosaur the way one shakes hands with a
dog; then she feeds it one of her tiny white shrimp. She says,
"Welcome to America, Reuben."

"Welcome to Romper Room," Felicia says. She and Amos and Karl and his wife have come up alongside our table.

Amos moves behind Ann and puts his hands on her shoulders. "You guys want to join us? They've got to have a table for six somewhere." He scans the room, still holding Ann's shoulders.

Karl starts to introduce his wife, but she stops him and says, "Hi, I'm Celeste Peters. You're Henry's Ann?" She reaches past her husband to shake hands with Ann, then nods at me. "Hello, Henry."

"Why don't you join us?" Karl says. "You can't work all the time."

"We're not working, Karl," I say.

Ann reaches up and rubs the back of Amos's hand. "We had to go see this Amy Irving movie," she says, looking up at Amos. "He's sick for Amy Irving."

Karl snickers and slaps me on the back. "What he needs is a visit from the Girl Fairy. No offense, Ann."

Amos moves back to Felicia and puts his arm around her waist. "Well, we can't stand here all night. Let's get a table and eat. I'm starved." He nods at me as he guides Felicia away.

The four of them follow a short Chinese waiter off toward one of the other rooms in the restaurant. The guy who's sitting immediately behind Ann turns around and frowns at me, then watches Amos and the others walk off. When he's made his point, he turns back to his table.

The food arrives, and we eat without saying much. Ann repeatedly glances over her shoulder; I push my snapper around on the plate, and after ten minutes I signal the waiter. He comes with the check and is very careful—sliding his little tray onto the thick white tablecloth—not to upset the dinosaur.

\*     \*     \*

It's two hours to Biloxi. I drive. The highway is white and
empty, and Ann falls asleep sitting sideways in the passenger
seat. The Ford seems to float on the road; I like the sound of
it—sealed and moving fast through the narrow landscape. I go
in through Gulfport, then along the water until the Broadwater
Beach sign comes into view. The parking lot needs repair; the
car hits a hole and the jolt wakes Ann, who yawns discreetly as I
steer into a space between two Volvo station wagons. When we
get out of the car, there's a terrific wind blowing in off the Gulf,
bending the palm trees and a big live oak that looks as if it must
be two hundred years old. The wind pushes our clothes around;
we have to lean into it just to get to the outer edge of the parking
lot for a look at the beach. Some cars go by. Out over the water
there's a helicopter with a police-type searchlight that flicks on
and off at intervals; now and then I hear the thuck-thucking of
the helicopter blades. High school kids run back and forth across
the four lanes between the hotel and the beach. They go by in
groups—mostly all boys or all girls—yelling to each other, waving beer cans. Some of them are wearing cutoffs, school jerseys,
and beat-up running shoes; others have on high-waisted white
slacks and open Hawaiian shirts. The wind is loud; when it hits,
it feels thick on my skin. A couple of blocks away, on the water
side of the highway, there's a large, turreted building, a souvenir
palace, bright against the dark sky, all lighted up with colored
flood lamps—salmon pinks and hot violets—and, surrounding
it, an elaborate miniature golf complex with castles and space-
ships, with monsters guarding the holes. On the roof, shuttling
back and forth over the tops of the letters in SOUVENIRS, a
hugely swarthy 3-D pirate in pirate boots and polka dots bran-
dishes a neon cutlass and cackles mechanically. Ann takes a look
at my face, then at the pirate's, loops her arm through mine, and
yanks me into the traffic.

# Shopgirls

YOU WATCH the pretty salesgirl slide a box of Halston soap onto a low shelf, watch her braid slip off her shoulder, watch like an adolescent as the vent at the neck of her blouse opens slightly— she is twenty, maybe twenty-two, tan, and greatly freckled; she wears a dark-blue V-neck blouse without a collar, and her skirt is white cotton, calf length, slit up the right side to a point just beneath her thigh. Her hair, a soft blond, is pulled straight and close to the scalp, woven at the back into a single thick strand. In the fluorescent light of the display cabinet her eye shadow shines.

She catches you staring and gives you a perfunctory but knowing smile, and you turn quickly to study the purses on the chrome rack next to where you stand. You are embarrassed. You open a large red purse from the rack and stick your hand inside, pretending to inspect the lining; then you lift the purse to your face as if the smell of it will help you determine the quality of the leather. The truth is that having sniffed the skin of the purse, you don't know what material it is, and for just an instant, that troubles you. You look more closely at the purse, twisting the lip a little so you can see the label, on which, in very small print, it says: MAN-MADE MATERIALS.

After what seems like a long time, you glance again at the perfume counter: the girl is not there. You drop the red purse back onto its hook and stand on your toes looking for the girl, then you start toward the center of the purse department for a clearer view.

"Can we help you with something?"

It's the salesgirl in Purses. She's thin, a brunette, with stylized makeup that seems to carve her face; she's wearing a thin black silklike dress—a sundress, and her shoulders are bare. She has caught you off guard and presses her advantage by putting a smooth hand with perfect red nails on your forearm.

"Sir?"

"Well," you begin, "I was looking for a gift."

"Of course you were," the girl says. The tone is patronizing; she has seen you staring at the blond girl in Perfumes.

"For my wife," you say.

"Something in the way of a purse," she says. "Or perhaps a nice perfume?"

"I'd better go," you say, but she tightens her grip on your arm and glances over a lightly rouged shoulder at a middle-aged woman who is standing impatiently at the far end of the purse department.

"I have a customer," the salesgirl says. "But why don't you wait a minute and talk to me? Jenny says you're very handsome but painfully shy—are you shy? Will you wait?"

You laugh self-consciously.

"I'll get rid of her," the girl says. "Be right back." As she turns away she draws her nails down on your arm, leaving thin white trace lines.

You watch her show the woman a purse, watch her arms move as she selects a second purse off a treelike stand, watch the way she cocks one foot up on its toe behind the other as she sells. The soft black skirt ripples and clings gently to the backs of her thighs as she moves, and when she goes behind the cash register to ring the sale, one of the straps falls off her shoulder, and she pulls it back into place routinely, smiling past her customer at you.

*    *    *

"Jenny says you followed her everywhere for weeks, is that so? All around here?" Finished with the middle-aged woman, the salesgirl has come back to you.

"I don't know Jenny," you say. But when the girl tugs at your arm and points over the tops of the displays toward the shoe section, you don't need to look. You know the girl she's talking about, the tall girl with the very short hair who works in Shoes. You trailed her around the store and around the mall for a few weeks, watching her shop, watching her eat, watching her sit by the garishly painted fountain in the center of the mall—you trailed her until you got worried. Then you stayed out of the mall for nearly two weeks, and when you returned you carefully avoided Shoes. That's not entirely true. Once you spent half the morning going up and down the escalator so that you could see her over the thickly forested juniors' casual wear.

"She likes you," the brunette says. "I think when you started in on Sally it hurt her feelings, Jenny's, I mean."

You nod to indicate that you have understood, then realize you shouldn't understand, so you say, "Sally?"

"Sally?" the salesgirl says, mimicking you, exaggerating your delivery until it is a high prissy whine. "Sally's the blonde you've been staring at all morning while playing with my purses."

"Oh," you say. You think you should have left when you had the chance, but the salesgirl has her hand on you again, her nails biting your skin, and to leave you'd have to jerk yourself out of her grip.

"Half the day," the girl says deliberately, "and that's a conservative estimate. That's this morning only. Then there's yesterday, and Saturday—you're quite a regular around here, aren't you? At first Sally thought you were the store dick, but she checked with Mr. Bo—he's our manager for this floor—and found out you weren't. My name's Andrea, what's yours?"

You don't want to tell her that. "Wiley Pitts," you say. It's a football player's name you saw in the morning paper. "I'm thirty-six years old." Instinctively you reach out to shake hands, then abruptly withdraw your hand and lift it to your forehead where a thin string of sweat has broken out along your hairline.

"Are you nervous?" she asks. "You shouldn't be nervous. Come sit with me." She guides you by the arm to a small round-topped stool in front of her sales counter. "I have to stick pretty close to this," she says, tapping the cash register with one bright fingernail.

You take the seat. You are inexplicably docile, obedient. You feel suddenly faint, as if moving about for the first time after a prolonged illness. Andrea is pretty, she smells pretty, she is being kind and gentle with you, and you are enjoying her attention. The sheen of her dress reflects the store light as she moves.

"The others think you're crazy," she says, twirling her finger near her temple and smiling. "I said you were just lonely."

"I suppose I am," you say. You cross your legs clumsily, then uncross them when you find it difficult to maintain your balance on the stool.

"We're all lonely sometimes," Andrea says. "I'll tell you what—I'll get the others and we can go to lunch together, would you like that? That way you can get a really close look at Sally."

"You're very pretty, too," you say. But as soon as you've said it you feel you shouldn't have, and you say, "I'm sorry. I don't know why I said that."

"Of course I'm pretty," Andrea says, laughing, obviously pleased. "We're all pretty. That's why they hire us. Do you think they want ugly girls out here trying to sell this stuff? We have to be pretty because that way the customers buy more so they can be pretty just like us." She tucks and smooths her dress for a minute, for your benefit, then says, "Well? What about it?"

Before you can reply, she's on the telephone. You realize she is talking to Jenny, the girl in Shoes. "Yes," Andrea says, fingering the curled cord and looking at you, "I'm sure he's the same one—you pointed him out, didn't you? No, not at all. Very nice. Yes. No, no—the first thing, yes. Right. Morrison's. You tell Sally—huh? Yes, she will."

You watch a young woman customer in very tight shorts and a lavender tank top glide up the escalator, which is directly across the aisle from Purses. Then Andrea is off the phone.

"Jenny's very excited," she says. "She didn't believe me at first."

You nod again, now staring at the empty escalator.

"Listen," Andrea says, "are you all right? You look very depressed." She tosses her hair over her shoulder and twists around on one leg to look at the store clock mounted on the wall above and behind her. "It'll just be a few minutes," she says. "You won't mind waiting, will you? Is your name really Pitts?"

"Robert," you say sheepishly. "Robert Caul. I'm sorry about the other." But Robert Caul is not your name either.

"Oh, don't worry about it, and don't look so forlorn, Robert Caul," she says. "You're going to have a great time, really you are. It'll be a dream come true."

"Yes," you say. Then you look away, around the store, seeing only colors and shapes and reflections in columns that've been turned into mirrors. Andrea moves off to chat with a customer, a young man in jeans who explains that his wife is pregnant and needs a new purse for when the baby comes. Finally, accidentally, you look toward Perfumes, and the blond girl is back, sitting primly on a tall stool inside her glass enclosure, talking on a black telephone and toying with the braid in her hair. She is looking at you.

At the cafeteria with Andrea, Jenny, and Sally, you take a thin slice of roast beef, three round white potatoes, a salad, and a shallow cup of peas. The women talk to one another as the four of you slide your trays over the polished aluminum rails attached to the serving counter. They are talking about you, whispering, being a little impolite, but you don't mind. You laugh too, and smile to yourself as if you are in on the joke.

When everyone is seated at the table by the window, Jenny says, "Why are you doing this?" The window is the size of a bathroom window, small and heavily curtained. It looks out into the center of the mall.

"Never mind that," Andrea says. "He sure is handsome, isn't he?"

"Within certain well-known guidelines," Sally says.

"Posh," Andrea says, smiling at you.

"You really scared me at first," Jenny says. "Following me like that. I didn't know *what* you wanted. But then I got used to it, and I wasn't scared anymore."

"You were going out of your skull," Sally says. "Admit it."

"Sure, at first," Jenny says. "After he'd followed me for a week, I almost went up and introduced myself one day."

"He wishes you had," Andrea says. "Don't you, Robert?"

"I don't know," you say. "Not exactly—maybe." You try to smile, but your lip catches on your teeth somehow, hooks itself there, and your smile feels horrible.

"I like a man who knows his mind," Sally says.

"Oh, leave him alone, Sally," Andrea says. "Can't you see he's nervous?"

"What's he nervous about?"

"You," Jenny says. "He thinks you're beautiful."

"He's right," Sally says. "But that doesn't mean I don't like him. I do like you, Robert. Really."

"Listen to her," Jenny says. "It takes her two hours every day to look like that, and she's so blasé."

"It's worth it," Sally says, wiping a small cone of mayonnaise off her dark lower lip with the tip of her third finger. "It makes me a more sensual person."

"If you were any more sensual," Jenny says, "you'd be an open sore."

"We had to go to school to learn how to look, Robert," Andrea says. "Would you believe that?"

"Some of us did," Sally says.

Jenny bobs her head and mouths some words to make fun of Sally, then turns to you: "We're professionals, like models. We make the women envious and we make the men feel cheated, and that's not as easy as it sounds."

"He doesn't talk much, does he?" Sally says, waving her fork in your direction. "What are we going to do with him?"

"*We're* not doing anything," Andrea says. "I'm taking him home with me." She drops her fingers over your wrist and pats you twice. "We all live in the same complex, Casa del Sol—ever hear of it?"

"I don't," you say. "I mean, I never heard of it, no. Sorry, Andrea."

"It's got a hot tub," Sally says proudly. "More than one, in fact."

"Six," Jenny says, smiling. "By actual count. Of course, some are hotter than others."

The three women laugh at this joke, then Sally says to you, "Jenny would know, she's a real hot-tub artist."

"Thanks, Sally," Jenny says.

"You know who he reminds me of?" Sally says. "He reminds me of one of the Dead Boys—I can't remember which one, though. I think it's the one they call Johnny."

"Jeff," Jenny says. "I saw them last week at the Palace, but he docsn't look much like Jeff, anyway."

You look down at your plate and see that you have cut your roast beef into tiny squares less than an inch on a side, and you have stacked the squares one on top of another in three small piles. You begin to play with your peas, lifting them onto your plate with the fork and then pushing them across the open center of the plate, encircling the stacks of beef.

Sally says, "You're not going to eat your salad, Robert? I'll eat it if you don't want it." She pulls your salad across the table, then turns to Jenny. "I wish somebody would tell me what we're going to do with him."

"Andrea's going to marry him," Jenny says. "The dear girl."

"Why don't we ask Robert what *he* wants us to do with him?" Sally says.

"We know what he wants," Jenny says, pushing a large square of lettuce from your stolen salad into her mouth. "He wants to lurk around the store watching you bend over."

"Or you," Sally says. "Or you, Andrea."

"We're just friends," Andrea says. "He can watch me at home."

"Well," Sally says, suddenly pushing back her chair and standing up, "I think it's me he really wants to look at. Isn't that right, Robert?" She comes around to your side of the table and leans over you and wraps her bare arm around your head, then pulls back and with her other hand opens her blouse slightly. "See, Robert? Isn't it pretty? Tell the girls I'm the one you really like."

"You're the one I really like," you say, but you don't think Andrea and Jenny hear you because you can hear them laughing, although you can't see them because Sally has your head in an awkward position, her upper arm almost covering your eyes.

"That's nice," Sally says, and she kisses you lightly on the top of the head.

"Doesn't prove anything," Jenny says, dragging a napkin over her lips. "If I showed him mine he'd swear he'd marry me ten times."

"He'd swear you'd *been* married ten times," Sally says, "if memory serves. You're a little lank through the chest, darling."

"Why, you cat," Jenny says. "You bitch."

Laughing, Sally says, "You guys ready to go?"

"Come on, Andrea," Jenny says, pushing her chair away from the table. "And bring your friend."

"You two go on ahead," Andrea says. "We'll be there in a minute."

Jenny and Sally walk out of the cafeteria together, and you watch them go, you watch the way each careful step causes a particular swing in the hips—they strut, their sleek clothes snapping precisely.

"That was fun," you say.

"Well, I'm sorry," Andrea says, looking at you over the rim of her coffee cup. "I didn't know."


In the living room of Andrea's Casa del Sol two-bedroom apartment there are identical white rented sofas facing each other. You sit on one of these sofas. Andrea is not home. Her television is small, white, balanced on top of a tall straw basket in front of the window. There is a white Princess telephone on the back of the sofa opposite you. The late afternoon sun slants into the room, cutting across the twin sofas and casting dense, hard-looking shadows. You have the feeling that you are the only one home at Casa del Sol.

When Andrea arrives she has two whole barbecued chickens, which she bought at the grocery store. The chickens are in aluminum foil pans, wrapped in clear plastic. You watch her unwrap the chickens and listen to her talk.

"My father," she says, picking at the skin on the breast of one of the chickens, "was a speedboat racer. Not for a living, but that's what he was really. I have home movies of him on Lake

Livingston, if you want to see. I've got lots of movies, in fact the
whole family—Dad worked real hard editing the movies, putting them all in order by year, you know the kind of thing I
mean. He even shot titles and put them in. He wanted so much
for everything to make sense."

You notice that the legs of each chicken are twisted together
so tightly that the bones have bent around each other.

"He wanted to know how things worked, even the simplest
things—the air conditioning, the movie projector. The first
thing he did when he got a new movie projector was take it
apart. Then he tried to improve on it, gluing little sticks of foam
to the lens mount to cut down on the vibration and, when that
didn't work, hooking rubber bands around the lens itself. It was
terrible the way all his improvements didn't work. But he didn't
notice that, or if he did he didn't talk about it. And he always
did it, no matter what. He busted the television trying to make a
better antenna, and he busted the stereo when he decided he
could make a spindle that would drop fifteen records instead of
the five the factory suggested. And the older he got, the worse it
was. I mean, he just kept busting things and busting things until
there was nothing to do but laugh, we all laughed, he even
laughed, it was so horrible."

You listen and nod, but she's finished. You don't know why
she's telling you about her father anyway. It has gotten dark
outside, and the only light in the apartment is a tiny night light
pushed into a socket on the kitchen wall. Andrea is crying.

You ask where Sally and Jenny live, thinking this will help,
and Andrea leads you to her front window and points across an
open courtyard, empty except for the brilliant green island of the
pool, at some apartments in another building. "They don't
know you're here," Andrea says. "Do you want to go surprise
them?"

"No," you say. "Not tonight."

"My grandmother is ninety-one," she says. "She lives in Palestine, Texas. She runs every day, she was running before everybody else started running, she was ahead. I don't know, around here everybody runs now. You go out at six o'clock, and it looks like one of those sports shows on TV. There isn't any reason to run, but they do it anyway. Bunch of goons. They think just because it's an apartment complex suddenly they're in California. I bought the shoes, but that's as far as it went. Are you getting hungry? If we don't eat I'm going to scalp this chicken."

She serves you a quarter of a chicken neatly severed between breast and thigh and two slabs of white bread on a bare plate. This makes you very happy. For the first time you stop wondering if you should have taken her key after lunch. Andrea sits on one sofa and you sit on the other, and both of you eat with your fingers, occasionally stopping to tear away a bite-sized square of bread. You smile at each other as you eat. The chicken is tender and spicy, the perfect meal. When you finish, you carry your plate into the small kitchen and drop the bones into the garbage sack under the sink. Then you rinse the plate and turn it upside down on the flecked Formica counter, then you wash your hands with her Ivory soap. As you run the water over your hands, you splash a little first on your lips, then over your entire face. You pull two paper towels off the roll alongside the sink and dry your face and hands. You throw the crumpled towels at the garbage sack, miss it by a full yard. When you return to the living room, Andrea is sitting in the semi-darkness, licking her fingers.

"Once, when there was a hurricane coming," she says, not talking directly to you but rather into the room and to herself, "my father required that we make all the preparations, and we checked the flashlights, counted the candles, drew clean water in the tubs

and sinks, bought bottled water to drink, taped the huge bay
windows in our house with gray duct tape, and nailed plywood
over the smaller windows. He carefully plotted the storm's
course on a chart he cut out of the newspaper. The storm moved
very slowly. My father called the weather service often, cursing
and slamming the phone down when he got a busy signal.
When the storm finally got into the Gulf it stopped dead in its
tracks for twenty hours, whirling itself into a two-hundred-mile-
an-hour frenzy, and as the storm got larger and more powerful
my father spent his time sitting silently by the radio, his head
slightly bent, a coffee cup balanced on the arm of his chair. He
wouldn't talk to any of us. He hushed us angrily when we tried
to talk to one another. He was intent on the storm, and he sat up
all night listening for new bulletins, marking and calculating on
the crumpled chart in his lap. The radio spewed instructions
about what to do in case of fire, what to do in case of flood, and
also history—the great and dangerous hurricanes of the century.
We were prepared, and as far as I knew the real danger to us was
minimal; nevertheless a silence spread over our house like nothing I'd ever felt before. The kids kept watch at the windows, but
the weather outside looked fine and breezy. At eight in the
morning the radio announcer read a bulletin from the weather
service: Elise had started to move again, but she had reversed
her course and was now headed southwest, straight for Mexico.
This news did not deter my father from his vigil, and seven
hours later, when the storm made landfall well below Browns-
ville, my father came to the door of his study and told us the
news. He was a big man, a powerful man physically, and I remember him filling that doorway between his study and the living room of our house, I remember the way his voice sounded
and how his eyes looked when he told us, and I remember
watching him retreat into his study and close the door. He shot
himself in the temple with a twenty-two-caliber pistol."

"Killed himself?" you ask, sure that you shouldn't, sure that you already know the answer.

"No," Andrea says. "Crippled himself. In a wheelchair the rest of his life."

"I'm sorry," you say.

"Me too," she says, staring at her red nails.


You notice for the first time that one of Andrea's eyebrows is plucked too much, and that the brows are not symmetrical with respect to the bridge of her nose. Her left brow, the one that is far too thin, also starts well over her left eye. Once you have seen this tiny imbalance, you cannot stop seeing it; every time you look at Andrea's face you see this odd-shaped patch of skin there above her nose. You stare at it. Her face looks wrong suddenly, almost deformed. You try to think of something to say about her father, but you can't think of anything. You wonder if you should ask Andrea about Sally and Jenny, but decide that that might hurt Andrea's feelings, so you say nothing. You sit with her until well past midnight—hours of occasional sound, occasional movement.

When she decides to go to bed you make no move to follow her into the bedroom, and she makes no special invitation. You sleep on the sofa, fully dressed, without even a sheet to cover you. You imagine yourself leaving the apartment on a sunny day in the middle of the week. Three beautiful women in tiny white bikinis lift their sunglasses as you pass them in the courtyard. They smile at you. You drive to the mall in a new car and spend two hours in Housewares on the second floor. You do not remember ever having been on the second floor before. Kitchen equipment is exquisite, you believe. You buy a wood-handled spatula from a lovely girl with clean short hair.

# Violet

KATHLEEN SULLIVAN is back on CNN, a guest on the call-in interview show. She's supposed to be talking about the boom in news, but the callers, who are all men, only want to talk about her bangs, and the new drab-look clothes she wears on ABC. Tonight she's wearing one of her old purple outfits, and her hair's messed up as it used to be when she co-anchored "Prime News 120." A caller who says his name is Toby, from Tennessee, says that he doesn't think she's the real Kathleen Sullivan, that the real Kathleen must've gone to heaven. "It's still me," Kathleen says, laughing prettily. "I look all right now, don't I?" Her not quite coordinated lip gloss, somewhere between grape and burgundy, is a nice touch.

The dinner I'm heating in the oven smells about ready, so I take the telephone receiver out of its cradle and drop it into a crack between the sofa frame and a seat cushion. A lock of Kathleen's hair has gotten crosswise with her part. I crouch in front of the set, tap the glass, and say, "Kathleen, Kathleen," but she goes on talking. I advance the color intensity and twist the hue knob to change the color of her lips to crimson. "That's better," I say to the television.

Somebody knocks at the door. I freeze in front of the set for a minute. When the quick, shy-sounding knock comes again, I decide it must be the landlady, and get up to see what she wants.

There's a girl outside. She's young—she looks about sixteen. Her hair is short, boyish, and she's thin like a stick, smiling at me. "Hi," she says, making a small move with her hand. "May I use your phone? I need to make a call."

"My phone?" It's silly what I've said—as if I had no phone, or didn't know what "phone" meant. I back away from the door and bump into the wall in the cramped foyer. "Sure. Come in."

"What're you burning?" The girl stops by the kitchen door, drops her brilliant green backpack, and stares at the stove. Without going into the kitchen, she bends forward and opens the oven. "I think it's too hot," she says, smiling at my dinner. She twists the temperature knob a couple of notches.

"I was in a hurry."

She goes into the living room. Her pants are Dickies, much too large in spite of the extra darts running from the top of each back pocket up into the waistband. "Oh," she says, seeing the telephone cord stretched out over the arm of the couch. "Are you on the phone?"

"No. I mean, I was, but I'm not now. Go ahead. You'll probably have to hang it up first."

She does a take to tell me I've said something stupid. The living room, which is ordinarily quite comfortable, suddenly seems cramped and shabby. The girl is six feet tall. As I look at her standing beside the couch, dialling numbers on the telephone, I realize that the pants are too big by design, a way to simultaneously disguise and exploit her thinness.

I excuse myself and go to close the front door. My neighbor, a thirty-year-old bookkeeper for K Mart, blond and not very popular with the other residents in the apartment complex, is sitting beside the pool with her Coors in a Styrofoam cooler. She's staring at the front page of the evening paper, just the way she does every night. It's the only time I ever see her.

The girl has come up behind me. "Who's that?" she asks. "I can't get through. Do you mind if I wait a minute and try again?"

"Sure." I close the door. "I was watching the news."

"Got any juice?" She backs toward the kitchen. "I love juice. Any kind. My name's Violet."

I follow her to the kitchen, reaching for her hand. "I'm Philip. Let's see what we can hunt up."

"I'm a runaway," she says. "I know it's old-fashioned, but my parents are intolerable."

There's a quart carton of orange juice in the refrigerator.

Violet takes the couch, sitting on it sideways, her back against the arm; I sit on one of the bentwood dining chairs. After an awkward silence, she raises her glass and says, "Cheers," and I raise my glass too.

"California," she says, anticipating a question. "Northern California, to be precise. It wasn't men or money, and nobody ever laid a hand on me. Not a mark anywhere." She swings a hand in front of her chest to show me where there are no marks, then looks at her glass, holding it up to the fading light outside the double sliding doors. "I wanted to see something, do something."

Her hair is thin, soft looking, and not much longer than mine. Her face is smooth, the skin tight and the cheekbones exaggerated by narrow scars of blusher. She's wearing a white T-shirt. She seems at ease in my apartment, on my couch.

"So you came South."

"Hitched," she says. "Yeah. It's O.K. Sometimes it's fun and sometimes it's scary. But it's not as different as I thought it'd be."

She grabs the phone and starts to dial again, and I stare at the television. On the eighth digit I turn around and watch her dial three more. She covers the mouthpiece with her palm. "I'm reversing the charges. Did you think I'd come in here and use your phone without paying?"

I smile weakly, push myself off the dining chair, and go into the kitchen.

*       *       *

In a couple of minutes she sticks her head around the doorframe. "Why don't we go out? We could eat somewhere good."

I've been leaning against the rolled edge of the counter, trying unsuccessfully to hear her conversation, moving pans now and then to make the kind of noise I'd make if I weren't listening.

"Go out?"

She picks up the Swanson frozen-food box from the counter, holds it in front of her chest, and points to the picture of the Salisbury steak, rubbing the cardboard with her fingertip. "See, this is a four-and-a-half-ounce entrée—we can't both eat it. We can go out and get a real dinner. I'll bet it's a month since you saw a vegetable. You can even have hot rolls and a dessert."

"I don't know," I say, looking around the obviously unused kitchen. "I don't think so—not tonight."

She frowns at me. "O.K., if that's what you want. What we ought to do is go somewhere you've never been, someplace you always wanted to go but never did." She stands in the kitchen doorway, hands on her hips, the T-shirt pulled tight across her small chest; she's scolding me with this pose.

"There's this funny place on the highway by the Knights Inn—I've never been there."

"See?" She breaks her stance and clicks the oven dial to "Off," all in one move. "Where's your car?"

"I've got to get some shoes first."

"Fine." She's already around the corner and on her way out the front door. "I'll meet you by the pool. Is it too cold for swimming?"

She doesn't wait for the answer. I go into my bedroom and sit in the oak swivel chair by the makeshift desk. I straighten my socks, slip my feet into the loafers I left there earlier, then get up

and look at myself in the mirror over the dresser. I bend close to
the glass and say, to my face, "Vegetable?"

Going out, I check the oven again, then go to turn off the TV.
Kathleen Sullivan is adjusting her lapel microphone, unaware
that she's on camera.


The place I had in mind isn't there anymore, so we end
up at Shoney's, with oversize, four-color, wrapped-in-clear-vinyl
menus in our laps. Behind Violet there are blood-red imitation-
bamboo slat blinds that the hostess had to wrestle with to lower.
Violet turns the big glistening pages of her menu, making little
noises as she looks from picture to picture.

"My treat," I say. "What do you like?"

"Oh, I don't know. Maybe the lobster. I could eat lobster for
breakfast. What do you think?" She flattens her menu on the tabletop and points to a picture of giant onion rings bathed in
thick ketchup. "Look at these," she says. "Aren't they amazing?"

On the windowsill beside her there are two dead flies, one on
its back and the other still standing but tipped forward, resting
on its nose.

"What about you?"

"I want pancakes," I say. "Ham and hash-brown potatoes and
a small glass of orange juice."

"No kidding? That's what you want?"

"I wonder if they serve pancakes this time of day."

Violet twists against the diamond-tufted seat and looks across
the room at the narrow pass-through between the kitchen and
the serving area. "Sure they do. Isn't that what their little man is
holding—a stack of pancakes?" She leafs quickly through the
menu. "There should be a drawing of him here somewhere."

"Look on the back."

She flops the menu on its face, rattling the silverware. "Nope."

The waitress wanders up to our table already writing something on her small pad. She's wearing a faded brown uniform and a gold, almost oval apron. "You ready to order yet?"

"Hi," Violet says. "Is the lobster good today? I'll have the lobster. Here." She points to the vivid picture on her menu. I order pancakes.

"So," Violet says, straightening her place setting. "How is it so far?"

"Excellent."

The restaurant is crowded with families. "Looks like they're selling a lot of chicken," Violet whispers. She's hunched over toward me with her arm out behind her toward the other diners.

"It's a hamburger. The boy on the sign is holding a hamburger."

"Those too," she says. "Look over here at the guy and his wife in the matching Bermuda-shorts outfits. Is that chicken or hamburger?"

I sit up and look over her shoulder. "Chicken. There was a bunch like that when we came in—all four in matching blue houndstooth shirts with huge collars."

"I don't think people should wear matching clothes," Violet says. "Except maybe at home it'd be all right."

"Even there," I say.

"Yeah. You're right. I don't think so at all."

I move my knife and fork around, then push the sugar rack back against the windowsill. I'm staring at a short, pretty waitress across the room when Violet taps my arm. "Philip? Look— food. Move your elbows so she can put the plates down."

I ask our waitress, who is teetering over the table with a large aluminum tray propped up on the fingers of her left hand, if she has any pure maple syrup. She bats her eyelashes at me and puts the plates on the table. "I'll see what we've got if you can hold your horses," she says. "I've got my hands full here just now."

When everything's on the table and the syrup has finally arrived—abruptly, smacking the Formica and sliding a few inches into the ketchup squirt bottle—Violet says, "Dig in, huh?" The pancakes are coaster-size and lapped on the plate like magazines on a coffee table, topped with scoops of white butter. The handle of the syrup dispenser is sticky. Violet's lobster is a pathetic flat thing, squat on the tan plate.

"Five pairs of legs," she says, catching my eye. "Of course, you don't eat them all. You could, I mean, but you don't have to."

After dinner, at the intersection outside Shoney's, we stop at a red light. Violet has a toothpick in her mouth, and her pale-blue running shoes propped up on the safety tray that is part of the dashboard of my Rabbit. A sedan pulls up alongside and the driver honks, two short blasts. The woman driving waves; I don't recognize her. She rolls her forefinger in tight circles to indicate she wants me to lower my window.

"Hi," she says, before the glass is halfway down. "I saw you coming out of the parking lot back there. Who's your friend?"

I look at the woman and point at myself. "What?"

"Hi," Violet says, pressing me back up against the seat. "This is Philip. Philip, that's Crystal."

"Hello, Crystal," I say, raising a hand in half salute. I watch the light for the left-turn lane flick from red to green.

"What've you been doing, Violet?" The woman has to shout to be heard over the engine of a truck turning out of the lane next to her.

"We ate at Shoney's," Violet shouts back. "He had pancakes."

"What? I can't hear you."

"Pancakes," Violet shouts. She makes a big circle with her thumbs and forefingers and holds up her hands for the woman to see.

The light changes. Crystal nods and shouts, "Be careful," then spurts forward past the buzzing sign of the all-night Texaco station, waving up behind her head when she cuts across the beams of our headlights.

I go through the intersection and turn right on the first cross street, Sugar Hill, then pull to the curb, cut the lights, and switch off the ignition.

"You want to walk some?" Violet says. "I don't mind. This is a good street. See, it's even got those new orange lights—look." She leans toward me, touching my arm, and points out the windshield toward the nearest street light. The street light has a rusty glow.

We sit for a few minutes without saying anything. Finally I say, "Who's that?"

"Crystal? Oh, she's a friend. Somebody I know."

"Somebody you know."

"Well, so what if I'm not a runaway?" Violet says. "So what? I had to say something."

I start the car, make a U-turn and then a left back onto Broadway, and go through a yellow light by the Shoney's. I expect Violet to explain, but she doesn't, and we drive in silence, watching the lights thin out, watching the street change from highway access to old neighborhood to just-built suburb. There are a lot of one-story strip shopping centers along the street, lit and empty. At a light after a couple of miles Violet points to a gas station that has been painted solid black and converted into a bar. "Let's stop," she says. "I want to go there."

"The Tip Top Club?"

She turns in the seat to face me. "Please, Philip, I want to see what it's like inside."

When the stoplight changes, I cut diagonally across the intersection and into a space in the parking lot between a silver van and a pickup. "If they ask, I'll say you're my daughter."

She pats my arm. "They won't ask, silly."

The room is dark and cold, and I almost trip on the carpet covering the three steps down to the dance floor. Violet tugs at my hand, pulling me to a small booth in the corner. The Tip Top Club is not crowded. Aside from the waitresses, who are gathered at one end of the bar, we're the only people there. Two empty tables away a stray blue flood lamp lights the surface of a table. A beat-up-looking woman in jeans and a tube top comes over to us and says, "Hi. What can we get you?"

"Scotch, please. Water and ice."

"Tomato juice," Violet says. "Thanks. And can you tell me what time it is?"

The woman bends around from the waist and looks toward the bar. "Nearly nine." She puts two napkins on the table and says, "I'll be back in a sec."

Violet says, "It's so old-fashioned, this place. You're not mad, are you?"

"I don't think so."

"It was the only thing I could think of, you know what I mean?"

The drinks arrive. Violet gulps half of her tomato juice, slides out from behind the table, and quick-steps across the room to the space-age jukebox. I finger my glass and listen to her quarters go down the slot. Then she's back at the table, standing beside me, reaching for her juice. With one hand on my shoulder she drains the glass in a single swallow. "Now," she says. She pulls on my arm until I get out of the booth. "This is probably against the law. I know. And it's tacky. But let's do it until they stop us."

The tune is a mournful cowboy song that I've heard a hundred times. Violet puts her arms on my shoulders, leans forward, presses her forehead to mine, smiles, then closes her eyes. I put my arms around her waist, and we shuffle around in a clumsy circle. It's wonderful; I haven't danced with anybody since high school. We go three times through the song without stopping. Then I notice the waitress standing by our table at the edge of the dance floor, obviously amused. I pull away, and when Violet opens her eyes, I raise my head toward the waitress. Violet looks over her shoulder. "We're fine," she says to the woman. "We don't need anything."


There's a guy the size of a tree peering in the driver's window of the Rabbit when we get outside. "Oh, hi," he says, straightening and slapping the roof a couple of times. "This yours?"

Violet puts a hand on my shoulder and presses close. I say, "Yes." Now that he's standing up, the guy is at least a foot taller than I am. The car only comes up to his elbows. He has huge hands, and fingers like breakfast sausages.

"I want to try it out," he says. "I want to go around the block."

I look at my watch. "We've got to get to the airport. My daughter's on her way back to college."

"She doesn't look old enough," he says. "I thought she was your girlfriend when I saw you dancing."

"Looks like he's got us," Violet says. She dances a little more in the gravel of the parking lot. "Let's give him a ride."

"That'd be real nice," the big guy says. "Maybe I could even drive."

He's standing alongside the driver's door; Violet and I are still in front of the car. "What do you want to drive for?" I ask.

"I never get to," he says. "I like to drive."

I shake my head. "Well, I'm sorry, but we're booked up. Sorry." I don't know what I'm going to do if he insists.

"Is he drunk?" Violet whispers, her lips pushed into the shoulder of my jacket.

He hears her and wags a meaty finger. "No, Ma'am. Not in the slightest. I don't drink at all, as a matter of fact."

Violet moves forward a little, still holding my shoulder. "Look," she says, "why don't you go to a dealership? We could take you to a dealership"—she turns back to me—"couldn't we? Do you know where one is?"

"I don't need to go to a dealership when I've got this Volkswagen right here."

Violet backs up a step and says, to me, "He doesn't need a dealership."

"I heard."

The guy takes a swipe at the door mirror, knocking it off the car. "Oops," he says, looking down to the ground and then back to us. "I busted it. I didn't mean to do that, honest."

There's no traffic, and I can hear the flicking of the electric switches in the box that controls the stoplight. The sky is muddy—no stars. We're in a standoff with this huge guy; he doesn't seem bent on violence, but he's very definite about wanting to drive the car. I don't want to give him the car unless I absolutely have to, so I say, "Let's go back inside, Violet," and start for the door of the Tip Top Club.

"Why don't you just let me have the keys for a minute?" the guy says. He isn't following us; I figure at worst he'll wait until we're inside and then take the car.

"Can't do that," I say, holding the door for Violet.

I wait just inside the entrance, looking out the diamond-shaped glass panel in the door. Violet says, "You want me to call the police?"

"I don't know. Hold on a minute." The guy is staring after us; he can't see us through the glass. He puts the door mirror on top of the car, then bends down and rests his head on the top too, like a man listening to railroad tracks. "I think we're going to get lucky."

"What's up?" It's the waitress in the tube top, stepping back and forth on her tiptoes, trying to get a look out between the beer decals on the glass. I back away and let her look.

"This guy's drunk, or crazy, or both. He wants my car. We're going to have to get the cops."

"Oh, Jesus, Mary, and Joseph," the waitress says. She starts to say something else, then puts a hand to her forehead and pushes out the door. "Sidney," she says sternly. "You get right back in the van. Now." She slaps her thigh and stamps a foot for emphasis. "Go on." She lets the door close about halfway and hisses something I can't hear. Then she opens the door for me. "Come on out. It's just my brother Sidney. He won't hurt you."

When we get outside, Sidney is climbing into the side door of the van next to the Rabbit. My mirror is gone.

"He's gentle as a lamb," the waitress says.

Violet and I get into the car. The waitress is standing by the front of the van, holding her brother at bay. He's sitting there in the open door, staring at us. Violet says, "I think we should take him with us."

"Oh, yeah?"

The waitress waves. Violet waves back and says, "We could at least take him around the block—that's all he wanted, really."

The waitress comes up to Violet's side of the car, hits on the window, and says, "What's wrong?"

Violet rolls down the window. "We were just talking about taking Sidney for a drive. We didn't know he was your brother. We thought he was a creep."

"Oh, you don't need to do that," the waitress says. "He gets plenty of rides with me. I take him everywhere I go."

"But we want to, don't we, Philip?" She pats my arm like a wife.

"Sure," I say, thinking maybe the waitress will kill the deal. "Can he drive? I mean, does he know how? He seemed to want to drive, for some reason."

"Sometimes I let him steer," the waitress says. "That's all. He likes your car because of the basketball-player commercial—have you seen that one?"

"Yeah," Violet says. "Sure. Maybe we'll just take him for a spin around town—you know, twenty minutes, no more. Would that be O.K.?"

The waitress bends farther down to look at me. "There's nothing wrong with him," she says. "He's just a little slow in the head. I don't know—what do you think?"

On my left, Sidney is sitting back in the seat of the van, smiling; I think he knows what we're talking about. "O.K.," I say. "He can ride in the front here. Violet, you get in the back."

"I'll tell him," the waitress says. "This is real nice of you people."

As Violet is getting into the back, she pulls herself forward and kisses my cheek. "It'll be fine," she says. We watch the waitress give Sidney his instructions as she walks him around the front of the car. He nods vigorously.

Sidney comes into the front seat head first. He grins at me. "Hi, Sidney," Violet says from the back. "I'm Violet. He's Philip."

"Hi," Sidney says, struggling to get all the way into the car. "I'm sorry about before. I wasn't really going to take the car, really."

"We know," Violet says.

The waitress, who is standing in the parking lot waiting to shut Sidney's door, says, "Now, you tell me when you get back, you hear? Just come in and tell Mike or Bub to fetch me. Are you listening to me, Sidney?"

"Yes," he says, reaching for the armrest. "I'll come in first thing."

Sidney's wearing black high-top sneakers and dark-green work pants. With the door closed, he has to sit with his knees apart, and his left knee is in the way of the gearshift. "I've got to get at this," I say, gently, tapping his leg with the back of my hand.

"Oh, sure," he says. He wraps a huge arm around the leg to keep it out of the way. "Where are we going?"

Violet sits up, leaning between the seats. "Where do you want to go, Sidney? We can go just about anywhere."

Sidney thinks a minute while I get the car out of the parking lot. "Which way?" I say. Close up, he's not so menacing. He points to the left, knocking the rearview mirror out of whack.

"Oh, I'm sorry," he says, starting to reset the mirror.

Violet reaches forward and tugs on his arm. "Don't worry about it," she says.

"There's a lot of room in here," he says. "Don't you think so?" He flattens his hand and wedges it between his head and the white padded headliner of the Rabbit. His knee falls on the gearshift and knocks the car out of third. "What happened?" he says when the engine revs noisily.

"Nothing," Violet says. She pats his shoulder. "How'd you like a big piece of cherry pie?"

He shakes his head. "I don't like cherry pie," he says. I shift into fourth gear.

"Do you like any kind of pie?" Violet asks. "I can get us all the pie we want, any kind."

"How's that?" I say.

"No," Sidney says. "I really don't like pie very much." He turns around in the seat. "But thank you anyway, Violet. You're being very nice to me."

"You're being nice too," she says. "I work at the pie store on Palmetto Street. I'm a pie girl."

I turn around to look at her.

"That's what they call us."

We drive around for half an hour seeing the sights. Sidney

spends a lot of time inspecting the car—asking about the tires and the seats and the gas mileage, running his thick fingers over the dashboard covering and the carpet, trying the horn and the air conditioning and the radio. Finally he says, "Can I drive now? Trish never lets me drive."

I look in the rearview mirror at Violet; she nods quickly and mouths "Please," so I make a turn onto an empty residential street and stop the car.

"O.K., Sidney. It's all yours."

"Really?" he says. "Now?" We switch places. He takes a few minutes practicing his shifting, and says, "Don't worry, Philip. I can do this." After a couple of stalls he gets us going, and he does fine. He has to bend his neck awkwardly to see out the windshield, and it's hard for him to release the clutch pedal, because his knee jams up under the steering wheel, but he gets it figured out, and we drive around some more. Violet compliments him lavishly on his driving, pats his shoulder and pushes his hair back off his forehead; she seems genuinely pleased for him. She asks him how tall he is, and he says, "Real tall," and laughs, looking up at her in the mirror.

"More than seven feet, I'll bet," she says, curling his hair back around his ear with her finger.

"I'm taller than Kareem too," he says proudly. "Seven-four."

"I think it's nice," she says. "I'd like to be seven-four."


At the club he parks in back, next to a chicken-wire cage and a bank of six steel trash cans. "Will you wait a minute?" he says, pushing himself backward out of the car. "I want to tell Trish we're here." He lopes around the front of the car and into the club through the kitchen door.

Violet punches the back of my seat. "See, that wasn't so bad, was it?"

"What's all this pie business?"

"That's where I work," she says. "Pie Country—you've been there." She's sitting forward on the rear seat, but we're not looking at each other—we're both looking out the windshield.

"I know I've been there. I go there all the time."

"After work," she says. "Usually." She punches the seat twice more. "Come on, let a girl out, will you?"

I unlock the door and open it, then turn sideways in the seat so that I can see her. She's got her hands on the seat's headrest, ready to pop out of the car. "Pie Country?" I say.

"You probably wouldn't know me out of uniform," she says. She shakes the seat back the way an infant shakes the sides of a crib. "Move it."

We're standing beside the car when Sidney and the waitress come out of the club hand in hand. "Did he really drive?" the waitress asks.

"Yes, Ma'am," Violet says. She gives Sidney a quick little hug, which he returns awkwardly. "He drove real well."

The waitress looks at me. "Perfect," I say. "Didn't miss a trick."

"See?" Sidney says to his sister. "I told you."

# *Fish*

SALLY MEETS ME in the driveway. "It's great you're back," she says. She's tall, willowy, tailored. "I'm going to a German movie at the university, but I'll be home right after. Will you be here?"

"Sure," I say. "You look great." I watch her get into her car, a red Audi four-door.

I've just rented a house from her younger brother and he's invited me to dinner. He comes out waving a rolled-up newsmagazine. "Already?" he says to her. "He hasn't even moved in yet, Sally." He kisses the magazine and waves it at her, and she gives him a drop-dead smile.

He comes down the concrete steps and stands alongside me in the drive. When she pulls away he puts an arm on my shoulder and pokes me in the stomach with the magazine. "There's a thing about elephants in here. You want to read it?"

"Sure. What's it say?"

It's cool for October, but Minor's wearing shorts. He insists we eat on the deck behind his house. His legs are bony and pink. "Go on and wear your coat if you're chilly," he says. "Sally's got everything set. All I've got to do is pop it in the microwave. I want to have a drink first, though." I follow him into the house and then out onto the deck. He puts a wedge of lime on the rim of his glass and points to the white director's chair next to his. "Check out the natural beauty," he says, waving toward the backyard.

A bug twice the size of my thumb is skittering up the side of the swimming pool. He hasn't filled the pool since last year, he tells me. He stares straight across the yard. There are pads of fat under his eyes. "So what do you think of the color?"

"Terrific," I say.

The walls of the pool are dark blue. He had it drained and painted by some kids from the junior high school, friends of a friend's daughter, he tells me. They worked a long time to get the color just the way Minor wanted it. They even built a model and painted it, then filled it with water to be sure of the color. "Sally can't pass up a movie. She says I should go with her." He sticks a couple of fingers in the waistband of the shorts. "You like elephants? You ought to take that article home with you. It's incredible what's happening to elephants."

"I want to read it," I say, pouring myself a glass of tonic. We sit on the redwood deck for a few minutes looking out into the yard.

"So, Ben, we haven't had a chance to talk. What've you been up to? What is it—ten years? Fifteen?"

"Seems longer," I say.

"Know what you mean," he says, nodding seriously. "Same here. I bought this place originally for Mama and Dad, but they moved to Tampa in seventy-eight, so I took it over. I had a restaurant and a shop, but I quit that—figured I could do better. I've sold a lot of glass animals, Ben. I started buying property in seventy-five. Sally lived in the yellow bungalow next to you there, after I bought it, but then she married this guy Paul, an art director, and they moved to Atlanta. She came back after the divorce."

"She looks good," I say.

Minor laughs and pulls at the leg of his shorts. "Always did."

I finish my tonic and pour another half glass. "So, how many houses do you have?"

"Six," he says. "You know, she wanted to marry you. Everybody got crazy about that—what were you, seventeen? So Sally threatens to quit school and get an apartment." He picks at the fly of his pants. "After you went to college there was this guy named Frank. He did better than you."

"What do you mean?" I stick my hands into my coat pockets, but I can't stop myself from shivering.

"You know what I mean," Minor says. "He got her right there in the garage. First time out." Minor squeezes his neck. "You chilly? It's cold out here, isn't it?"

"I'm freezing, as a matter of fact."

He snorts and stands up, tossing the ice from his drink out into the pool. "I felt bad for you when I saw that," he says. "Really."


The kitchen is a narrow room with a four-bulb fluorescent light fixture mounted on the ceiling. The wallpaper is marigolds and buttercups. There's a round butcher-block table pushed into one corner of the room. "It's easier to eat in here, I guess," Minor says. "Anyway, I want to keep an eye on the microwave. You know about microwaves?" He hustles around the kitchen, selecting dishes, checking the food already in the oven. In a couple of minutes he serves two pale-looking steaks and some cut green beans that have golden spots all over them. "Think I overdid these," he says, rolling beans onto my plate. "They should taste O.K. though. See if they're crunchy."

I spear a couple of beans, avoiding the splotched ones. "Good," I say. "What about cable? You get cable out here?"

He picks a bean off my plate and chews thoughtfully. "Crap," he says. "This ain't crunchy." He scrapes my beans back into the casserole. "You go ahead and start. I'll do up something else." He plants a shoe on the garbage can pedal and dumps the beans into the can.

"Sure," I say, cutting the steak. "We had this great cable TV in Ohio—thirty channels. Incredible stuff. The Playboy channel, three superstations, everything. Twenty-four-hour sports—you get that?"

"Nope." He touches the microwave key pad, setting the oven to defrost and cook frozen broccoli. The oven chirps every time he touches a number.

"I guess I'll get by without it," I say. "I didn't use it that much."

He points at the microwave. "We're interfering at the molecular level," he says. "You're going to love this broccoli."

The phone rings. Minor takes the receiver off the wall and says hello, bending to look inside the oven. He listens for a minute, then puts his palm over the mouthpiece and says, "It's Sally. She and her friend left the movie and they want us to go eat at Cafe 90."

"Sure," I say, waving my fork. "It's up to you—you haven't eaten yet."

"Forget it," Minor says into the phone. "We're staying put."

By the time he's ready to eat I'm on my second cup of coffee. He puts a sprig of broccoli on a butter plate for me.

"Very nice," I say, trying the broccoli. "Very tender."

"Does anything," he says, his mouth full of steak. "Anything. Bacon, eggs—bake you a potato in five minutes. You want a potato?"

I hold up my hands. "Not tonight, thanks."

"I'm not pressing," Minor says. "You don't want a potato, that's fine with me. I'm just being polite." He finishes the piece of steak he's chewing and cuts the rest of the meat on his plate into bite-size sections. When that's done he looks up, stares at me for a minute as if he's trying to recall who I am. "You probably don't even like broccoli."

"Sure I do. Broccoli's one of my favorites."

Minor's face is bloated and tight. "Crap. That's crap. You're almost squirming there, you know that? Doesn't make any difference to me. I'm set up. I got my houses, Sally—you're the renter." He wags a hand at me, wiping his mouth with a yellow napkin. He gets a quart of Miller beer from the refrigerator and takes a drink, then points the bottleneck at me. "You want beer?"

"Yes." I dump the last of my tonic into the sink and start to rinse my glass.

He looks at the ceiling. "Why don't you just get a new glass, huh? We've got glasses. Check the cabinet."

I get a mug out of the cabinet, and he pours the beer.

"You want to sit in here?" he says when I sit down again. "We don't have to sit in here. Why don't we sit in the other room?"

"Sure. Great. Let's sit in there. What the hell. You don't want to go to the bar?"

"No," he says, heading into the den.

The only light in there is green and comes from a twenty-gallon fish tank under one window. Minor climbs into a recliner and a small footrest pops out from under the seat. He points to the matching sofa. "She'll be home quick enough."

I sit on the sofa arm and look into the aquarium. The filtering system is bubbling, but there aren't any fish. "Hobby?" I say, touching the glass.

"She won't feed 'em. I try, but sometimes I'm late getting home, this and that." He twists his head to look at the aquarium. "I've got one angel left, stuck in the castle—see the castle? Went in a month ago and now he can't get out. I drop food on him but I figure he'll belly-up pretty quick." Minor wipes his forehead and takes another drink from the quart. "Look on the side there, see if you can see in that window in the turret or whatever it's called."

The castle is four shades of green and two of pink. There's an

opening as big as a stamp in one side, and through the opening I
see the stripes on the fish, which is tilted at about forty-five degrees. The gills flap a little. "He's breathing," I say.

"Look at his eyes."

"I can't see his eyes. All I can see is his side."

"Bang the glass."

I tick on the glass with my fingernail and the fish jerks a couple of times. Then one eye appears in the hole in the castle wall.
"There he is," I say. "He looks sick."

Minor sighs. "I told her to get him out of there last week, but
I guess she didn't."

"You want me to do it?"

He squints at me, then shrugs. "I guess you'd better leave him
alone. He's probably grown or something." He gets up and
comes over to the aquarium. "I don't know why she couldn't
just take care of this," he says, sticking a hand into the water. He
uproots the castle, and the fish slips out and into a tangle of
aquarium grass, its body still leaning.

"Hiya, pal," Minor says, looking down into the tank. He re-
places the castle, twisting it into the dirty white rocks to seat it
securely. "Looks like a little dead guy, doesn't he?" He pinches
some food into the tank above where the angelfish is swimming,
then closes the cover and returns to his chair. "He wasn't the
pretty one to start with. Really. You know what I'm saying?"


Sally is four years older than Minor, my age. "I'm glad you
stayed," she says when she comes in. "He told me you were taking the house, but I thought he was messing around."

"Who's this 'he' you're always talking about?" Minor says.

She ignores him. "Minor says he feels very close to you. He
says you might as well be family."

"Not quite what I said, Piggy."

"Oh hush, Minor." She pulls her sweater over her head and

arranges her hair with her fingers. She's wearing a white T-shirt with "Girl" stitched in red above the small pocket. "He always calls me Piggy when he gets mad," she says, looking at Minor. "It's his way of telling me that I'd better watch out. Anyway, Betty wanted to come back with me, to meet you, but her boy has a fever so she couldn't. I told her we'd have you and she for dinner one night soon."

"Betty's your class-B divorcée," Minor says.

Sally makes a small ticking sound with her lips and rolls her eyes. "This one," she says, pointing a thumb toward Minor, "wouldn't know a divorcée from a koala bear." She reaches under the shade of a floor lamp and turns on the light. "How come it's so dark in here?"

"I let the fish out," Minor says, motioning toward the aquarium.

"Well thank God for that," she says. She goes to the aquarium and bends to look inside. "Poor baby's nearly dead, it looks like."

She reaches for the fish food but stops when he says, "I already did that."

"Fed him too?" She looks at me. "He's a take-charge kind of guy, my brother." She waves at the angelfish, then turns around and shakes her head. "I'm getting something to eat before I faint. You want anything? A sandwich?"

"Nope," he says.

I pick up the magazine that has the elephant story in it. "We just ate, thanks."

"He explained the microwave, I'll bet," she says.

Minor makes a face at her back as she disappears into the kitchen. "How was the movie?"

"The seats were hard and the sound was awful," she says. "The guys behind me were arguing with the guys behind them about smoking grass in the theatre. That's why we left. This one guy leaned over to me and whispered something, and I thought he said he was going to burn my hair off. He must've had a speech defect. What he said was could he borrow a lighter. What's with the beans in the garbage?"

"We had a bean problem," Minor says. "I did broccoli instead."

"It was very tender," I say.

Sally comes out of the kitchen carrying a tiny glass of milk and a plate of crackers, cheese cubes, and apple slices. "I hate broccoli, but my friend Ann makes me eat it because she says it kills cancer. I just love Ann. She's so great even he likes her, don't you?"

Minor crosses the room to look at Sally's plate, then wags his head. "Maybe we should get her and Betty over together and let Ben take his choice, how's that?"

"Maybe he'll want both of them," Sally says. "How come you ate so late?" She balances a cheese cube on a cracker and puts the cracker into her mouth. "Oh, never mind. I don't want to know."

"You," he says. "Ben and you. That's the reason."

"Too bad we didn't stick together," she says to me. "Paul was a lizard."

"She hates her ex-husband," Minor says. "She likes to hate people."

"Uh-huh," Sally says, holding the milk glass close to her lips. "Pete Rose I totally hate."

"That's so easy," Minor says. He's standing in front of the aquarium.

"I'll bet Pete Rose smells funny," she says.

Minor yawns. "I'm real tired."

"Now wait a minute," she says. "I just got here. I haven't had a chance to talk yet."

"I ought to go on," I say, flipping through the magazine. "I've got elephants to do."

Minor squats and leans his forehead against the aquarium. "I hate this fish," he says. "Can we get rid of this fish? He's driving me nuts."

"Maybe we could give him away," Sally says.

Minor rubs his nose on the glass and starts to say something but then stops and swivels around on his heels, looking at me. Sally looks too. The two of them look at me as if I'm the answer to their prayers.

# Moon Deluxe

YOU'RE STUCK in traffic on the way home from work, counting blue cars, and when a blue-metallic Jetta pulls alongside, you count it—twenty-eight. You've seen the driver on other evenings; she looks strikingly like a young man—big, with dark, almost red hair clipped tight around her head. Her clear fingernails move slowly, like gears, on the black steering wheel. She watches you, expressionless, for a long second, then deliberately opens her mouth and circles her lips with the wet tip of her tongue. You look away, then back. Suddenly her lane moves ahead—two, three, four cars go by. You roll down the window and stick your head out, trying to see where she is, but she's gone. The car in front of you signals to change lanes. All the cars in your lane are moving into the other lane. There must be a wreck ahead, so you punch your blinker. You straighten your arm out the window, hoping to get in behind a van that has come up beside you, and you wait, trying to remember what the woman looked like.

Half an hour later you pull into the parking lot of the K & B Pharmacy. Inside you look at red jumper cables, a jigsaw puzzle of some TV actor's face, the tooled-leather cowboy belts, a case of cameras and calculators, the pebble-surfaced tumblers on the housewares aisle. At the medical supplies you try on several different finger splints, then stare at a drawing on a box containing some kind of shoulder harness designed to improve the posture. You look at toolboxes, opening the fatigue-green plastic ones, then the cardinal-red metal ones. You pick up a plumber's helper and try it out on the floor, surprised when it pops loose by itself—it reminds you of a camel getting off its knees. Near the stationery, you face a shelf of ceramic coin banks shaped and painted like trays of big crinkle French fries smothered in ketchup.

"Go on—buy one," says a girl walking by.

You turn and watch her shoulders; you do want something, suddenly, so you go back to the medical supplies and select Curad bandages, because the package is green. On the way to check out, you pick up a red toolbox. You buy these things.

Leaving the parking lot, you drive too fast and nearly hit a teen-ager, whose hair is straight down her back to her knees. She glares and gets into a grape-colored Porsche.

At The Creekside you go in through your patio gate, because it's closer to the assigned parking.

"Edward?" says a voice from outside the patio. "It's Eileen." You knew it was Eileen, a neighbor two apartments down, a divorcée. She's older, and you like her because she's easy to get along with.

"Hello, Eileen," you say, turning to face her, not sure exactly where she is along the cedar fence.

The slats wobble, and then Eileen's stiff hair, like a giant black meringue, rises over the top of the fence. "Bad traffic?" she says.

"Not good," you say, stooping to pick up the paper, which is stuck upright in the dirt of the flower bed.

She is teetering a little; you wonder what she's standing on to look over the fence. Then, glancing quickly over her shoulder, she almost whispers, "Do you want to come over later? I mean after you get settled? I have a friend for dinner. Two friends, in fact."

"Can I leave early, Eileen?"

She grins and nods rapidly several times, shaking the fence. "I knew you were the answer. See you at seven-thirty?" She waves and drops abruptly out of sight.

Inside, you spray a lettuce head with cold water and strip away the outer layer, dropping the brown-edged leaves into the Disposall. You pull fresh leaves, rinse and sugar them the way your mother did when you were a child, then eat, looking at the local news.

When you finish, you drop the small lettuce into the crisper at the bottom of the refrigerator and go upstairs. You look at your teeth in the bathroom mirror. They need brushing. You strip, start the water for a bath, and carry your clothes into the bedroom. You stand in front of the full-length mirror for a few seconds, looking at your skin.


Phil, Eileen's boyfriend and the owner of a local Mexican restaurant, opens her door. "Hello yourself," he says. "Come in. Ivy says you haven't been around much. Why'd you wear a coat— trying to make me look bad?"

You don't know why he calls her Ivy.

She is sitting on the arm of the couch, turned toward the door. "Hi," she says, her body so twisted, her arms and legs so tightly intertwined, that you think it must hurt her to sit that way. "Come and meet Lily."

As Eileen stands, you see Lily, her blond hair smooth around her head like a soft hat. She wears green slacks, a red belt, a shiny violet undershirt, a white jacket. She quickly slips one hand into a baggy pocket and extends the other. "Amazing," she says. "I'd swear I've met this man somewhere before."

Phil and Eileen laugh; you shrug in what must look like an odd way and take her hand.

"She moved into Carmen's apartment," Eileen says, eyeing

you. "He and Carmen had a thing," she says to Lily. "Only a small thing, but definitely a thing."

"Well, congratulations, son," Phil says, hitting you on the back. "Let's hope the record goes unblemished." He widens his eyes at you.

"Yes, let's," Lily says.

Phil wraps an arm over your shoulder, steering you to a glass-topped cart crowded with new liquor bottles. "Let's see," Phil says, grabbing a bottle by its neck and twisting it around so he can see the label. "Is it Scotch?" He turns the bottle so you can see the label.

"That'll be fine."

"You need to try bourbon, son." He twirls his stubby forefinger around in your drink and thrusts the glass at you. "Drink up. The night is young."

Phil retires to the kitchen to prepare his part of the dinner; Eileen gives you a little shove toward Lily, then follows Phil, who is opening and closing cabinet doors.

Rain starts popping on the patio, and you go to the window, pushing the drapes away from one edge of the glass.

"My roommate knew Carmen," Lily says. "That's how we got here."

"Your roommate?"

Lily turns toward you, and there's something odd about the way she looks you over. "Yes—Tony. Antonia, really. She loves this place—the palms, the walks, the tilework. Tony's an architect. It's all junk, but she likes it anyway."

The two of you watch bubbles slide down the window. In the background Phil and Eileen are laughing.

Finally, she says, "We can probably leave right after dinner, don't you think? I stayed the last time—Phil's magic tricks were funny."

✳     ✳     ✳

At the table, Eileen hands you a bowl heaped with discs of fried potato—Phil's specialty. "Lily's just back from England," she says.

"Oh, yes?" you say, inadvertently passing the potatoes to Phil without taking any for yourself.

"Visiting my brother," Lily says.

"Lily's brother is one of those music types," Eileen says. "He has a band and pink hair."

"One of my people has *blue* hair," Phil says, putting a circle of potato into his mouth. "Nice kid, actually."

"Rudy doesn't have hair anymore," Lily says.

Phil belches agreement through his napkin and nods his head vigorously, like a horse. "Know what you mean," he says. Then, to Eileen, "Tell them about your sister, Ivy."

"Well," Eileen says, balancing her fork on the edge of her plate, "my sister's always been a bit of a problem in the family, you know—nothing serious, just a little more difficult than the rest of us. She has Raynaud's disease: circulation. Last winter, Mother noticed that Heather's palms were discolored—they were orange. Mother got very worried. She urged Heather to go to the doctor; Heather wouldn't go. Mother was telling us about this on the telephone all the time, and pretty soon she had us thinking Heather was going to lose her hands—that's what you have to do with Raynaud's, amputate. This went on for almost two months. Telephones ringing all over the country. My brother calling me, and me calling Mother, and Julie—that's my other sister—calling, and David and Mother—"

"They get the idea," Phil says.

"So finally Mother forced Heather to see Dr. Shigekane, this tiny Japanese surgeon who did Mother's stomach, and do you know what happened?"

"Carrots," cracks Phil.

Eileen nods. "Shigekane told her to quit eating carrots."

"See," Phil says, "the orange from the carrots was rubbing off

on her hands, into the skin." He holds up a thick palm and pops
the first finger of his other hand into it. "It was just too many
carrots."

After coffee, Phil takes off his shoes and urges you to do the
same. "Feels great," he says.

Lily says she has to get home and asks if you want to walk
with her.

"I'd walk her myself," Phil says, "but Ivy'd never forgive me."

"I may not anyway," Eileen says, forcing a crisp little smile.
Then, to you, "Now Edward, remember, she's just a young
girl."

At the door, Lily kisses Eileen's cheek; Eileen laughs.

"Good to see you," Phil says, waving from the couch, where
he's slumped, his green-stockinged feet propped on the glass
coffee table.

Outside, the air is sweet and dense after the rain, the side-
walks are still wet, and as the two of you bend to go under a tree
limb that hangs low over the path, Lily slips her hand into yours.
When you turn to look, she lets go. All around you the building
lights are glittering, reflecting through and off slick trees. Coming to a set of steps and a branching in the path near the pool,
you say, "Sorry. Not thinking again. Do you want to walk?"

"You're not anxious to rush to my apartment and keep your
record intact?"

"A persuasive argument. But we could walk first." You pluck
some red berries off a bush that presses out over the sidewalk,
then flick the berries, one by one, like marbles off your thumb.

Lily watches their flight, then drops quickly down the four
steps and catches one of the berries in the air. Out of Eileen's
bright apartment, framed by the bushes and the curving walk,
Lily seems more comfortable.

"Sure," she says, juggling the berry in her hands. "Let's take a walk. You can give me the tour. I haven't taken a walk with a man for God knows how long."

"We don't have to go."

"Don't be silly." She stops playing with the berry and motions for you to come down the steps. "It's a lovely night. Besides, I have something to tell you about as we walk—me. Can you stand it?" She loops her arm inside yours when you reach the bottom of the steps, then marches you off along the path leading away from the swimming pool. "Now, I don't want you to get upset by this," she begins, patting your encircled arm, and then she starts a rambling account of where she was born, what her parents were like, where she went to school, how much she loves her brother Rudy. You walk on concrete and through wet grass, across parking lots, up and down steps, into more than one cul-de-sac, along the tiny creek after which the site is named. In all of Lily's story—which is punctuated by tugs on your arm, jokes, and laughter—there is nothing upsetting.

You're lost when you emerge from a tunnel of crape myrtles into a courtyard glowing with green light from the pool.

"You knew," you say. "You tricked me into taking you home."

"Isn't ours," Lily says. "The pool, I mean. This is the big one; we're next to the small one. Anyway, you're supposed to know this place better than I do."

You look at the staggered wood-and-stucco buildings. "Well, they all look alike. It's part of the charm, isn't it?"

"And confusing. We go this way," she says, skirting the deeper end of the pool.

"My feet have begun to squish," you say, stopping her. "Don't move—listen." You take several steps, exaggerating the movement like a mime.

"I don't hear them," Lily says.

"They didn't do it that time. Wait a minute."

But as you try to make the watery noise, Lily walks away. "You can dry them at the house," she says. "Come on. I told Tony I'd be back by nine, and it's already ten."

"So you're a little late," you say, jogging a few steps to catch up with her. "What's the big deal?"

"Tony," she says. "That's what I've been trying to tell you."

Antonia is the woman you saw in traffic; she's huge, extraordinary, easily over six feet. Taller than you. Her skin is glass-smooth and her pale eyes are a watery turquoise. Her hair is parted on one side and brushed back flat to her scalp. She answers Lily's abbreviated knock wearing khaki shorts and a white T-shirt with "So many men, so little time" silk-screened in two lines across the chest.

"Irony," Lily says, pointing at the shirt. "Tony, meet tonight's Mr. Lucky."

"Come in," Antonia says. "Oh—I saw you today. You remember? In the car?"

Her thick lips are burnt red, pouting, traced with little cracks—she's stunning.

The apartment looks like the inside of a fifties'-movie spaceship. It's almost empty. The few pieces of furniture are curiously placed, the walls are washed with light from track fixtures in the ceiling, and a serving cart stands in front of the sliding glass door. Two thick aluminum poles lean dumbly into one corner. A grainy photograph, the size of a window, shows a man with a black fedora and cane rolled up in a rug in a small room whose only other occupant is a wolf. At the far end of the apartment there are speakers the size of steamer trunks. There are no magazines or papers anywhere in the room.

"Would you like a drink?" Antonia says. "This is wonderful."

"His feet are wet, Tony," Lily says. She stands on her tiptoes and pecks the taller woman on the cheek. "He needs to take his shoes off."

"How about brandy?" Antonia says. She guides you to the squat Art Deco sofa, which is upholstered in fabric that looks like a yellow satin packing quilt. The sofa is squarely in the center of the room, facing the brightly lighted patio.

"Fine," you say. "Good."

"I'll bring a towel down when I come," Lily says from the foot of the stairs. "I'm going to change real quick."

"Don't be silly," you say, but she's already going up the steps.

"If they're wet, you'd better take them off," Antonia says, heading for the white wood cart, which has giant platter wheels on one end.

"What is that?" you ask, watching her bend to pull a bottle off the cart's bottom shelf.

"Just some junk cognac we got last year."

"No, I mean the cart there."

"Oh. It's a famous table—do you like it?"

"Certainly is crazy."

She laughs, stepping back to look at you. "I suppose it is. Maybe it's good." She hands you the snifter and pours a half inch of cognac. "That enough?"

"Fine," you say.

She looks at the label. "You always seem so fierce. You stare at me, you know. In the car sometimes. Have you been with Lily all night?"

"Don't answer that," Lily says, coming back into the room. "It's the brandy routine." She takes the seat beside you on the sofa and looks at Antonia. "Two years ago Tony's grandfather, who was a war correspondent or something, sent us this bottle of cognac—very fancy, very special. Both of us hate the stuff, so we've lugged the damn bottle with us everywhere, waiting for the chance to use it on some bobo. The trouble is, the stuff is too fancy, nobody every heard of it."

"It's very nice," you say.

"Might as well be Ripple," Antonia says mournfully. Then she laughs. "I wouldn't drink it if I were you. Maybe you should put it on your feet."

"She's flashy," Lily says, shoving her friend away. "Isn't she flashy?"

"I can take a hint," Antonia says. "You two want to be alone, I can see that." She returns the bottle to its place on the cart, then goes to the turntable. "Young love, true love," she warbles softly as she thumbs through a stack of records.

"Funny, Tony," Lily says. "Why don't you come over here and sit down like a normal person?"

"I'm trying to find the *right* record for this moment," Antonia says. "If I don't find it, I'm going to have an episode. Oh, this is horrible, I think it's happening, Lily, I can't stand it. Lily—what record? What music? What? Quick, grab my hands, grab my feet."

"Tony," Lily says, smiling at you. "We have a guest."

"I know it, I know," Antonia says. "Quick! I can't touch another record. I'm slipping away."

Lily gets up and goes to the turntable, takes Antonia's wrists, walks her robot style back to the sofa, and sits her down.

"I feel better," Antonia says. "I definitely feel better now."

Lily stands beside the sofa, gently straightening Antonia's boyish hair. "That's the whole show," Lily says. "Another great performance."

"I don't know what I'd do without you," Antonia says. "Edward's not a threat, is he? You're not a threat, are you, Edward?"

"I don't guess so. To my dismay."

"What a wonderful thing to say," Lily says. She combs Antonia's hair with her fingers, drawing it into funny points behind the ears. "Maybe I'll go out with Edward more often."

"What about me?" Antonia says, reaching up for Lily's hands. She looks at you. "Or say I can come too—otherwise I'll feel left out."

Lily presses her fingers over Antonia's eyes, bends forward, and whispers, "You'll be the guest of honor, Tony. You'll have the best seat in the house."

"I feel better," Antonia says. She pulls Lily's hands away, turns them, then kisses the sharp nails.

"I'm going," you announce. You get up from the sofa, brush the thighs of your jeans, then push your hands into your coat pockets.

You wonder what it would be like if they invited you to stay the night, to sleep on the splendid yellow couch, to have a hurried breakfast with them before work, to be part of their routine.

For a second nobody moves and then Antonia falls sideways on the sofa and turns onto her back, her knees folded over the sofa arm farthest from you. She reaches up and grabs your wrist through your coat, looking at you upside down. "I should have smiled, I guess," she says. "I should have just smiled." When she releases you, her arms fall behind her on the couch and the T-shirt pulls out of the waist of her pants, showing the dark curves of her stomach, the lemony hair at her navel.

Both women walk you to the door, lead you out into the courtyard, walk ahead of you a few steps toward the pool. You follow, looking at their backs, then at the low sky. "This is crazy," you say when they stop by the small diving board.

"I see that," Lily says.

"You do?" Antonia says.

Then, one after the other, the women kiss you with their lips awkwardly, resolutely shut. You circle the diving board, turn and walk backward across the courtyard, watching Lily and Antonia, hand in hand, vanish into their apartment. There is a moon. You can definitely feel the water in your shoes. Pool lights are waving on the sides of the buildings.

# The Browns

HAROLD GOT in a fight with the neighbors' dog and won, so we had to apologize, which is something I don't mind doing, usually, because I don't take it too seriously and it seems to make everybody feel better. The fight started in our front yard, but we didn't get the dogs apart until they'd fought their way into the Browns' driveway. I walked Harold home and locked him in the garage while Allison talked to Pilar Brown about the cuts on her dog, which was wrapped up in a ball under a bush at the edge of the drive. When I got back, Allison was saying how sorry she was it had ever happened.

"This is terrible," I said, walking up the slope of their driveway. "I feel rotten—we may have to do something about Harold, Allison. This is ridiculous." I shook my head and shrugged at Pilar. "I'm really sorry. I thought those two dogs liked each other."

The Browns have two BMWs and a chocolate-brown house with pale-blue trim. She's an architect and he's a lawyer, and they're both about thirty. She went to school in San Francisco, and she says everybody out there paints houses interesting colors. "People aren't afraid of color on the Coast the way they are here," she said when we first met. I said I liked lavender a lot, and that I might paint our new house lavender. Allison just shook her head. Then Pilar brought out the cocker spaniel named Jupiter. "We named him after the planet. Duncan's crazy for planets."

We'd moved into the neighborhood because we got an assumption on a ranch-style brick three-bedroom. It was our first house, although we'd been together for years. We were in the middle of our argument about friends—Allison wanted some. "You just hide out all the time like a palooka," she said the first night in the new house. "You got away with it at the apartment, but you've got a house now. You've got neighbors."

I told her I was ready for anything. I thought that sounded pretty good—wry and romantic, something from a modern movie full of wood-sided station wagons and blue-green pools, the kind of movie Hollywood started making in numbers about five or six years ago, in which ordinary life is made fun of and made mysterious and beautiful at the same time. Those are my favorite movies now, which is why I thought my line was pretty good. It didn't thrill Allison. "What about the Browns?" she said. "Let's have them over."

"Did you think it was odd that both her name and her house were brown?" I said.

"No," Allison said.

"Oh. O.K.," I said. "Call her up. She has a kid, doesn't she? Didn't she say she had a kid about Cory's age?"

"Yes," Allison said. "A boy. Del."

"Del?"

"That's what she said."

"It's O.K., really. Invite them over. They can be our first friends. They'll probably mess up the floors, sit in the chairs, stuff like that, but call them anyway."

Three months later we'd had the Browns to dinner twice, and they'd had us twice. Then the dogs had this fight.


One of the Browns must have called the ASPCA. In the middle of the afternoon a white city truck pulled up in front of our house and two guys in identical orange shirts found Harold, whom I'd let out of the garage, in the flower bed by the drive- way. Harold is named after Allison's brother, the hard-luck case in her family. He sells chain-link fencing door to door in Big Spring, and he's always getting attacked. We hear a lot of stories from Harold about dogs ripping off people's limbs. Anyway, I watched the guys check the dog Harold's tags, then walk him up to our door. When I answered the bell, the taller of the two in- troduced himself and told me he was going to have to take Harold to the pound for tests. He didn't call it the pound. He called it the shelter. "Routine stuff," he said. "Nothing to sweat."

"This about the fight?" I said.

"Yep," the shorter one said. He had a face like a football— dark tan and bad skin. He flapped open an aluminum clipboard. "Reported by Mrs. P. Brown." He poked his finger on Harold's skull a couple of times and said, "He don't look rabid, but the city says I got to check him out." Harold twisted his head around to look at the short guy, then took a swipe at the finger with his tongue. "Naw, hell—we look all right," the guy said, tugging on Harold's ear. "See that tongue? That's the best- looking tongue I had in weeks. Right, Hondo?"

"Right," Hondo said. "That's a swell tongue. So let's go. We've got the chow on Barna Place to get." He gave me a re- ceipt and snapped a leash on Harold's collar. "You can get him any time after four-thirty," he said. "They close at seven. Bring ten bucks. Cash, no checks."

They put Harold in the back of the truck. I stayed on the porch and watched a guy across the street three houses down who was washing his house with a hose and push broom.

Allison had gone for the car pool. When she got back, I told her about the ASPCA. She got mad and called Pilar. "What in the hell is this?" she said. "You had them come get Harold?

We're supposed to be neighbors, friends. I don't believe you people." She slammed the phone into its cradle before Pilar had a chance to say anything, and then she went to the bedroom to rest. I went to get Harold.

The pound was a low concrete-block building diagonally across from the abandoned rail terminal. In the lobby a line of construction-paper sheets with glitter letters on them, one to a sheet, was tacked to the wall. The message was PETS ARE PRECIOUS, and it was signed on the last sheet by the fifteen members of the Doxiama Elementary School second grade. That included Debra, Bart, Nikki, Rosalie, and Spider, among others. I was reading the names when a guy who looked like Bruce Dern came through a tin-covered door and asked me what I wanted. I told him.

"Oh, yeah," he said, stripping off the oversize black rubber gloves he was wearing. He pulled an open Baby Ruth out of his shirt pocket and took a bite. "Kind of spotty? Looks like a hound dog—that him? Real friendly?"

"Sounds like Harold," I said.

We walked through another tin-covered door and into a narrow, concrete alley between two rows of damp, Cyclone-fenced pens. Most of the dogs didn't look too bad, but the building looked like something you might see in an exposé on "Nightly News." Harold was in the next-to-last pen. "This Harold?" the guy said, slapping the gloves against the gate.

I said it was.

"Well, let's get him the hell out of here, what do you say?" He opened the gate and Harold came out running and jumping. At the same time, a ratty little monkey skittered out from behind a dark-green fifty-five-gallon drum that was alongside the last pen, and the Bruce Dern guy gave the monkey a hand up

onto his shoulder, then followed me and Harold all the way out
to the parking lot. He was petting the monkey and feeding it bits
of chocolate from the Baby Ruth. "Twenty bucks," he said,
after I'd gotten Harold in the back seat.

I reached for my wallet. "Twenty?"

"You got a hearing loss?" he said. "Twenty."

I pulled two ten-dollar bills out and handed them to him. The
monkey grabbed the bills and started chewing on them. The guy
grinned. "Hungry monkey," he said.

After dinner Duncan Brown called and said my wife shouldn't
yell at his wife. "Besides," he said, "*I* called the ASPCA. She
didn't."

"They took Harold, Duncan."

"I know. Maybe I overreacted. I probably made him sound
worse than he really is."

"I had to go over there. I just got back. Have you ever been to
the pound?"

"Sorry," he said.

"It's not Harold's fault they got in the fight," I said.

"I know, I know," he said. "Look, let's forget this one, O.K.?
Let's just put it behind us. You people want to come for drinks
Friday? We're having Jake and Linda Mars."

Jake and Linda owned the local Scandinavian-import store.
They were clients of Brown's. I put my palm over the telephone
mouthpiece and asked Allison. She frowned, but then whispered, "I guess we'd better go," so I got back on the phone and
said, "Fine. Sounds fine."

"Tell him we'll bring Harold," Allison said. "Turn it into a
get-together for the dogs." She nodded seriously and pointed at
the phone, so I asked Duncan.

"That a joke?" he said. "If that's a joke, it's not funny."

"No joke," I said. "I mean I think it's a good idea. Maybe they'll learn to get along."

He went to ask Pilar, and then he was back on the phone saying she thought it might work but why didn't we come early, because if it didn't work she didn't want the party screwed up.

"If there's any trouble," I said, "we'll just take our dog and go home."


I watched a made-for-TV movie about a Southern sheriff who was involved in white slavery, emphasis on thin young girls, and then I went out to the kitchen, where Allison was making a Black Bottom pie for somebody at her office. "This Friday thing," I said. "Taking Harold and all that. He'll probably chew up Jupiter."

Allison was grating a big semisweet chocolate bar. "I don't see how you can get out of it now, do you?"

There was a knock on the kitchen door. I opened it and Pilar was on the porch, in the yellow light that's supposed to discourage bugs. Pilar looked bad. She was swatting at a moth that seemed to want to land in her hair.

I said, "Hi. Come in. What's the matter?"

"It's Jupiter," she said. "I think he got some infection from Harold, where Harold bit him." She made a little mouth with her hand and bit herself on the neck with it. "It's a mess. It's all swollen and purple. Duncan says I'll have to take Jupiter to the vet tomorrow."

"It's probably not serious," Allison said. "You want coffee?"

"He'll be all right," I said. "I know a vet we can call tonight if you want."

Allison put a red mug of coffee in front of Pilar, who sat at the kitchen table thumbing through a magazine. "Jupiter is so important to us," she said. "I know it's dumb, but he is."

"It's not dumb," Allison said. "Not at all. We know exactly what you mean, don't we, Bill?"

I looked in the drawer by the refrigerator for the card with the emergency numbers on it. "Sure do," I said. "When we first got Harold, I wouldn't let him out of the house."

"It's just after what happened to the other one," Pilar said. "Blitzen. You remember?"

"That was horrible," Allison said. "I don't know why the men didn't notice that he was in that can."

"Must've been asleep," I said. "The way they toss those things around. He barked at trucks, didn't he?"

"Not the garbage truck," Pilar said. "He never barked at a garbage truck in his whole life."

"Don't worry," I said. "Dogs fight all the time."

"I hope they don't shave him," Allison said. "Shaved dogs give me the creeps."

Pilar looked up from her coffee.

"Oops," Allison said. "That was dumb."

I nodded at Allison and went to get my address book. Harold was on the bed, sleeping with one paw over his nose. "You're cute," I said to him. I got the address book and shut the bedroom door on my way out. Pilar was telling Allison about Key West. The Browns spent a week there last winter. They took Jupiter, and he had a wonderful time in the sand. Duncan got sun poisoning and had to stay in the whole time, but Pilar and Jupiter and Del went for long walks on the beach, waving as they passed back and forth in front of Duncan's room.

"I put the pie in the freezer," Allison said. "We can have a piece in a few minutes."

"I thought it was for your co-worker," I said.

She ignored me. "Do you want to call Duncan? See if everything's all right?"

"He's in bed with his sinuses," Pilar said. She looked at her watch, then pulled the stem and reset it. She was a small woman with shaggy black hair and pale-green eye shadow. Her wrists were the size of paper-towel tubes.

"Poor Duncan," Allison said. "Sinuses can really blow your face all out of condition." She went to the sink and ran water into the bowl she'd used for the chocolate.

"Between him and Jupiter I've got my hands full," Pilar said. "You think he'll be O.K.? Jupiter?"

"Sure," I said. I waved the address book. "Or we can call Wenzel. He did some work for us when Harold had his gallbladder."

"Harold had a gallbladder? I didn't know that."

"Well, it wasn't the bladder so much," Allison said. "It was a worm or something, wasn't it?" She looked at me.

"Don't look at me," I said. "You told me it was gallbladder."

"Stones, maybe it was stones," Pilar said. "That's not uncommon in today's dog."

"Is this pie ready yet?" I went to the refrigerator and opened the freezer door. The pie was lopsided on a tower of three or four Birds Eye lima bean packs. "Looks ready."

"He can tell by looking," Allison said to Pilar. "A rare gift." She crossed the kitchen and closed the freezer door. "Not ready. I think it was stones, now that I remember it. Two little stones no bigger than wood ticks. I thought he was going to die, swear to God."

"Harold?" Pilar said.

"No," Allison said, taking the address book from my hand and going back to the table. "Rocky here." She shot a thumb over her shoulder at me. "Get me a pencil, Rocky." She leafed through the book, shaking her head. "He was crying. I found him kneeling over Harold and crying. Had to call my sister to get Wenzel's name. He's expensive."

I gave her a red felt-tip pen, and she wrote Wenzel's number on a corner of the evening paper.

"I wasn't crying," I said. "I was listening, trying to hear something."

"He's always trying to hear something," Allison said. She tore off the corner of the paper and handed it to Pilar.

The phone rang. It was Duncan, calling to see if Pilar was with us. I told him she was and held the receiver out for her, then watched her face as she talked.

Cory, our five-year-old, came in through the back door carrying a jar with a toad in it. "I need an icepick," she said. "I've got to get some holes in here before this guy dies. Hi, Pilar." She started opening and closing drawers next to the sink.

"Third one up," Allison said.

Pilar was whispering into the receiver. She'd turned her back, and she had her forehead pressed against the small green chalkboard on the wall next to the phone.

Cory got the icepick and squatted in the middle of the kitchen, struggling to push the pick through the jar top.

"You have to hit it," I said. I took the pick, steadied it, then popped it with the heel of my hand. The jar busted. Glass scattered all over the place. Cory fell over backward.

Allison shouted, "Oh, crap, Bill. Did she cut herself?"

The toad hopped toward the living room. Cory went after it. "That's great, Dad," she said. "That's really great."

"Well, help her, why don't you?" Allison said.

I started out of the room and heard Pilar say, "Bill tried to stab Cory's frog with an icepick."

We chased the toad around the living room for a few minutes, finally trapping it under the sofa. I whispered to Cory that I was going to lift the sofa and she should grab the toad. But when we tried that, she missed, and the toad went into the hall leading back to the bedrooms. Harold started barking and scratching at the bedroom door. Allison came down the hall from the kitchen. "Oh, get out of the way," she said. She picked up the toad by one of its back legs. It jerked a couple of times as if it were trying to hop away, but then it gave up and hung limp in her hand.

"Don't hurt his feet," Cory said.

"I'm not hurting his feet," Allison said. "Get me something to put him in." She carried the toad back to the kitchen.

"What?" Cory said. She ran around her mother and into the kitchen.

"How about a bowl?" I said.

"I don't want this frog in one of my bowls," Allison said. "Get the Tupperware thing out of the cabinet."

"Oh, yeah," Cory said. "Great."

"You want me to put some holes in the top?" I said.

"Sure, Dad."

"I'll do the holes," Allison said. Pilar was still on the telephone. She turned to see what we were doing, and the toad somehow jumped out of Allison's grip and landed on Pilar's chest. She jerked away, banging her head against the range hood. "Shoot," she said, rubbing the spot.

"Shoot?" Cory said.

Allison picked up the toad.

"I've got to go, Duncan," Pilar said into the phone. "Allison put a frog on me."

Harold was still barking. "Shut him up, will you?" Allison said. "I don't know why he thinks he has to bark at everything. What good does it do?"

"Jupiter's getting worse," Pilar said. "He went under the house and Duncan had to go under there after him. I think we'd better call the vet."

"Take care of him, please," Allison said to me, waving toward the bedroom.

I yelled down the hall at Harold to be quiet.

"What's the vet's number?" Allison said, dropping the toad into an orange Tupperware bowl Cory was holding. I handed her the paper she'd written the number on, and she started for the phone.

"Is the pie ready?" Cory said. "I want some pie to watch TV with."

"The pie's not ready," Allison said.

"Maybe you could take Harold out in the backyard for a run," I said to Cory. "He sounds like he wants to go out."

"He wants to eat my frog like last time, remember?"

"I'm going to eat your frog if you don't get it out of here," Pilar said.

Wenzel had on a Jim Morrison T-shirt when he rang the Browns' doorbell. He was about twenty-five, with a carefully trimmed gray stubble on his chin and thick glasses with red frames. "Where's the pup?" he said. He hoisted a bag big enough for a couple of bowling balls off the rubber mat and followed Pilar into the kitchen.

"Forget Friday," Allison whispered to me. "It stinks in here. I don't think these people ever wash anything. We'll pretend we forgot. Maybe we'll go away for the weekend."

We sat in the Browns' living room and waited for Pilar and Wenzel to reappear. They'd just redecorated, with thickly padded furniture, heavy drapes, deep-pile carpet. I counted six different floral prints, including two on the walls. Even the cocktail table had a flower motif around the edge. Everything in the room had been wrapped in foam or flowers. I was looking around and Allison was staring at the single uncovered window when Duncan came in bundled in a gold sheet.

"Howdy," he said. "The doc here?"

"With the patient," I said. I pointed toward the hall that led to the kitchen.

"I've been napping," Duncan said. He stood in the open arch between the living and dining rooms holding the sheet from underneath with two hands. I could see his fists outlined in the cloth. "I guess Harold's had his shots this year?"

Allison and I nodded.

"I was sure he had," Duncan said. "It's really not all that serious. Just a lump on his neck, right about here." He brought the lower hand out from the sheet and made a biting motion on the back of his neck. The sheet came open. He was wearing boxer shorts, tan with a double pinstripe. He glanced down and quickly closed the sheet by turning his body to one side. Then he drew his hand back under the sheet and said, "Sorry, Allison."

"It's O.K.," she said.

"Can I get you something? Beer?"

She shook her head and I said, "No, thanks." Then the three of us were quiet for a minute.

Allison got up. "We're not much good here." She looked at me, and I got up too. "I'm going to see if I can help. Wenzel didn't look at the peak of his game." She started for the kitchen.

Duncan shuffled across the carpet. "Good idea. Me and Billy need to talk anyway."

When Allison was out of sight, he grabbed my arm and pulled me back onto the couch. "All the women I ever slept with were lousy lovers," he said. "That's a terrible thing to say, I know. I asked Bert and he said it was the same for him, but that's the kind of thing he always says."

"Bert?" I said.

"My analyst," Duncan said. "You met him at dinner once, I think. Short guy with a mustache? Remember? Plays racquetball?"

"He's your analyst?"

"Yep. Bert says celibacy's O.K."

"I suppose," I said.

"You know," Duncan said, "when I was a kid, I played priest all the time. I made altars out of cardboard boxes covered with sheets. My mother had this pewter cup I used for a chalice, and

I used the *Columbia Encyclopedia* for a missal. I had vestments, salad-dressing things for cruets, smashed bread for the host. You do that? Cut bread slices with a glass and smash them flat?"

"I did that," I said. "Sure."

"I spent a lot of rainy afternoons mumbling over the encyclopedia and raising the host, genuflecting—once I went for a week holding my thumbs and forefingers together the way priests do. Mother didn't discourage it. I think she figured it was cowboys-and-Indians."

I nodded and smiled and looked at the backs of my hands, then at the hall leading into the kitchen.

"Priests have it good," Duncan said. "They walk around in those robes all the time—do they still do that? I always envied priests."

"I don't think they do that anymore," I said. "Reforms. Modernization."

"God lifts those bastards right off the planet, you know what I'm saying, Billy?" Duncan put his hand on my knee for emphasis. "They go around feeling good all the time—I mean, what are a priest's problems? A priest wants a good meal, a couple of drinks, and a television for his favorite sport."

"Basketball," I said. "They always like basketball."

"Right. Right. You know, we have Del in St. Pius, but Pilar's not happy. I guess we'll look at some other schools. I wanted him in a Catholic school, but I get the feeling they aren't what they were. I mean, I had to go to class for six weeks in the convent in the fifth grade because I threw an eraser at this pig of a nun who lied to the Mother Superior about me, told her I'd made remarks about her 'sexual apparatus'—no kidding, that's what she called it. They assigned me to a room in the convent for the next six weeks. Somebody brought me the lessons every afternoon, and the next day I sat in that dark little room staring out the window at the baseball diamond. It's a good thing I hated baseball."

The dog squealed in the kitchen, and Duncan winced. I said, "You think we ought to see what's going on?"

"Naw," he said. "You know this guy, right? Anyway, it isn't that bad." Duncan waved the sheet around his legs a couple of times, then grabbed my knee again. "I had a teacher named Miss Phantom when I was in school; Del's got Sister Susie. What good is that? Nuns used to sneak around in those habits, and now look at 'em."

I shrugged and stood up. "I know. There's some terrible stuff going on."

"You said it," Duncan said. "And I don't like it, either."

Allison and Pilar and Wenzel came into the living room single file. Allison pulled her thumb over her shoulder. "Let's go, Rocky," she said. "The worst is over."

"Is Jupiter all right?" Duncan asked. He stood up beside me.

"Perfect," Wenzel said.

Pilar put her arm around Duncan. "Wenzel gave him a shot so he could sleep. No problems." She patted her husband's shoulder.

I sidestepped the cocktail table and shuffled out the door with Allison and Wenzel.

"Nobody wants to stay for coffee?" Pilar asked when the three of us were on the porch.

We thanked her and said no, and she thanked Wenzel, and Duncan said it was real nice to have somebody to talk to once in a while, and then the three of us started for the street. The door closed behind us, and the porch light went off. We stopped at Wenzel's car to thank him for coming, and he said, "You'd better bring Harold in to see me. He's got a lot of distortion in his molars. He's not getting all the power he should."

# Gila Flambé

THE WOMAN with the menus stops me by the cash register because the restaurant is crowded and she doesn't think she has a table for one. I'm soaked after running across the jammed parking lot in the hot rain, so I'm not sympathetic when the woman, whose lips are a juicy red, shakes her head and gazes forlornly around the room. "Nobody ever comes in alone," she says.

I point to a small man sitting by himself in a corner.

"Oh," she says, straightening the menus on her arm. "That's Mr. Pelham. I forgot about him."

"Well, maybe he'd like company?" I don't want to sit there, but it's better than nothing.

"No. He always eats alone."

Mr. Pelham occupies a small table near the kitchen doors—not a good table at all, but it has two chairs, one of them empty, and there isn't another unoccupied chair in the room. The restaurant used to be a hardware store; now it's all done up in cheesy L.A. late-thirties gear, the hard-boiled version—palms, ratty paintings, neon, ersatz columns, colored lights, pale-salmon walls in bad plaster, black tile floor. The waitresses slink around in period evening dress; the blondes make an effort at Veronica Lake. There's a lot of smoke-colored taffeta and lamé in evidence. This is my first trip.

"Why don't you ask him," I say. "He looks like he could use a friend."

The woman with the menus doesn't want to do this, but after

another look around she agrees, and slides across the room toward his table, narrowly missing a waitress in a shiny dress who's carrying a tray of squat cocktails.

There's a commotion in the corner; abruptly Mr. Pelham gets up and pushes the menu woman aside. He's short. He stands awkwardly, bent forward, his fists planted on the table, his black raincoat still tight around him, and he stares across the room at me. I point at him, then at myself, then back at him; he says something to the woman, then sits down. She flaps her hand at me, telling me it's all right, I should come over.

Pelham looks fifty. At the neck of his raincoat—only the topmost button is undone—the bright, starched, tightly buttoned collar of a white dress shirt is visible. He isn't wearing a tie. On the table, half covering the chrome wire rack of sugar packets, there's a black hat with a ribbed band. I remove my raincoat and drop it onto the floor next to the second chair. "Thanks," I say. "I didn't want to bother you, but"—I turn and look quickly around the room—"there's no place left to sit. My name's Harold. Sometimes I'm called Zoot." I stick out my hand, but Pelham doesn't look up from his soup. He's bent over the shallow dish, blowing on the soup, pulling away occasionally to whisk his spoon around the rim. "I'll move if something opens up, O.K.?"

Pelham's hair is thin and sticking to his scalp. "I'm waiting for somebody," he says. "You'll have to move when she comes."

A woman who can't be twenty hands me a glassy scarlet menu. She's wearing a black dress with thin straps and a feather motif in sequins up under the bodice. She looks good. I ask her to keep an eye out for a vacant table, but she doesn't seem to understand.

"Mr. Pelham has been kind enough to let me join him until another table becomes available."

"Oh," the waitress says, reaching for the menu she's just given me.

"I'll keep it." We have a little tug-of-war over the menu, very quick, which she gracefully allows me to win. She's not sure about the water glass she's holding, but finally decides to leave it.

Pelham says, "Don't stain the table," so I open the menu and slide the glass onto one corner of it. There's an eight-foot-high potted palm behind him, and every time the kitchen doors swing open, one of the largest fronds sways, brushing the back of his head, and he jerks out of the way.

"I'm not alone all the time," he says. "I've got people come to see me night and day." He's looking very carefully through his soup, picking up spoonfuls, twisting them to catch the light, then dripping the soup back into the dish. "Don't get the idea that I'm bad off."

"O.K.," I say, and drink my water. There's a dark, irregular stain on the corner of the menu; I try to put the glass back exactly where it was. "You come often? Here, I mean?"

"What're you, an accountant? You run a small store or something? You're not from the Board of Health, are you?"

"No." I wish I'd waited at the door. "No, I just came to try the food."

He laughs and drops the spoon into the saucer. "Yeah, and I love yams," he says. "Slinky's food is nothing. She goes off to Vassar or someplace and suddenly everybody's stiff for her."

"The desserts—somebody said they were good."

"Her aunt. Slinky's idea of dessert is a weekend with wet hair in a station wagon." He presses a hand to his forehead, then slides the fingers back over his scalp, gluing new points of dark hair to the skin. He rolls his eyes. "Look at these people—why the hell don't they go home? Go to Bonanza, for Christ's sake."

Looking around the room, I wonder the same thing. Bonanza's not so bad, and you can usually get a table.

Pelham looks at me for the first time since I sat down. "What're you doing here, Mac? You're out of town and it's raining and you're here alone—don't that beat all. Where's your beautiful wife? Where's your beautiful house?"

I grin and shrug stupidly, aiming for camaraderie. "No wife, no house. My beautiful car's in the lot outside, only it's a Chevrolet."

Pelham shreds four crackers into his soup, which must be room temperature by now. "Zoot? What kind of name is that? That's a stupid name."

I nod and study the menu, trying to decide whether I want to stay. I've been called Zoot since I was a kid—my father played lousy saxophone and loved Zoot Sims. "It's all tongue, boy," he used to say while we listened together to a Sims record so loud it rattled the figurines in my mother's china cabinet. "Tongue and breath." And we sat, listening, my father's open saxophone case on the sofa, the horn a light, glistening gold, until late into the weekend nights. As nicknames go, Zoot isn't so bad. "My dad was a musician. He gave me the name."

"I know a guy named Stick," Pelham says. "And I used to know a guy named Nipple, but he got his throat cut on a rig in the Gulf. Stick's a bowling champion somewhere—Little Rock, maybe. He's got himself set up with a bar called the 7–10 Club, something like that." Pelham flakes more crackers into the dish. His soup is beginning to look like day-old cereal.

"Stick," I repeat.

Two couples come in together and are seated at a table against the far wall. I catch the eye of the woman with the menus, and she tosses her head a little to indicate that she gets the message.

"Yeah. Stick. And you're Zoot. And I'm Blink, because I never do. Ain't that wonderful."


I eat a small steak while Pelham watches, still nursing his soup. The steak isn't bad. The waitress with the sequins says she's sorry ten or fifteen times, talking, it seems, more to Pelham than to me. She suggests a dessert that turns out to be a circle of fresh pineapple embedded in a square of white chocolate and topped with curled almond shavings.

"I need a ride," Pelham says while I add the tip on the Visa slip. "Hot young thing like you can afford to give me a ride, can't you?"

"Sure. Where're you headed?" It's a reflex; I don't know why I'm agreeing. Maybe it's the way Pelham looks—the eyebrows and the sallow skin and the disdain. Maybe I want to prove I'm not such a rotten fellow.

"It ain't far," he says. "I'll buy gas if you want to be pissy about it. I've got to meet somebody, and my Lamborghini's in the shop."

"Fine. O.K."

"Course if you're too busy I'll just crawl." He pushes his chair back from the table, deposits the hat on his head, then falls to his knees and crawls toward the entrance. For a minute I think he's crippled, but at the door he gets up and gives the menu woman a hug, then brushes his knees. He signals for me to hurry up. I'm still seated at the table, trying to figure out what's going on, when he shouts, "Let's move it, kid," as if we were Marines in a movie.

The first thing I do when I get the car started is look at the gas gauge: half a tank, plenty. Then I turn on the windshield wipers and turn off the radio. Pelham jams his hands in his raincoat pockets and says, "That way," jerking his head to the right. "How old are you, thirty? Thirty-five?"

"Two," I say, wheeling out of the parking lot. "Where're we going?"

"I'll tell you where to turn." he stares straight out the windshield. "I'm fifty today. When you're fifty, it goes very fast. You people don't know that."

We drive through town, which is eight blocks of two- and

three-story buildings, then go out a winding road past the indus-
trial section, past some kind of all-lit-up oil refinery, and out
onto an old highway that used to be a truck route; it's raining
heavily, so I can't see much except the occasional brights of a
passing tanker truck.

"I'm going to help you out, kid," Pelham says after we've
been driving a few minutes in silence. "I'm going to introduce
you to Melba."

Oncoming lights make the rain on the windshield look alive,
the way the water pops off the glass and flies into midair. I wait
for Pelham to tell me about Melba. Suddenly he says, "Here.
Turn here."

I spin the Chevrolet onto a red clay road full of potholes
and brown standing water. We buck and heave in the front
seat of the car, and there's nothing to see but the hood, the
rain, the almost pumpkin-colored road. We go a little way,
and I start to say something but Pelham pulls his hand out of
his raincoat pocket and grabs my arm. "O.K.," he says. "Here.
Stop. Cut the lights and sit tight." Then he yanks the hat
down over his forehead, opens the door, and pushes out into
the rain.

I do what he says. With the lights off I can't see anything at
all; at first I can't even see the steering wheel in my lap. I know
where we are, how far we are from town, but when lightning
cracks somewhere in the distance to the left, I'm too slow to
catch it, and see only empty space, a field—no trees or buildings—before the blackness closes in again. Pelham's only been
gone a minute or two, but it seems longer. I pull the knob that
turns on the instrument lights so I can read the clock: nine-
eighteen. It's ridiculous—I can't leave the poor bastard in the
rain in the middle of nowhere. There's no place to turn the car
around anyway; I'd have to back up the three-quarters of a mile
to the highway. I feel stupid for getting into this. I start the car,

snap on the lights, and punch the horn button a couple of times; he doesn't show, so I lock all four doors, then turn the engine and lights off and listen to the chatter of the rain.

Pelham knocks on my window, and I roll it down. "Come on out, kid. It's O.K." He's got an umbrella—one of those oversize golf umbrellas with alternating wedges of color, red and white. "Got to get you inside, get you into some dry clothes."

"Inside what?" I say. "There isn't a place for miles. I'm leaving."

I begin to close my window, starting the car at the same time. He shouts, "Wait a minute, kid. Hold on."

"You want a ride back to town, Pelham?" He's got on different clothes—a red checked shirt under the raincoat. "I'm going."

"Sure, kid. Sure. Hold on a minute. Let me get Melba." He goes off again, and I sit there with the motor running. It's nine-thirty-seven.

Melba's a dog—coal black and the size of a small pony. When we get her into the back seat, she shakes herself off, throwing water all over the inside of the car. Pelham hammers on the passenger window; that door's still locked. "Fifty yards up, there's a drive," he says, getting into the car. "You can turn there."

I go out a lot faster than I came in, the car bouncing and sliding through the holes and the slop; when I make the highway, we head for town, driving fast. Pelham is talking to the dog, which has vanished from the rearview mirror. "I knew right where you'd be, Melba," Pelham says. "Came for you just like I said I would, didn't I?" He talks all the way. When I take the turn into the parking lot outside the restaurant too fast and slide the rear end into the back fender of somebody's white Mercedes, Pelham says, "Attaboy."

"O.K." I say, pushing the shift lever into park and turning off the engine. "Get the dog out." I go around to the back of the car to see how bad the damage is. Pelham eases the dog out of the rear seat, holds her on a tight chain, and heads for the restaurant, twirling the bright umbrella. People are lining up at the windows of the building, rubbing the glass and peering out. It looks as if my bumper is caught in the Mercedes' rear wheel well, and the tire there is flattening fast. I jump on the trunk of my car, trying to free the bumper, but the jumping doesn't do any good; the cars are hooked tight.

At the cash register inside I tell the woman what's happened and give her the Mercedes' license number.

"That's Miss Landson's car," the woman says. "You sure know how to pick 'em. Wait here and I'll get her."

I look around the restaurant. There are lots of empty tables now. Back toward the corner where I ate dinner, Pelham comes out of the kitchen carrying what must be a new bowl of soup, the huge dog right behind him.

Miss Landson looks twenty-five and calm, like a hippie girl who suddenly got rich. Her hair is long, straight, thin, and brown. She comes out through the swinging doors of the kitchen talking to the cashier; she's wearing Levi's and lime-yellow running shoes—Nikes, from the look of the decoration—and a denim jacket. As she passes Pelham, who's sitting at the same table playing with the soup, she taps him on the back. She extends her hand when she's still ten feet away from me. "Ericka Landson," she says. "We had a wreck?"

"Only a small wreck, but you lost a tire. I'm sure there's no problem—I mean, Allstate will take care of it."

"Maybe we ought to have a look." She smiles at me and walks toward the door. "It's still raining, I guess." The tail of the jacket is curled at the bottom in back; she doesn't seem to have a shirt on underneath. "Betsy," she says, turning to the cashier, "bring a couple of umbrellas, will you?"

"I'm sorry about this. I was going too fast coming in. It got away from me."

Ericka stands with the door slightly open, looking out into the parking lot. "I heard that. My husband tells me you were mad at him for making you go get Melba."

"Excuse me?" I heard what she said; I just need a minute to get used to the idea. "Oh, yes. Pretty dog. Big."

She laughs. "Dumb. She's afraid of the rain. That's why Warren wanted to go get her, although I don't know why he didn't drive himself." She lets the door close, then looks at her watch, which is black and digital, like an underwater watch. The cuffs of her jacket are rolled twice; she has small, masculine hands, long fingers, clear nails, no wedding ring.

"I sat with him at dinner. Your husband, I mean. Only I didn't know he was your husband."

Ericka looks across the room at Pelham. "He likes soup," she says. "Today's his birthday."

Betsy comes out of the kitchen with Pelham's red-and-white umbrella and a second, tan one. Pelham looks up as she passes him, then looks at the two of us standing inside the front door. He seems to chuckle to himself, a vague grin creeping up on one side of his face. "This is all I could find, Miss Landson. This brown one is busted. Carlos has a good umbrella, but he couldn't find it."

"Take one," Ericka says, pointing to the umbrellas. I take the tan and follow her out into the rain. Her shoulders are broad; she's a big woman but not heavy—like an athlete, a runner.

Our cars are awkwardly banged together at the edge of the now almost empty lot. A street light hanging off a telephone pole just beyond the entrance to the lot throws a ghoulish green-white light on the wet cars, and they glisten. The Mercedes is covered with thousands of mirrorlike bubbles. Ericka squats between the cars to assess the damage; the tire on her Mercedes is spread out like a pool of tar under the chromed wheel. She fingers the lug nuts as she surveys the situation.

"I tried jumping on mine, but it didn't help."

"No. It wouldn't," she says, standing. "It'll come out when we jack this one up to replace the tire. The fender's torn a little." She comes out from between the cars, fishing in a breast pocket, from which she pulls a ring of keys. "Let me check the spare. I don't want to get somebody out here if the spare's no good."

She opens the trunk of the Mercedes, then bends under the lid and flips up the carpet to get at the spare. When she closes the trunk, she looks at my car and says, "You didn't do so badly, outside of the taillight. It's Warren's fault, really—he likes intrigue."

We go back inside. She suggests I sit down at the round table near the cash register while she takes care of the cars. "I'll bring coffee in a minute," she says, heading for the kitchen. Pelham watches me strip off the raincoat, shake it lightly, and drape it over the back of a chair. When I sit down to inspect my shoes, Betsy arrives with two cups of coffee. "Miss Landson'll be out in a minute," she says. "Did you want something else? A nice dessert?"

"I don't know." I look past her at Pelham; he's working on the soup. "No. I guess I'm fine."

Betsy turns to look at Pelham too, then whispers to me, "It's his birthday today. He's a nice man—he really is. I don't think it makes any difference that he's so much older than she is."

"No," I say, nodding. "I agree with you. Thanks, Betsy."

The last diners are leaving, pushing arms into raincoats, picking up purses, straightening clothes. A small fellow in a navy chalk-stripe suit, coral shirt, and regimental tie stops alongside my table and hands Betsy a ten-dollar bill. She says, "Thank you," and folds the bill twice, then slips it under her wide patent-leather belt.

The guy turns to me. "What, you staying all night?"

I look at Betsy; she raises her eyebrows and rolls her eyes in a quick half circle. The guy looks at me as if he expects an answer.

"What's that mean? Who're you?"

Ericka slips up behind him before he has a chance to answer. "Hello, Bill," she says. "Did you enjoy dinner?"

Bill grins uncomfortably and catches up with a weak-faced woman who is waiting for him in the aisle.

Three Chicano busboys are noisily stacking dishes in spattered gray rubber trays. Betsy and two waitresses cluster around the cash register, smoking and counting the evening's receipts. Pelham has put his soup on the floor for the dog, which laps hungrily at the dish while Pelham watches, expressionless.

"You dance?" Ericka says, holding her coffee to her lips with both hands. Her eyes seem very bright.

"Not much. You?"

"Sometimes I go to this cowboy bar out on the bypass— Boots, it's called—and dance all night. I love it. It's going to take a while for the Triple A people to get here—maybe we should go out?"

"I don't think so, thanks," I say watching Pelham and the dog. "We've got no cars."

"Oh, I've got a truck in back. Warren can stay here and take care of the accident."

"He'll love that."

"It's O.K." She turns and looks over her shoulder, her elbows still planted on the table. "Hey, Warren. We're going out to Boots; you come out when the wreckers get finished, O.K.?"

Pelham looks up from the dog, then closes his eyes and drops his head maybe a quarter of an inch. He reaches into his coat pocket and pulls out two car keys on a thick yellow string.

"Toss it," Ericka says. He does, and she shoves her chair back, leaping off the floor to make a one-handed catch. "Come on, buzzard," she says, grabbing my arm. "I'll teach you every dance I know. Let me have your keys for Warren, so he can bring your car out."

I give her my keys, and she takes them across the room and hands them to Pelham, then squats down and cups the dog's ears. The dog stops eating long enough to look up and lick its lips, soup drooping off its black jaw. Ericka says something to Pelham, then pats his calf, and they both laugh.

I put on my raincoat. For a minute I leave the collar of the coat turned up, but then decide it looks too stupid that way, and fold it neatly down.

"Let's go, youngster," Ericka calls. "Don't be shy, now."

The truck is parked in a narrow alley in back of the restaurant; the passenger side is so close to the brick wall that I can't even squeeze between the fender and the wall, much less get into the truck. The rain has let up.

"I'm already having a good time," Ericka says. "You want to drive?"

"I don't want to go."

"Listen to the man, will you? The man's got 'Born to Bop' tattooed on his neck and he's talking about retirement. Try this side over here, Slick." She does a little two-step, opening the door for me.


Ericka Landson did a year at Sarah Lawrence, hated it, and went to Georgia Tech, where she took bachelor's and master's degrees in chemical engineering. She delivered the diplomas to her father on a Thursday and bought the building for her restaurant the next day. That was almost a year ago; since then her father died and left her half a million dollars in cash and three times that in land.

"So I married Warren," she says while we're sitting in the cab of the Ford Ranchero waiting for the attendant at the Sinclair station to return with her credit card. "I'd been in love with him since I was a kid. He had a lot more money than I did, so I figured I was safe."

The attendant, a boy with wet blond shoulder-length hair and giant lips, stops in back of the car to write the license number on a charge slip, then pushes the green plastic clipboard in Ericka's window. "I like this weather," he says. "Brings out the bugs. Get me plenty of food for my Gila monsters."

"I want those lizards," Ericka says. "I need them for my menu. The palates of the customers demand monster."

The boy grins messily; the grin distorts his face, drawing the lips tight over a row of brown teeth. "I believe you'd try it, too, Mrs. Landson," he says. "But they gonna come dear."

"And go dearer," Ericka says, passing the clipboard back out the window. "We'll call them Bobby Murtaugh's Gila Flambé—how's that sound?"

"Put a little spinach around the edges too, huh? I love spinach." He tears her carbon of the slip from between his copy and the company's copy and hands her the tissuey sheet. "And some melon balls, all different colors."

"We'll leave the heads on. Let the customers see what they eat."

"They gonna have to pay, though," Bobby Murtaugh says. "Gilas ain't easy to copulate, know what I mean?"

Ericka starts the engine, then holds up her hand in a stiff salute. "Amen. Things is tough all over. Thanks, Bobby."

The kid takes a step back and watches us pull out; when we get to the edge of his station, I turn around and see him crawling around the pump island, hunting for bugs.

The highway heading out of town is the same one Pelham had me on earlier, but the thunderstorms have moved off to the east, where they sit like huge colored cliffs, made visible by the diffused lightning. The rain is so spare we drive with the Ranchero windows open. "I don't feel like dancing," she says after we've listened to the tires on the wet road for a while. "I dance all the time. Dancing makes me sick to my stomach." She turns to look at me in the headlights of a passing truck. "This isn't routine. I made it sound routine, but it isn't."

I shrug, then put my right arm out the window parallel to the ground, palm flat, and play that kid's game of flying the hand as if it were the wing of an airplane.

"Sometimes I hate it out here," Ericka says. "Living out here away from everything." She puts her hand out the window and does the same thing I'm doing, makes the hand swoop and dip in the air by slight twists of her wrist. "Warren helps."

One headlight of the Ranchero is out of whack, aimed upward and off to the side, and as we slip down the highway the light glitters on the telephone wires.

"He reads everything," she says. "He gets papers from all over the country and reads them; he reads books all the time; he subscribes to forty-seven magazines. When he goes to Houston, we have to buy new luggage to bring back all the stuff he buys. He's got three computers at the house—three. You'd think one would be enough."

"More than I've got."

"Ask him for one, he'll give it to you. They're a lot of fun at first." She slows the truck and points out the window at a clay road cutting out into the field on my side of the highway. "That's where you were earlier, when you came to get Melba. Warren has a trailer out there in the woods. We live back toward town."

"How long will it take to untangle the cars? I mean, maybe we should turn around here somewhere?"

"I don't know your name—what's your name?"

"Harold Ohls."

"What are you, French?" There's a Union 76 station ahead, and Ericka slows as we get near. The place is a diner too—white wood siding and a big horizontal window like a lozenge. One of the rounded pieces of glass is badly cracked; struts of two-inch tape have been stuck on to hold it together. "Let's get something inside before we go back, O.K.?"

Ericka orders chicken-fried steak, cream gravy, mashed potatoes, green peas, toast, and iced tea, then looks up from the greasy vinyl-sleeved menu. "What about you?" I order Coke and lemon pie, then nod agreeably when she says, "I always eat late. Want me to put something on the jukebox?"

The waitress, a pudgy woman wearing a purple satin-look bowling shirt with "GlueSlingers" in gold script across the back, gives Ericka a handful of quarters in exchange for some bills and disappears through the swinging door into the kitchen. Ericka pushes the coins into the jukebox, then hovers over the selections, pressing big colored buttons. By the time she gets back to the table, the room is filled with rock and roll. "The original Doctor Funkenstein," she says. "You like it?"

The diner is no bigger than a single-car garage; all three tables have red linoleum tops with rippled chrome strips wrapped around the edges. The chairs don't match the tables or each other, except that everything in the room seems to have pitted tubular chrome legs.

"What's Pelham going to do when he gets to that place and we're missing?" I ask, leaning back so the waitress can deposit my pie, which is perched on thick restaurant china with cordovan triangles in a circle around the rim.

"Warren won't go to Boots—he never does. He'll just go to the house and wait. He's long-suffering—remember that word? He didn't want to marry me, but he'll kill you if you hurt me."

My fork is wrapped tight in a paper napkin. "That's funny. Is he going to kill you if you hurt me?"

"Eat your pie, why don't you?"

"Happily," I say, pulling the fork out of the end of the rolled napkin. One of the tines is missing. I show this to Ericka and then start on the pie. "We're not doing so well, are we?"

"We're not supposed to," she says. "How is it?"

"Pretty good. You want some?"

"Dessert is later." She grabs my free hand and yanks it across the table, then pins it to the red linoleum and bends over to inspect the fingernails. "These are a mess. I can clean them up if you want me to."

"Maybe later."

Her food arrives on a brown oval plate with portion dividers; the dirty-whitish gravy has been liberally applied so that it seeps from one section to the next in an uninterrupted flow. Ericka starts with the toast, plunging the corner of the first piece into the thick pool on top of the potatoes. I finish the pie and then watch her eat. She asks a couple of questions—what do I do, where was I born?—but then she loses interest and concentrates on the food. We go through the rest of the dinner in silence. I'm tired.

"Now," she says, when she's finished. "Now we dance." She tears a couple of napkins trying to get a whole one out of the chrome-faced dispenser screwed to the table just under the window.

"Please—no dancing tonight, O.K.? Tonight let's go home."

She unbuttons one of the pockets of her denim jacket and brings out a five-dollar bill. She puts the money on the table and gets up. "No dancing?" she says, affecting a hurt expression. "You seem like kind of a drip, Harold."

"Thanks."

In the car she says, "We'll have cake with Warren and then you can go, O.K.?"

\*          \*          \*

The house is modern, white as ice and lit up like a circus. My car is parked in the U-shaped drive next to the Mercedes. Warren is inside watching a bank of three Sonys; he's wearing a black silk robe with scarlet piping, and under that he's got on green pajamas. Melba is asleep beside his chair. "You have fun?" he asks his wife.

"We decided to have cake," she says. "You need cake."

"What's on?" I ask, motioning toward the televisions.

"A movie, Tom Snyder, and 'Love Boat.' "

"I got the truck filled up," Ericka says. "Harold didn't have such a great time. We went out to the diner. I don't think he knows what's going on." She sits on the arm of Pelham's chair, facing the televisions. She rubs the back of the dog's neck.

"We don't have any problems," he says. "That's easy enough. Slinky's looking for a companion because I wear out fast."

"Me too," I say. "Sorry."

"I'll get the cake," Ericka says, heading for the kitchen. "I made it myself, Harold. It's really good."

"Her aunt made it. I've had it before," Pelham says when Ericka's out of the room. "It's pitiful looking."

I laugh sympathetically. "What about the cars? How're we going to work that out?"

"Don't worry about the cars."

"I won't if you'll send me something I can give the insurance guy."

"Yeah, well," Pelham says, waving at the sofa, "it just isn't necessary. What you're supposed to do is distract Slinky, but I don't guess you're going to."

I drop my raincoat over a ladder-back chair near the door, then take a seat at one end of the sofa. We sit there in silence watching the televisions. All three of them have the sound on, so that what we hear is a garbled, random mix of talk and music. Pelham pets the dog and looks from one screen to the next, his eyes shifting from left to right with habitual precision. Then all three stations start commercials at the same time—a Pepsi ad, a car ad, and an ad for perfume—and all three look the same: dramatic silvery colors, surreal spaces, glittering sexy women. "Look at that," I say pointing.

"I know," Pelham says, without turning around. "Good."

Ericka comes back into the room carrying a tray on which is a large flat cake stuck full of lighted candles. The icing is sherbety orange. She puts the tray on the coffee table and starts to sing "Happy Birthday," gesturing for me to join in. I'm embarrassed, but I sing along. Pelham hangs on to his composure for a minute, then grins and starts singing. When we finish the chorus, Ericka starts it again, and everybody sings loudly this time, complete with conductor's gestures, vibrato, and three-part homemade harmony. The singing wakes Melba, who yawns and shakes, then steps up to the coffee table waving her big tail and rips a four-inch hole in the cake's fruity icing.

# Trip

HARRY LANG'S company Chevrolet breaks down on the highway fifteen miles outside of Dallas. He gets the car to a small old town called Cummings, leaves it at the gas station, and calls Fay, a woman he met at a corporate sensitivity workshop in San Antonio last year and the reason for his trip. They have spent the last six months having long and wistful and detailed telephone conversations on the company WATS line, talking about everything that they can think of, even business, and sometimes nothing at all, just sitting on opposite ends of the line, allowing the delicate contact between them a few extra minutes; finally, they agreed that he should come for a visit.

Now, from the garage in Cummings, he tells her that he will not get into town until the next day, because of his car. Two hours later he's at the Starlight Motor Hotel watching television when there's a knock on the door. It's Fay, standing on the other side of the screen, fidgeting with her shirt cuffs. "May I come in?" she says.

He pushes open the screen and steps back so she can enter the room, which is small, panelled, dark. It's dusk; the only lights outside are the star-shaped motel sign and the yellow neon ringing the eaves of the buildings.

Fay sits on the bed. "It's real clammy in here."

He clicks on the table lamp. The base of the lamp is a bronze cowgirl on horseback twirling a lariat. "You look wonderful," he says. "How'd you get away?"

"Easy," she says. "I can't leave you alone. After an hour I decided I should come to you. You got a Bufferin?" She looks around the room. "What's that music?"

He listens, but doesn't hear any music. Fay is thirty-five, small, and pretty. She's wearing white shorts, a Polo dress shirt with a tiny round-tipped collar, and brown-striped espadrilles. She bounces on the bed, testing it.

Harry opens his suitcase, brings out a bottle of Anacin. "Will these do?"

She picks two pills out of his palm and points toward the open bathroom door. "Use your water?"

He tucks in his shirttail and uses the window as a mirror to fix his hair. When she comes out of the bath, she's patting her face with a small coral towel that has "Starlight" stitched into it in awkward brown script. "You want to eat something?" she says.

They go in her car to the Spur station to check on his Chevrolet. The station owner, a mechanic named Gorky, is on his back under the car. "Lucky you don't live out here," he says. "Toss me a five-eighths. Second drawer."

Harry finds the socket the mechanic wants and drops it into his palm.

"Don't get into Dallas much," Gorky says. "I don't mind, though. We got fishing and women. It doesn't matter really— for an old son like me the fish don't bite and the women don't either. You see a lock washer out there somewhere, about so big?" Again the hand shoots out from under the car, thumb and forefinger spread.

Harry hands him a washer, but the mechanic drops it; when he tries to turn over onto his stomach, he can't make it because the Malibu's not jacked up enough. Finally, he says, "Crap," and rolls out from under the car. He sits up, his back against the door, and wipes his hands on a red rag, then rubs the rag around on his puffed, stubble-covered face.

"So, what do you think?" Harry asks. "About the car?"

"I'm happy you're spending the night is what I think." Gorky tells a kid who looks like a young TV actor to watch the gas islands, then motions toward a primered GMC pickup with a bed full of tractor tires. "I can let you borrow this one, but maybe you don't need it since you got this woman here."

"He hasn't got me yet," Fay says. She loosens her thin leather belt, then refastens it, taking it up a notch and centering the buckle above her fly.

The mechanic stares at her for a minute, then laughs. "Anyway, I'll have yours tomorrow. Maybe one or so, huh?"

"Fine," Harry says.

"Go to Nick's if you want to eat." Gorky scrubs at his palm with the rag. "I mean, if you don't go in town. It's just up here a mile. Good chow. Dottie get you set?"

Dottie is Mrs. Kiwi, the owner of the Starlight, a tiny woman with a barrel chest and a dwarf's face. This afternoon she was wearing a fuchsia muscle shirt.

"I got a nice room," Harry says. "Thanks."

"I told her about you," Gorky says, waving a hand at a circling bug. "Me and her's kinda, you know"—he takes a long time thinking of the word, getting it right—"acquainted."


At Nick's Sandwich Shop Harry orders a Kingburger and Fay has a salad with Green Goddess dressing. Afterward they go to the Odeon Theatre to see the movie. There's a crowd of a dozen people out front, but there's no one in the box office. Harry stares at Fay's eyes, which are mismatched in a becoming way. Two teen-agers in line behind them are talking about a girl named Rose Ann they both seem to be in love with.

"I saw my neighbors making it in the driveway," Fay says, bending to look past him at the teen-agers. "I watched out the bedroom window."

Harry sticks his hands in his pants pockets, then brings them out again and folds his arms, admiring the crispness and neatness of Fay's clothes.

"This woman does the dishes in a bikini, you know what I mean? Then she's out in the driveway moaning like a cow. I envied her."

The kids are listening; they've gotten very quiet. Fay points a finger at him. "I wear a fair bikini myself"—she pauses for emphasis, wagging the finger—"but mostly on the beach."

Two teen-age couples join the line. Harry says, "Uh-huh."

Fay puts her hand on his side, on his ribs. "Last Christmas I helped Melody—that's her name—last year I helped her build shelves in the downstairs bath, a couple of little four-inch shelves, nothing big. Then, in June, what do you think I found in there?" She pauses and looks at him triumphantly, as if he'll never guess. "It was the saw, the electric saw, tucked in alongside the toilet. If it was me, I'd have had the thing back in its place before it stopped turning."

He folds one hand inside the other and starts to crack the knuckles, but she frowns, anticipating the sound. "Oh, sorry," he says, and puts the hands back into his pockets.

"No," she says. "I want to hear them. Go on."

"I don't think so," he says, shaking his head.

"She plays this music all the time. You're trying to sleep, or read, or sit in the tub—sometimes I spend a whole afternoon in the tub—and here comes Nat King Cole into your life."

The kids have started their conversation again. They're brothers, and they're trying to be sensible about this thing with Rose Ann, but they're having trouble deciding who's going to get her.

"I like music," Fay says. "Don't get me wrong. I even like Nat King Cole, once every forty years or so." She digs into her boxy purse and then turns around holding a Polaroid snapshot of a man in a bathing suit. "This is my husband, Tim. I thought you ought to see him." She pokes the picture at Harry. "Take a look."

The man in the picture is overweight. He doesn't have much hair, and his legs are peculiarly thin for the rest of his body. He's standing alongside a Buick sedan holding a hose with water running out the end. Behind him in the picture there's a two-car garage and, off to the extreme left, the shoulder and leg of another man, also in bathing trunks.

"He looks fine to me," Harry says, handing the snapshot back to her. "He's a good-looking man."

She takes the picture and holds it very close to her face. "You think so?" She moves the picture up and down, examining her husband. "He does have eyes," she says, snapping open the purse and dropping the photograph inside. "I think I married the eyes, really. That's the first thing I noticed about you—eyes."

A kid on a girl's bicycle rides up beside them. "You all on line?" he asks. When Fay says they are, the kid says, "You want to give me a cut? I'm only ten."

Fay nods, so the kid gets off the bike, puts it down on the sidewalk where he's standing, and gets into line.

"I love kids, don't you?" she whispers. "I don't like to think about not having any. I suppose it's my fault. You don't mind me talking, do you?"

"I guess not," Harry says.

In the flickering light of the theatre marquee Fay's face is all white planes and sharp shadows; she looks like somebody vulnerable in a forties' movie poster. Her hair is tight to her scalp in dark knots.

"Maybe you should call the police or something," Harry says. "About this woman."

"Not on your life, Buster." She pulls a thread away from one of the belt loops of her shorts. "Melody's one of the highlights of my life. A role model for me." She snaps the thread off her waist. "Besides, she's gorgeous to look at. The husband ain't bad either."

Harry reaches for the thread, which she has rolled into a tiny ball between her fingers.

"He runs the Bonanza out by us. He likes me, but I don't have the guts to sleep with him. I guess I don't want to."

One of the brothers has bumped Harry several times trying to hear Fay's story. He says something to the other one and the brothers both laugh.

Fay glances at the boy. "He's a handsome kid, isn't he?" she says, loud enough for the boy to hear. "Maybe he needs some attention."

"Excuse me?" the boy says. "Were you talking to me?"

"What?" she says, as if she's been interrupted. "Oh. No, I was talking to Harry—this is Harry."

"Howdy," Harry says.

"Howdy?" the brothers say to each other, exchanging silly looks.

She twists back toward the ticket booth. Looking over her shoulder, she says, "Rose Ann probably loves you both, you're so cute." She pulls Harry forward in line. "Howdy? Oh, never mind. Let's talk about something else—are you hot?"

"No, I'm O.K."

"I perspire," she says, opening her arms and glancing at her chest. "I admit it, Harry. And I won't wear those teeny satin tops, those thin ones you see everywhere." She sighs, then smiles and straightens her blouse.

"I don't think we'll ever get in here," Harry says.

"I mean, I could if I wanted to. And plum lips and metallic underpants—you interested?" She laughs and fingers some of the curls over her ear. "It's not that I wasn't trained, you know. I was trained just like everybody else. I can do the business—here, I'll show you." She wraps an arm around his neck, moistens her lips with her tongue, then tightens her grip and pulls his face close to hers, her eyes flashing.

"Hey," Harry says, tugging free. "That's pretty good."

The line is moving. They're halfway to the ticket window. Three boys with big portable radios go by, heading for the box office. The radios are tuned to the same station and the area in front of the theatre is suddenly full of Mexican polka music. "What are you guys doing?" Fay shouts. "The line's back here."

At the Starlight after the movie Fay gets into Harry's bed. "I'm going to stay all night, O.K.?" She twists around under the spread for a minute and produces her shorts and sandals, which she deposits on the floor by the telephone. "I think I'll keep this on for now," she says, pinching her shirt and tugging it a couple of times.

"Great," he says.

Harry's up first, at noon. He takes a shower in the metal stall, being as quiet as he can, but when he comes out Fay is gone and Mrs. Kiwi is banging on the screen. "What do you people think I'm running here, a bordello?"

Harry jumps. "Just a minute, I'm coming."

He just gets his pants on before she's in the open door brandishing her passkey. Her muscle shirt is cranberry this time.

She sighs and rolls the key between her fingers. "I've been running the Starlight twenty-two years and I've seen it all. Her creeping out of here like that—you should be ashamed."

He points toward the parking lot. "We're together."

Mrs. Kiwi pockets the key in the stretch trousers she's wearing. "Yes. I see that." She nods gravely, then puts on a grin and pats Harry's arm. "I understand perfectly, Mr. Lang."

"We work together. I mean, she works here in Dallas, and I work in Louisiana, but for the same company."

"Sure," Mrs. Kiwi says, patting more solicitously than before. She makes a sucking noise between her teeth, then laughs. "There's a lot of that around is what I understand. More and more." She shades her eyes and stares through the white dust at her office, then puts her fists on her hips and looks at his bare feet.

Fay pulls the screen door open. "Harry? What's going on?"

"Nothing, darling," Mrs. Kiwi says, shooing Fay with the backs of her hands. "You go on outside before the Baptists see you. Maybe we all ought to go outside." She turns back to Harry. "I was a girl myself—fourteen brothers. You don't get so many families like that anymore, what with the economy and the state of things. All of them died, too. One after another. I had dead brothers all over this country for a while. I would've had a big family if Mr. Kiwi, God rest his soul, hadn't passed on so sudden. That's a long time ago now, forty years." She snorts and does a little twist with her head, then says, "Well, now, that's about enough of that." She reaches into her pocket and gets a folded piece of note paper. "A.D. called earlier on and said the car's gonna be late. I've got the number here if you want to dial him up."

She shakes the paper at Harry. There's a telephone number in blue ballpoint in one corner, but the rest of the sheet is covered with foreign words and phrases. The words "buena" and "bueno" appear repeatedly in block letters at the center of the sheet. "Maybe I'll give him a call," Harry says.

Mrs. Kiwi wipes at the perspiration stuck in her eyebrows, then looks at her fingers. "I think you kids better come on for some lunch—I mean, once you get straightened away." She points over her shoulder with a thumb.

"Let me check with her," Harry says. "O.K.?"

She nods and turns to look at a passing long-haul truck that has huge limes painted on its side. "But you're welcome." She nods several more times, her crinkled gray hair springing in the noon sun, then abruptly starts off toward the office, kicking up dust. "Got biscuits," she says over her shoulder. "Plenty of biscuits."

Fay brings a slimline briefcase when she comes back to the room. She undresses and quickly showers, then puts on a slip and a white shirtwaist dress that clings to her legs when she moves. Walking back and forth at the foot of the bed, she says, "I think I'd better call Tim soon." She looks at the nails on her left hand, holding the hand very close to her face and popping the tips of the fingers out from under her thumb. The nails are the flat orange of flesh-colored stockings. "I don't want him to think I had a wreck and died on the highway. I want him to know where I am." She sits on the bed, keeping the telephone between them. Her hair's wet. "I mean, he still likes me and everything."

"He should," Harry says.

"Damn right," she says. "I like him, don't I?"

Harry goes into the bathroom while she calls Tim. The conversation is quick; Fay's part is full of half sentences and short silences in which he can hear her flicking her fingers.

When they drive out, Mrs. Kiwi is behind her counter, and Gorky is there too, playing with some kind of phonograph record, spinning it on a pencil. He waves. His GMC is parked up close to the back of the office, mostly out of sight.

"I feel like going somewhere," Fay says. "Somewhere pretty. I wonder if they have a zoo out here. We could get hot dogs—you like hot dogs? We could feed the seals."

Harry points out the car window at a one-story shack that has a dozen glittery brown vinyl booths piled up on the porch and PEACOCK CAFE stenciled in silver on the door. "We could go there."

"I don't want to go there, Harry. I want to go somewhere where there are seals, but I guess there aren't any seals out here. I probably should've waited for you in town. You don't seem to be working at this."

He taps on the dashboard and looks at the scenery for a minute; the road is lined with empty lots full of tires, hundreds of automobile tires. "I agree," he finally says.

"What do you agree?" The dress is pulled over her knees, bunched at her thighs, fanned awkwardly around her on the seat.

"Why don't we just get a burger?"

She steers the car into a gas station where a guy in a business suit is looking at a small John Deere tractor. Fay smiles and says, "Excuse me," out the car window to the guy, and he has to step up on the pump island to let her through. "Looks like he sells rats, doesn't he?" she whispers.

They go back to Nick's. She wants to sit at the counter, so they get stools between a huge man wearing bib-style overalls and a kid who's picking his teeth while he waits for food. The big guy takes a look at them when they sit down, then goes back to his smothered chicken.

Nick's is sixty feet deep and twenty feet wide. On one side it's a low counter and a kitchen, on the other a row of wooden booths. In between are a few school cafeteria tables.

"Well, so tell me about yourself," Fay says after they've ordered hamburgers. "You eat here often?"

"Here come the burgers," he says, pointing at the cook who's slipping meat patties on two fat buns.

There's a whine from the doorway, and a girl in an electric wheelchair comes in. Everyone seems to know her. She slaps left hands with some of the customers as she steers herself to the back. She has shoulder-length hair, dark skin, puffy lips, big eyes. She's wearing a soft-blue pullover. The waiters, kids in jeans and short-sleeved shirts, dote on her, bring silverware and napkins and water, and stay to talk. She teases them with sexy laughs and white smiles. The waiters stand by her table, straddle the oak chairs. Harry catches the girl's eyes once, between the turned backs, and she stares at him as if they were old, loving friends.

"O.K.," Fay says. "This isn't so marvelous. No more burger for me." She drops her hamburger on the paper plate and shoves it away from her, accidentally knocking it off the counter.

The big guy next to Harry says, "Jesus." He pushes himself up on the counter and peers behind it to see where the hamburger landed. "Hey, Manny. Take a look." He points toward the floor.

The old man doing the cooking shuffles over, picks up the hamburger, and stands right in front of Harry. "What's wrong here? You get a bad one?"

"It's fine," Fay says. "It really is good, but we've got an emergency." She pushes off the stool and opens her purse.

"Look, lady. If it's bad, just say so. We get a bad one now and again."

She puts a five-dollar bill on the counter. "No," she says, smiling. "It's good. You ready, Harry?"

Manny picks up the five and holds it out to Harry. "Take it," he says, waving the hamburger back and forth between Fay and himself. "I can understand this. Take the money."

The guy in the overalls wipes his face on the sleeve of his T-shirt, leaving a strip of coleslaw like a green worm on his shoulder. He and Harry slide off their stools at the same time and the guy is at least half a foot taller. He looks at Fay, then plucks the bill out of Manny's hand and puts it in hers. "You heard the man," he says.

Outside, Fay goes straight for her car. They drive to the Starlight without talking. She looks determined and lovely steering with one hand, propping her head on the other. Mrs. Kiwi is on her knees in the tiny horseshoe-shaped flower bed by the office; she goes up like a squirrel in the foot-high tulips and waves as Fay and Harry go under the portico.

The bed in Harry's room has been made and there are new towels in the bath; the air conditioner, which he left running, has been turned off, so the room is stuffy. Fay stands in front of the open door, her legs dark against the light fabric of the skirt; she's fiddling with her pale sunglasses. Harry sits on the edge of the bed and looks at the knees of his pants. She opens her purse, looks inside, closes it again, then comes away from the door and stands in front of him.

"I don't know how to explain all this," he says, smoothing the skirt at her hip with his fingers. Mrs. Kiwi is coming across the oyster-shell lot swinging a plastic bag full of biscuits.

Fay slips her glasses into place. "When's your birthday?" she says. "I want to get you something nice for your birthday."

# Pool Lights

THERE ARE things that cannot be understood—things said at school, at the supermarket, or in this case by the pool of the Santa Rosa Apartments on a hazy afternoon in midsummer. A young woman wearing pleated white shorts and a thin gauze shirt open over her bikini top introduces herself as Dolores Prince and says, "You have a pretty face." Automatically, you smile and say, "Thank you," but, looking up at her, wonder why she selected that particular word, that adjective.

She is small, already tan, delicate but not frail. Her dark hair is in a braid tight against her scalp. "I mean it," she says, dropping her canvas tote on the pea-gravel concrete apron of the pool. "It's all soft and pink." She steps out of the shorts and snaps the elastic around the leg openings of her swimsuit.

"It's the shirt." You pluck at the collar of the faded red alligator pullover, then point at the sky. "Bounces off the shirt."

"You're at the school, aren't you?" she says. "You're the swimming teacher?"

"Two years, yes. How did you know?"

"Mrs. Scree told me. She tells me everything."

Alongside the edge of the pool, ten feet away, Dolores spreads a black towel laced with salmon, peach, and gray-green flowers, then pulls things out of the tote—a tall red plastic glass and a can of Sprite, a pack of cigarettes in a leather case with a lighter pouch, a rolled copy of *Cosmopolitan*, a ribbed brown squeeze bottle of suntan cream, a thin silver radio the size of a wallet, a pair of square-lensed sunglasses with clear frames; she arranges these items around her towel, on the perimeter of her new territory, at the ready.

"It isn't the shirt," she says after she's in position, on her back on the towel, her knees up, facing the open pagoda next to the pool. "I know enough about color to know that the shirt would turn you brown, not pink."

"Oh." The sureness in her voice is startling. "Then maybe it's the clouds?"

"Clouds are white," she says without opening her eyes.

She's probably not right about the shirt, and she's wrong about the clouds—they're undefined and sulphur yellow.

"You new at Santa Rosa?" she asks, wiping the backs of her lotion-slick hands on her belly.

"I'm in 281 over here." You gesture sideways across the courtyard in the direction of your apartment. "Two months, but I don't come out much—out here, I mean."

She pushes up on an elbow and twists to look. "That's too bad. I'm out here all the time."

"You like it."

"Who doesn't?" she says. She sits up and spins around on her rump, wrapping her long dark arms around her knees. Her fingernails are pointed and chocolaty.

Your sprung metal chair rocks a little. "I imagine all these people looking out their windows at me. It makes me nervous."

"Oh, you can't think about that," Dolores says. She scans the buildings surrounding the pool. "If they look, they look—who gets hurt?" She says this with a coy smile, as if she suspects you watch poolside parties from the apartment window. She wipes more lotion on her thighs. "Some Saturday afternoons in summer the sunbathers are irresistible, I guess, especially through a slit in the curtains."

"I look. Sometimes I start to watch a ball game on TV and

then end up watching people out here all afternoon. Don't you do that?"

She adjusts the thick braid at the back of her head. "Not really. I just come out."

"I like watching them talk to each other. The way they move around, gesturing, making faces—it's interesting."

"I know what you mean. And the women aren't bad either."


Because the floral brocade furniture the landlady had to offer was unacceptable, the apartment looks almost vacant—as if someone is moving out. Buying a round card table at Wilson's seemed dumb, but now that it's in place in the bedroom, it seems right. It's sturdy and large enough to hold the twelve-inch Sony, with room left to eat or work. The two pinkish-brown steel folding chairs that came with the table are uncomfortable but serviceable. The only other furniture in the bedroom is a queen-size bed pulled out into the room on the diagonal so it floats, like a great lozenge, on the harvest-gold carpet.

At midnight Friday you go into the small living–dining room and click on the overhead light. There, in neat low stacks along three walls, is the summer project: piles of *Time, Rolling Stone, Sports Illustrated, Money, Road & Track, Stereo Review, American Photographer, Skin Diver,* and *Vogue.* All from American Educational Services at a terrific discount. When they started piling up unread, they became a collection. After better than a year, the subscriptions got cancelled. And after two moves—one across country, one across town—the project was born: Look through the collection, maybe save an article or two, a peculiar picture, a curious headline, and toss the rest. Reading every word seemed at first a possibility, but finally the idea was exhausting.

The project isn't far along. The first thing was to strip the

covers off all the issues of *Time* and put them together with
Acco fasteners. Then the same for the other magazines. These
"books" of covers are on the floor between two natural-wood
deck chairs bought at an import store. The chairs and the covers
and the magazines are all that's in the living room except for a
huge pencil cactus, easily six feet high, which stands just inside
the sliding door to a three-by-eight-foot balcony.

Picking up copies of *American Photographer* and the latest
*Vogue* in the stack, dated January 1981, you take these into the
bedroom, put them on top of the telephone book next to the
TV, then go back and water the pencil cactus, straighten the
pile of *Road & Track*—looking at the contents of the topmost
issue to see what cars were road-tested that month—and switch
off the light on the way to the kitchen for cornflakes to take into
the bedroom. The first issue of *American Photographer* has lots
of small ads. The featured pictures seem to be of the edges of
things—buildings, cars, furniture, streets; another portfolio, in
color, is of women's backs, taken from down low so that the
backgrounds are all blue sky. Some of the pictures are attractive,
but fooling with them seems like too much trouble, so you push
the magazine back onto the stack and take the cereal to the
kitchen, put it in the sink, and run the faucet until the bowl is
full of gray water.

Undressing in the bathroom, you watch the mirror above the
lavatory, then drop the clothes in a tall plastic basket kept in the
hall closet for outgoing laundry. You floss, thinking of the den-
tist. His assistants wear matching Cheryl Tiegs jeans and T-
shirts; he pipes Willie Nelson's "Stardust" into the cubicle; he
makes jokes about the color of teeth, and he talks to the mouth
when he's working on it. "How's Mr. Mouth doing today?" or
"Would Mr. Mouth like a club sandwich?" All this and he tries
not to punish. Still, you avoid him.

At one-thirty a movie called *Berlin Correspondent*, starring
Dana Andrews, starts on Channel 17.

\*     \*     \*

At noon on Saturday, Dolores is already arranged flat on her stomach near the deep end of the pool, almost directly below your window.

She waves. The phone rings. Your brother in Taos wants to know what has been said to so seriously alienate your father. You tell him you love your father. He says he knows that, but what was said? You just woke up and don't remember. He urges that the family try to understand the father. "He wants us to think he's wonderful."

"He is."

"He's sad. I'm trying to help."

The glistening sliver of Dolores is visible through the curtains. She's wearing a dark Danskin. "I didn't want to upset him. I tried to talk to him. I tried to tell him to take it easy."

"Just be sensible about it. We've got to stop jumping all over him."

This view of the situation is not as correct as he assumes it to be, but when told this, he does not back away from his assertion. You promise to think about it, and ask what is going on in Taos, to which he replies, "Nothing." You agree to call him later, after breakfast.

"Talk to you," he says, and hangs up.

In the kitchen you turn on the coffee, then fill a pan with water to poach eggs, and put the pan on the stove.

Later, when the eggs are ready, shaking gently on crisp muffin halves, you carry plate, flatware, coffee, and napkin back into the bedroom. Getting the one-bedroom apartment overlooking the pool was lucky—so Mrs. Scree said when she agreed to show the less expensive one-bedroom, which overlooked the Santa Rosa parking lot and the laundromat. "The drain backs up sometimes," she said. "I gotta tell you so when it happens you won't go yelling at me." It is hard to imagine—yelling at Mrs. Scree:

after twenty-four years, by her account, managing apartments, she knows how to handle dissatisfied tenants.

By one o'clock Dolores has been joined by several other tenants: a balloonish young husband and his skinny wife, a single girl named Beverly who works at Sears, a plump woman in an emerald terry-cloth slit-to-the-thigh bandeau-top sundress, an older man named Wilkins, whose chest is covered with bright silver hair, and on the fringe of the group, standing near the corner of the pool in conversation with a young couple who are obviously apartment hunting, Mrs. Scree, dressed in her usual dark-blue slacks and sleeveless flowered blouse.

You stand at the window for a few minutes, watching the party. When Mrs. Scree finishes with the apartment hunters, she pulls a long aluminum pole from behind the redwood pagoda and starts to scoop multicolored miniature plastic bowling pins out of the pool. She is not very good at this, and after she makes several passes at a bright-red pin painted with an Air Force insignia, Wilkins pushes himself out of his lawn chair and, with a flourish, wrests the pole from her. The others are immediately drawn into the action, giving directions, cracking jokes, pointing and laughing as Wilkins tries to capture the bowling pin. He walks to the long side of the pool and eases the pole into the water so its small net dips just under the pin. When he tries to lift the pole, the bowling pin topples off the frame of the net and slides away on the surface of the clear water. Everybody laughs. Even Mrs. Scree, who ordinarily laughs only at her own jokes, punches her tenant playfully on the arm, points at the floating pin, and laughs heartily. Dolores, who sat up when Wilkins took the pole, turns away from the pool, shades her eyes with her hand, and with the forefinger of her other hand beckons you downstairs.

You jerk the two edges of the curtains together, lapping one over the other, certain that she couldn't actually see, that she was just guessing. Getting back into bed, head wrapped in a towel because of wet hair from the shower, you pull up the sheet, lie there, and leaf through the magazines.

Later Dolores catches you by the mailboxes, says she wants to go for a drive, and hustles off to her apartment to change. The afternoon is hot.

"You hid earlier," she says, getting into the car. "I'm ashamed of you."

"I almost came out when Mr. Wilkins was going for the pin."

"I signalled you."

"It was hard to resist."

The interstate takes you fifty miles to a small coast town, Conklin, population 8,528. It's almost five o'clock.

"Let's buy something," Dolores says. "There's a market. Let's get shrimp to take back."

"What's special about shrimp?"

"Nothing." She's got a wraparound skirt over her thin plum suit and she looks sexy.

The butcher is busy with a customer who looks as if she has never had anything but shrimp in her life—crisp clothes and crisper hair. The butcher holds up a half dozen lamb chops on a piece of white paper for her, and at the same time nods at Dolores to indicate that she's next. Dolores squats in front of his case to get a closer look at the shrimp, which are half-buried in ice. The woman wants to inspect the chops; she tells the butcher to put them on top of the counter for a minute. The clock says it's five of five. The butcher drops the paper onto the case and the chops teeter for a second, then tip over the edge and slip one by one down the sloped front, piling up at the lower edge of the glass.

The woman isn't upset. She bends over and sticks her face

very close to the meat. Abruptly she straightens and says to the butcher, who is standing behind the case with his hands on his hips, staring at the ceiling fan, "I don't know, Carl. What do you think? They don't smell too good."

"Lady," the butcher says, moving toward the end of the case and wiping his hands on his apron. "They ain't supposed to be gardenias."

The woman turns. "Sir?" she says. "Would you help me with these chops? Would you take a look?"

"I will," Dolores says, popping up from her crouch in front of the shrimp. She takes a close look at the lamb chops, picks up one and squeezes it, then pokes it against her nose. The butcher comes out in front, pulls the paper off the top of the case, and stacks the other chops on his hand again.

"What do you think?" the woman says.

"Yeah," the butcher says. "What do you think?"

"I think they're fine," Dolores says, placing her chop on top of the others. Then she whispers, "Let's get out. It's dog food."

After a wrong turn trying to get back to the interstate, you end up on the old highway, a two-lane job, but it's got signs pointing toward home and Dolores says she wants to stick with it. An hour later the terrain begins to look familiar.

"See. That wasn't so bad."

She's right. With twilight the temperature goes down fast, and the old highway is more interesting to drive, because of the towns, roadside signs, and animals.

"Better than trees," she says.

At the crossroad that goes back to town she sees a motel, one of those old places with two-room brick bungalows back off the road in a cluster of pines. Its neon sign says GOLDEN GABLES MOTOR LODGE in purple, VACANCY in pink, and BASS POND in lime green.

Dolores points at the sign. "You game?" she says. "I've never been in one of these. Let's try it."

"I don't think so." But you brake and pull over next to the entrance anyway, in case Dolores is dead set on seeing the inside.

She is. The office is an Airstream trailer jacked up on cement blocks. The registration desk is a free-standing panelled bar with a thick black pillow of padding around the edge. A man shorter than a ten-year-old boy pushes through a beaded curtain and walks across the small room as if he has a spring on his right foot.

"Can we see a room?" Dolores says.

Only his shoulders and head stick up over the bar. He looks at Dolores, then pokes a knobby forefinger into the collar of his starched white shirt. He tilts his head when he talks. "You staying long? A night? A week?" His voice is high, nasal.

"We don't know," Dolores says, grinning. "First we want to look at the room."

"How come you don't try in town? They got everything in town. Television, food, Magic Fingers—the works." He crawls up onto a barstool with a swivel seat.

"No bass pond."

"Right," Dolores says. "No bass pond—where is it, anyway?"

"You drove over it coming in. Sucker dried up on us last summer."

"How much per night?" Dolores asks.

"You going to use the kitchen?"

"Not tonight."

At this the little man catapults himself off the swivel stool and limps to the front of the trailer, where he steps up on a wooden box draped with a yellow rubber car mat. He looks out the small round window. "This your car?" he says. "Registered in the county?"

"We live in town," Dolores says. "We just want to see what the rooms are like."

He hops off the box and looks hard at Dolores. Sweat as thick as Vaseline is collecting on his neck just above the tight collar. "You bring your tiger-skin drawers?"

"Let's go, Dolores. I don't think the man wants to rent a room."

"Oh, I want to rent one, all right." He's cleaning the finger-nails on one hand with the thumbnail of the other. "Sure I do. I want to rent twenty. Just don't much want to show one, see what I mean?"


On Sunday at half past ten in the morning, going down to pick up the paper—which the deliverywoman has gotten in the habit of placing, unrolled, on the third step up from the bottom of the stairs—just out of bed, wearing jeans and a terry-cloth bathrobe, hair sticking out in all directions, you meet Dolores. She's coming around the corner of the building carrying a cream-colored plastic garbage bag full of sharp-edged objects— boxes, it looks like—that give the bag a set of curiously geometric surfaces.

"That was fun last night," she says. "That guy was really short, wasn't he?"

The morning light in the apartment courtyard is strangely cheerful. The palms around the pagoda shift a little with the wind.

"Sure was." The newspaper slips down two steps.

She laughs and props her bag against the side of the stairs. "Housekeeping," she says, pointing to the bag. "Maybe we can get together later?"

"Sure."

Mrs. Scree follows her dog out of her apartment and, seeing tenants in conversation, rumbles across the courtyard. "Dolores, I forgot to tell you yesterday that they're coming to do your carpet tomorrow."

"Finally. That's great."

"And what's he dressed up for? That your samurai outfit?" She laughs.

"We're discussing cocktails by the pool this evening," Dolores says, smiling lavishly.

"A new romance right here in the complex," Mrs. Scree says. She acts as if she knew it all along. "Well, I'll keep Raymond inside if that'll help—he's such an old gossip." Raymond is her husband.

Then Wilkins backs out of his apartment in tennis shorts and flip-flops. He's got a thick purple towel bunched around his neck, and his sunglasses are balanced on top of his head. In one hand he has a tall glass of tomato juice and in the other a portable radio.

"There you are," Mrs. Scree shouts. "With weather like this I expected you out at dawn. Now, where's that dog got to? Here Spinner, here boy." She crouches down to look across the court for her dog.

Wilkins waves his tomato juice and then points at one of the squat palms around the pagoda. "I think he's in there," Wilkins says. "I see his tail."

"So do you want breakfast or not?" Dolores says.

"Don't go too far, honey," Mrs. Scree says without turning around. She falls forward on her hands and knees, trying to look under the sagging fronds of the palms; she's wearing something like boxer shorts under her black knit slacks. "Making breakfast is serious."

"I had breakfast already, thanks."

Mrs. Scree is crawling about on the grass at the foot of the stairs, occasionally dropping her head to the ground to check another opening in the foliage. Wilkins drags a recently painted steel lounger out into the morning sun, aligning it for balanced distribution of the tanning rays.

"Just let me get set up here, Peggy," he says, "then I'll go in there after him."

"Don't be silly, Fred," Mrs. Scree says. She pushes herself upright on her knees and, with some effort, gets to her feet. "He'll be out of there the instant I go back inside."

An older woman who lives in the apartment directly beneath yours comes out dressed as if for church.

"Good morning, Mrs. Talbot," Mrs. Scree says, brushing at the whitish stains on her pants. "How's the knee these days?"

"Much better, thank you," Mrs. Talbot says. "The hot-water bottle you gave me helps a good deal."

"Your neighbor here been behaving himself?" Mrs. Scree says.

The older woman nods and says, "I'm Irene Talbot." She switches her purse and gloves around, then extends her hand. "I'm very pleased to finally meet you; after all the times we've said hello, I feel as if I already know you." She turns to the landlady. "He's quiet as a mouse, although with my hearing I'm not sure I'd know if he wasn't. Anyway, it's very reassuring to know that there's a man nearby, in case something should happen."

"And a man with such a fine face," Dolores says.

"Now that you mention it," Mrs. Talbot says, eyeing Dolores. "The face and skull *are* very good." She smiles faintly and toys with her gloves.

"A new romance," Mrs. Scree says, winking broadly, making her face a parody of collusion.

"Morning, Mrs. Talbot," Wilkins shouts from his place by the pool. "You look mighty handsome today."

"Thank you," Mrs. Talbot says. Then, when Wilkins turns away, she grins at Mrs. Scree.

Backing up the stairs, you say, "I think I'll go on up and read this," then flap the newspaper a couple of times at no one in particular. "A pleasure meeting you, Mrs. Talbot."

Mrs. Talbot nods, gives a short wave of her gloves to Mrs. Scree and Dolores, and walks off toward the parking lot.

"Well, I'll leave you two alone," Mrs. Scree says. "Raymond's going to need breakfast soon and I just wanted to get Spinner done." She calls the dog again, and Spinner, so named because he likes to chase his tail, pops his head out from under the edge of the pagoda. "There he is," Mrs. Scree shouts. "Come here, Spinner. Right now."

The dog wipes his nose on his paws but does not budge from the spot under the building.

"Don't forget tonight," Dolores says. She hoists the milky plastic bag onto her shoulder. "He's so pretty," she says to the landlady. "It's embarrassing."

"What's tonight?" Mr. Wilkins says, propping his chin on the carefully folded towel at the end of the lounger.

"Never you mind, Fred," Mrs. Scree says. "You weren't invited. This is a private affair."

Wilkins frowns, and Dolores says, "Oh, sure you are, Mr. Wilkins. We're having cocktails by the pool at six."

"Cocktails?" he says, blinking furiously.

Mrs. Scree pads across the concrete and playfully pushes his face back into the towel. "Fred doesn't need any cocktails today," she says. She reaches behind her, under the tail of her blouse, to scratch her back.

"We could even have a barbecue," Dolores says, following Mrs. Scree. "If we had anything to barbecue."

"I'm going to barbecue that dog if he doesn't come over here right now," Mrs. Scree says. "And tell your young man not to come dressed that way—he looks like Karl Wallenda."

Inside, you drop the newspaper on the kitchen cabinet, go into the bedroom, take off the jeans and the bathrobe, and get back into bed.

\*      \*      \*

The telephone wakes you. "Look," your brother says, "I want to clarify something. I'm not accusing you of being stupid and insensitive about Father, I'm just reporting what it was like there last week. How he sees things. It seems to me at his age we've got to think about that—I mean, how *he* sees things. You know what I'm saying?"

"Yes." Your arm is numb and tingling.

"I'm not saying you're not right. He can be a butt sometimes."

"Uh-huh."

"But that's not even the point. The point is, you have a tendency to jump on him whether he's being a butt or not. I mean, if he wants to play Lord High Executioner, where's the harm?"

"I don't want to humor him." With all the curtains closed, it's dark in the apartment. "Listen, what time is it?"

"Three," he says. "About." He shouts to his wife for the time, then says, "Three-thirty. I didn't mean humor him. It's just that he isn't always wrong."

"Sure."

"Talk to you," he says.

You toss the receiver at its cradle, miss, shove it into place, reach across the table to switch on the television, and then, when the picture appears, twist quickly through the channels until there's a movie. When the sound is fixed so the actors can just barely be heard, you hunch forward in the metal folding chair, naked, elbows on knees, flexing the left hand and watching. At the commercial you make toast and pour orange juice into a large glass of ice, then go back to the bedroom.

There are shouts from the courtyard. Dolores and the others from yesterday, along with a few more tenants, are gathered in a loose group at one end of the pool. You shut the curtains, sit down at the card table, and eat breakfast.

By five, most of the tenants have returned to their apartments.
Mr. Wilkins and Mrs. Scree are the last ones by the pool. They
sit at a round green table under the pagoda, sipping drinks from
mismatched glasses. You straighten the bedroom, then bathe
and shave; at five-thirty the courtyard is empty. In fresh Levi's, a
checked shirt, and a black corduroy jacket, you pour a small
glass of milk and watch the end of the local news.

At six the court is still empty. The lights in the pagoda have
come on early, as have the yellow lights at the front doors of
many apartments facing the pool. The sun is almost gone except
for a reddish glow reflected from low clouds, which are gray in
the eastern sky and shiny scarlet in the west.

Dolores hasn't come out. Mike Wallace interviews a California man who stuffs pet animals for their owners. Harry Reasoner
reports on the Florida drug trade. It's not clear whether Dolores
intends to come out or was just playing. To be sure, and because
talking to Dolores outside in the courtyard might be pleasant,
you turn off the television and go down to the pagoda. All the
chairs and tables are painted the color of the lighted water in the
pool. For the hundredth time, water seems beautiful. The palms
around three sides of the pagoda make it feel secluded, even
though it isn't really. The apartment windows where there are
lights have drawn curtains; the dark windows could hide people.
Still, it's comfortable outside, and if Dolores doesn't show, it's
not a total loss.

Two young girls go by carrying two plastic baskets of clothes.
The overweight young husband and his skinny wife come in
from the parking lot—from an early dinner perhaps—and say
hello before entering their apartment, switching on the lights,
and hastily drawing the curtains. Someone passes between the
pagoda and the pool and says, "Aren't summer nights incredible

and amazing?" A large tree roach runs along a floorboard. In the distance several dogs howl. Mr. Wilkins, whose front door is almost on a center line with the pool, opens his door and stands on the threshold. There's enough light to see him, even though his porch lamp isn't on. He's wearing shorts and a square-tailed shirt.

"Hey," he says, shading his eyes with a hand. "That you? How's it going out here?"

"Fine, I guess."

"How's that?" he says, moving the hand from over his eyes to cup his ear. "Where's the party?"

"It's a slow starter."

"Well," he says, waving. "Sometimes that happens." He goes back into his apartment. His porch light snaps on.

Upstairs, you toss the coat on one of the deck chairs in the living room, then take a Coke out of the refrigerator, go into the bedroom, and drink the Coke, thumbing through an issue of *Stereo Review* devoted to mini-components.


At nine you pull the slim telephone book out from under the stack of magazines and look up Dolores Prince, writing her number on the inside back cover of the book. There is a knock at the door.

Two kids, a boy and a girl, neither older than ten or twelve, are on the landing. Below, on the sidewalk, a man is silhouetted against the pool.

"We're working for Jesus," the kids say in imperfect unison. The boy wears a blue suit and the girl a lilac dress, black pumps, and taut white socks.

"Aren't we all."

"We have Jesus is our hearts," they say. "We have subscriptions to *Spirituality*, *Aspire*, and *The Beacon*, and we're trying to win a trip."

"Thank you, but no." You hold up your hand like a crosswalk guard in after-school traffic.

They continue, though the young girl, as she speaks, turns and looks toward the foot of the stairs. "Wouldn't you like to have His message come into your home each month? Only twenty-six dollars for twelve issues." Then the girl adds, "Please? Two more and our whole family gets a chance for a trip to Six Flags."

"Yeah," the boy says. "Dad has a chance at a boat, too."

Apart from their clothes, the children are quite ordinary looking, like kids at the school, or at the shopping center, or on bicycles going down Park Street in the afternoon.

"No, thank you." The man below moves forward slightly to consult a piece of white letter-size paper in his hand, and you call to him, "No, thank you."

The kids turn uncertainly and look down into the dark courtyard. The boy grabs the frame around the door as if he's lost his balance.

"O.K.," says the man downstairs.

The children turn around, obviously disappointed, and say, "Thank you, sir. May the Lord Jesus come into your heart." Then the girl goes down the steps, her heels clacking on the metal, and the boy, much more cautiously, follows her, his hand a tight fist around the railing.

When the door is closed and the kids and the man have stopped talking outside, and the kids are knocking on Mrs. Talbot's door, the telephone rings.

"Hi," Dolores says. "I tried to call earlier, but you're unlisted. I have to apologize about tonight."

"How'd you get the number?"

"Mrs. Scree. Listen, I got into something I couldn't get out of—you know how it is. Sundays are bad for me."

"We'll do it another day."

"Sure," she says. "I'm out there all the time. Just come on out whenever you're ready."

"Whenever I'm ready I'll just come on out." The telephone book is still creased flat on the table in front of the television.

"Did the kids get to you?" she asks. "They must've thought I was Mary Magdalene, the way I was dressed when I opened the door. But look, are you busy? Why not come for a nightcap?"

The TV is making a curious high whine, even though the sound is off. Outside there are people talking, and there is the sound of a chair being pulled across the pebbly concrete, then Mrs. Scree's loud, sudden laugh, like the bark of a monkey. "I don't think so. Not tonight."

There's another pause, and then Dolores says, "Well, suit yourself. If you want me you know where to find me."

"You're in the book."

"Right."

She hangs up. You hold the telephone to your ear until the dial tone returns, then replace the receiver. Some people are running back and forth across the television screen. The voices are coming up from poolside. After a few minutes you go into the living room, put on the black coat, take a Löwenbräu out of the refrigerator, and go outside. You sit sideways on the diving board and listen to Mrs. Scree and her husband, Raymond, and another tenant—the plump woman from Saturday. The subscription kids go out the front gate. Mrs. Scree wags her arms like an explorer in a jungle and introduces you as the king of the crawl.

# Grapette

MARGARET SEAVER comes around the corner of the swimming pool carrying a paper plate in front of her. On the plate is a frankfurter so big it sticks out both ends of the bun. "I was going to fold it up," she says. "I even tried it, but the thing wouldn't stay put." She reaches into her apron pocket and produces a pink plastic knife-and-fork set, which she presses into my hand. "You can cut off the extra parts if you want." Then she tucks a pink-and-coral party napkin between two buttons of my shirt. "Okeydoke. That ought to fix you." There's a raised line of mustard along her forefinger, which she wipes on her apron. She's fortyish and built like a seal. We're standing on the combed-concrete apron of the Seaver swimming pool, celebrating the seventeenth birthday of Margaret's daughter, Carmel, who's at the opposite end of the pool, surrounded by her friends.

"Here," Margaret says, grabbing her husband's arm as he passes. "Herm, take your old friend to the garage."

Herman paid seventeen thousand dollars for the water-blue Peugeot, a present for his daughter. "It's a beautiful Peugeot," he says proudly.

"Sure is."

"She's a good girl," he says. "She's earned this."

I nod. The garage is amazingly clean; it looks like a living room—windows and a couch, wall-to-wall patio carpet, and in the corner a huge ficus in a crimson plastic pot. "Nice garage," I say, waving my hand too generously, tossing the frankfurter off the plate and under a rear tire of the car.

Herman is a real estate developer. He's six and a half feet tall, wearing bright-orange slacks with a pleated stretch waist and no back pockets. His shirt is white knit. Out the garage window I see the teen-agers in their narrow bathing suits clustered around the diving board. "You want me to take that wiener?" Herman points under the Peugeot's rear tire. "You go on back."

He turns along the wall of the house toward the buffet table, and I go between the low, square-cut bushes of the garden to the pool.

Carmel is looking at me over her boyfriend Duane's shoulder. Duane seems to be telling a story; the others are standing and smoking cigarettes and nodding to each other. Carmel's wearing a metallic-finish two-piece swimsuit and jewelry—a tiny gold chain around her waist.

Margaret catches my elbow. "I don't know where she gets those mugs," she says, throwing her head back to indicate the group surrounding her daughter. "Let's have a drink." She leads me to a white iron table with a glass top. "So how's the business?" Margaret says, but before I have a chance to answer, a woman in a black uniform is at the table for instructions. I nod when Margaret points to me and says, "Gin?," then look at the lawn, the pines, the shaped bushes that dot the property. Then I look at Carmel.

I've known her since she was two. When she was thirteen and I was thirty-three, we had a little romance. Margaret and Herman wrote it off as a crush, but I wasn't so sure. Carmel looked twenty then; I took her to galleries and movies, and we slept together. One of Margaret's therapist friends wondered if it was such a good idea to encourage this; I told Herman that it was wearing on me, too.

\*    \*    \*

Margaret has to take a telephone call inside—the pool phone is out, and Herman's cordless is upstairs in his bath—so I sit at the white table with my gin. Carmel whispers something to Duane and pats his sleek lavender bottom, then joins me.

"I've got to get out of here," she says, pulling a chair around the table so we're sitting side by side. "It's crazy—Herm's crazy for doing it. I don't think Maggie wanted him to do it, but he did anyway. Did you see it, the car?"

"He showed me. It's very nice."

"Jesus." Carmel thumbs her navel, removing a glossy deposit of suntan lotion. "I've only had my license a year."

Since she was thirteen, I haven't seen her more than half a dozen times, and never alone. We stare at her friends. "How's Duane?"

"Duane drips, to the max," she says. "Duane has discovered his immensely gorgeous body and he loves it. You look dumb with a mustache."

"That bad?"

"You could manage a Penney's."

"Anything else?" I turn to look at her face, then her breasts; she doesn't look older than she did four years ago, only smoother.

She smiles and rubs some of the oil off her belly, then wipes her palm on my forearm. "I want a birthday present from you. You know Jeremy Stein? In Herm's office? I was seeing him for a while, but he wanted to get married—can you imagine that? He must've been forty."

"I'm close," I say, twirling the remaining cube around the wall of my glass.

"Men are dorks at forty. They don't know what's good for them."

"Thanks."

"Jeremy went to California and took off his socks. A personal breakthrough." Carmel pulls on the soft white string that seems to hold the top of her swimsuit together; the string comes loose, but the halter stays put. "You still like to talk on the phone? Herm put a phone in the car—maybe I'll call you."

She's looking at my wrist, wiping lotion on it and making the hair stick to the skin.


Three engineers share a four-bedroom apartment near mine in the huge Low River complex. The day after Carmel's birthday they're having a Saturday-night party. They have lots of parties. They always invite me, but I never go. The engineers are from Michigan; each owns a new black Toyota Celica—the Supra model—which he keeps in showroom condition. The oldest engineer is Morgan Zwerdling. He couldn't be more than twenty-five.

I'm having a sandwich and reading the newspaper when Morgan rings my doorbell and asks if he can stash a couple of chairs for the evening. "Tonight you gotta come," he says. "Tonight is the end of the world as we have known it."

I help him get four dining chairs and a recliner into my living room. He thanks me, then waves at the chairs and says, "These aren't going to be in your way or something, are they? If they are, just blast 'em to smithereens." He laughs.


I'm trying the recliner when Carmel calls and wants to go to dinner. She's out riding in her new car and she wants some company. I hear car horns over the phone; then Carmel says, "Out yours, too, Buster."

I struggle to get the recliner upright. "I guess I could watch."

"That's great," she says. "Bring a camera. I'll get you in two minutes."

On the narrow blacktop highway headed for Mobile, she pulls

down a metal flap under the dash, revealing the telephone. "Have at it," she says.

"Some girl at your party told me I looked bad. She meant sick, I think. She pointed at my chin."

"I don't see anything wrong with your chin." Carmel's wearing a thin white dress and a silver-and-turquoise choker; she looks pretty, and she's more comfortable than I am.

"So what's happening since four years ago?" I turn around in my seat, bumping a knee into the phone-compartment door. "All right if I shut this?"

"Sure." She points to the glove box on my side of the dashboard. "Hand me a cigarette out of there, will you?"

I open the glove box and fish around inside for her cigarettes. "I've been to Mobile a couple of times," I say. I hand her the package of Kools.

She pulls the dash lighter out of its socket and plants it on the tip of her cigarette. "Jeremy was a freak for Mobile—the history, everything. You just sit tight."

"Right."

"I might get an apartment. Maybe where you are."

"What about Herm and Margaret?"

"What about them?" She points out the window at an abandoned gas station we're passing. There's a red horse nosing around inside the office of the station. "Sucker's going to get his pretty head bashed if he's not careful. Look at the roof." Carmel snaps her ash onto the straw floor mat, then turns on the headlights; I stare out the window on my side of the car, watching cows in fields.

Ten minutes go by, and then there's a truck crosswise in the road. The truck is carrying tree trunks thirty or forty feet long, but only a few remain on the bed; most of the load is spread out over the highway. I put my hand on top of the dashboard and point toward the wreck.

"Not for me," Carmel says. She slows quickly, then turns onto a white gravel drive in front of a sign that says MODERN NED'S CATFISH THIS WAY. She looks at me and I can tell she's not having fun.

"Want to go back?"

"What, and give up? We've got dinner to eat. We've got to get to know each other again. We've got to do business."

"Right. I forgot."

The gravel stops about a hundred feet off the highway, and then we're on a dirt road with a steeply peaked center; Carmel drives on the right of the road, so I'm pushed up against the passenger door. It feels as if the Peugeot is ready to tip over.

"You O.K.?" Carmel asks after a couple of minutes.

"Great. You drive in an interesting way."

"How come you never called?" she says, struggling with the steering. "I've been ready." She puts a hand to her neck and the car dips suddenly to the right, kicking up a spray of whitish dust. Rocks ping against the sheet metal. She grabs the padded steering wheel with both hands.

I brace myself against the dash.

"Sorry," she says. "I have a friend in New Mexico who makes jewelry. You think this collar's too much?"

"Yes."

"I wondered about that. I think I'm still young."

We're a mile into the dirt road. It's dusk, and grayer than it was out on the highway. "You like catfish?" I ask.

"Why, you don't?" She seems satisfied that she can handle the road now and reaches into her lap, where the cigarette pack is lodged.

"No."

She stops digging for a Kool long enough to glance at me. "Here," she says, steering the car up onto the center of the road, "I'll slow down some and maybe you'll feel better—how's that? Punch that lighter."

She resettles in her bucket seat and drags her dress a little higher over her knees. There's a small square of white on a tree a couple of hundred yards up the road—a sign of some kind. When the lighter pops, I pull it out of its socket and hand it to her.

The sign says POSTED—KEEP OUT. Carmel sighs, filling the car with smoke. "I'm beginning to think Ned's doesn't exist anymore."

"You've been here?"

"Once, with Jeremy. I had white beans." She downshifts, then wipes the palm of her hand up over her forehead and stops the car in the middle of the dirt road. "This road isn't going anywhere. Let's take a walk—what do you say?" Without waiting for an answer, she gets out and slams the door. I follow her. She looks very strange in this setting, like a woman on a hand-painted billboard; I track her for a few steps, then change my mind and sit on the Peugeot's front fender, watching Carmel walk.

It's dark when we get back. Even in the kitchen, which is the part of my apartment farthest from the engineers', we can hear the thump of the bass and the noise of the guests who have taken to the patio. Carmel is eating a peanut-butter-and-jelly sandwich, and I'm searching for the Tostitos. She's taken off the choker; there are thin abrasions on her neck where the silver bit into her skin. I watch her eat.

"Good," she says, finishing the last corner of her sandwich. She points to her plate, which is dotted with bubbles of shining jelly. "Let's go out."

"We just got in. Where do you want to go?"

"Let's get something at the store."

"What store? What kind of something?"

She takes her plate to the sink and runs the hot water. Her

skirt is flawlessly smooth in the back. "I don't know—just a store. We'll go to a store, look around, buy something. I always find things I want when I go to the store, don't you?"

"Not every time," I say. Carmel fills a new yellow sponge with water, wrings it out, and starts to wipe the dark wood-grained doors of the kitchen cabinets. "But if you're going to housekeep, I'll go."

She stops what she's doing and looks at the sponge in her hand as if it had suddenly turned into a fish. "Jesus," she says. "I didn't even think—this is your apartment." She drops the sponge on the lip of the sink, rubs her hands together, and reaches for her purse. She removes a small bottle and taps a curl of hand cream into her palm, then screws on the bottle top before rubbing the cream into her skin. "I really do want to go out. Are there any good stores around here? Is that surplus store still open? What time is it, anyway?"


The man behind the platform counter at Fuji News looks as if he should be out buying a Mr. Turtle swimming pool for his kid. He grins when Carmel pushes through the slatted saloon-type doors into the adult-books section.

"We're browsing," I tell him.

"Look at this." Carmel pulls a shrink-wrapped magazine off the rack and hands it to me, tapping the close-up on the cover with her fingernail. "That's love." She hands me another magazine, a tabloid stapled shut twice in the middle of the front cover. "Names and addresses," she says. "You'd be surprised who's in here. Herm and Maggie and their friends. Really. They've got it at home. I've seen it."

The back room of the newsstand is smelly; it has black wire racks for the paperbacks and wooden racks for the magazines. Up on the cashier's platform, which spans the two rooms, there's a glass case of films and sex toys. "I'm going out front," I say to Carmel, bending close to her so that the other customers—a fellow who looks like an Olympic swimmer, a man in a plaid shirt who looks as if he just woke up, and a kid who's hunkered down in an alcove in back—can't overhear. "You be O.K.?"

"I'm finished anyway. This stuff is sleazoid, isn't it?"

"You want something special?" the counterman says as we go through the swinging doors.

"Nope," Carmel says, smiling at him. "We got what we came for."

A very tan guy in tennis gear looks up from his Italian architecture magazine when he hears Carmel. "Hi," he says. "You on patrol?"

"Oh—Chuck. You win?" She points to his clothes. "I got a Peugeot."

I can see what's on the cover of the magazine he's looking at: an interior, done in new-pastel green satins. Carmel introduces us.

"Chuck's an ex," she says. "He worked on Herm's Omni Centre."

"And look at me now—an old married man with one in the bucket and one on the way."

There's shouting in the back, and the swimmer leaps through the double doors. He grabs Carmel's shoulder and shoves her to one side, then pushes past Chuck and runs out. The plaid-shirt guy catches the swinging doors and shouts, "Try it again, Muscle Face, and I'll teach you mush." He pulls the doors shut, glaring over them at me. "He's a friend of yours?"

"C'mon, Billy," the counterman says. "Ease up."

"We never saw him before in our lives," Carmel says. She grabs my wrist and twists it a little. "Quit shoving, will you? I'm not ready yet."

Chuck has closed his magazine and now he slaps it on his bare thigh several times.

"I'm a welder," Billy says, still looking over the doors. "I work out in Bayside. Nights."

Chuck says, "Oh? I worked on a bank in Bayside, on Dot Street."

Carmel squats down in the aisle and pulls a copy of *Interface Age* off a fresh stack. "Look at this," she whispers to me, pointing to a photograph of an integrated circuit in the magazine.

Billy comes out from behind the doors, his hand pushed at Chuck. "What're you, a designer? You worked on First Bayside? Me and the boys did that lobby fountain. My name's Billy Farrar."

Chuck and Billy shake hands.

"Yep—that's you, all right," Billy says, pointing at Chuck's magazine. "This where you get all the ideas? The boys were laughing all the damn time about that fountain. And it looked good, too." He grabs Chuck's shoulder and gives it a stiff tug. "No, really—it's real pretty." He shakes his head as if he's not certain he'll be believed, then points toward the door. "Little girl tried to grope me. You get that in a place like this." He shrugs and looks at Carmel. "I'm on my way to work. It ain't that bad a drive. All you got to do is come up here and catch the Loop"—he starts drawing a map in the air—"then swing on around by 59 there, and get off at the Dictionary Street exit, there by Cross Tool—it don't take long."

On the sidewalk outside the store Carmel slaps Chuck's backside. "Hey," she says. "Just like old times."

He takes a swipe at her with his magazine, which is rolled tight like a baton in his fist. "My Frank Lloyd Wright imitation."

We walk down the sidewalk together until Chuck steps off the curb to unlock a gunpowder-gray Audi 5000. "So where's this Peugeot?" He stands up on his toes and looks down the line of cars.

"Over here," Carmel says. "Want a look?"

Chuck has to lock the Audi again; then the three of us go for a look at Carmel's car. When Chuck's just about finished examining it, she pushes him into the front seat and shows him the telephone.

"Oh, Jesus," he says. "Sweet everlovin' Jesus."

"Yeah," she says.

We walk Chuck back to his car, and stand on the sidewalk and wave as he pulls out.

"He's O.K.," Carmel says out of the side of her mouth. "But his wife's a twit."

The newsstand is in a strip shopping center on a six-lane feeder for the downtown freeway and the Loop that Billy was talking about. The street is bordered by silver poles and greenish street lights and blinking nudie-bar signs, the temporary kind that are always stuck in weedy lots—a red edge outlined with clear blinking lamps and a message that says CIRLS GIRLS CIRLS.

A startlingly thin black woman in skintight lamé jeans and a string top passes us on the sidewalk, headed for the bar next to the newsstand. She says hello to me; she's got glitter all around her eyes and she's wearing some kind of plastic-jewel headdress that comes down her nose and then drapes in shallow arcs over her cheekbones and back above her ears. Carmel pokes me in the arm, then looks over her shoulder at the woman. "I thought you didn't like jewelry."

We get halfway into a parking space in front of my apartment before two young guys who are standing in the space, obviously drunk and having a discussion, look up. They don't move out of the way. One of them, a frail-looking kid with coarse, dark hair and a satin windbreaker open to the waist, waves us away, shading his eyes with a long-neck beer bottle. He's one of the engineers; I don't know the other guy. Carmel rolls down her window, holding the car on the very slight incline of the parking space by alternately engaging and disengaging the clutch.

"Give me a break, hey?" she says, leaning her head out the car window.

The two guys talk another minute, gesturing toward the car, and then step awkwardly out of the way, pressing themselves up against the burgundy Plymouth parked next to the space we're trying to get into.

"Hi there, Peugeot," the engineer says. He bends forward from the waist and rests his folded forearms on Carmel's window. "You want a beer? Good beer—Lone Star." He shoves his bottle halfway in her window, neck first.

"Never heard of it," Carmel says.

He turns to his partner, who's still leaning against the Plymouth, and says, "She never heard of Lone Star."

Carmel opens her door a couple of inches. The engineer jumps back and wobbles.

"Damn," he says. "Scared the pee out of me, woman."

His friend pulls him by the shirt sleeve. "I told you, man, you got to go slow, you got to tattoo her memory pan, slow and easy"—he pokes his friend deliberately on the arm—"bap, bap, bap, bap—like that." Then he reaches forward and opens the door for Carmel. "I'm Vern. Everybody calls me V.O., but my name's Vernon—Vern for short. What's your name?"

"Sugar," Carmel says.

Vern glances at my neighbor, then back at Carmel. "Can I call you Sugar?"

"Maybe," Carmel says. "Good party?"

"The best," the engineer says, stumbling forward. "Light-Emitting Diode City, really. I mean totally killer." He grins at me through the corner of the windshield, then slips and vanishes below the car's fender.

"The women are short," Vern says, looking down at his friend. "All these teeny little women in there." He swings his bottle hand over his shoulder toward the engineer's apartment. "Is everybody suddenly shorter than they used to be?"

"Not me," Carmel says. She gets out and slides between Vern and the front fender of the Peugeot, stepping around the fallen engineer. "Maybe we'll come over."

"Straight?" Vern says. "I mean, you telling me straight?"

"Sure," she says, patting the shoulder of his pale-blue shirt. He's wearing red gym trunks and this pale-blue shirt with a sailboat painted on it.


"That's better," Carmel says, her face smushed in a plump off-white cushion. "You've got a great couch."

I turn on the television, crouching in front of the set to leaf through the *TV Weekly* book that comes with my Saturday paper. "There's a George Raft movie. You interested?" I spin around on one foot, still in a crouch, and almost fall over backward into the wire TV table.

"George Raft? What else? Why don't we go to the party?" Carmel rolls onto her side and slugs the pillow a couple of times to make it fit comfortably under her arm. "What's all this furniture?" She looks at the dining chairs and the recliner.

"They brought it over to make room," I say. "I may get me one of those La-Z-Boys."

"Sure. I know—I can't go to the party because I'd just get sick after. I hate being sick, really." She stares past me at the television.

I go into the kitchen. "You want something to drink?"

"Cream soda," she says.

I open the refrigerator, then stop and look around the door. "What?"

"Do you have any cream soda? What I'd like more than anything else in the world is a cream soda."

"Sorry." I pull a sixteen-ounce Coke out of its plastic holder. "How about Coke?"

"Gimme a Dew."

"What? Oh—Mountain Dew. Fresh out." I unscrew the cap of my drink, take a swallow, and stand in front of the refrigerator, straightening the cold eggs in the door rack. "You might as well just go ahead and ask for a Grapette."

She turns back onto her stomach, then pushes up on her elbows and presses her forehead into the cushion. "I never heard of it."

She lifts her head and looks across the room at me; her face is shadowed, because the only light in the room is above and behind her, but the pose is familiar. I shut the refrigerator door and go to the recliner, pushing it back until I'm horizontal, floating in the middle of the living room. "No Grapette," I say, scanning the ceiling.

"What is it?"

"The end of the world as we have known it."

"Oh."

"Little purple bottles, six ounces." I wave my hand and twist my head to one side so I can see her on the couch. "Grapette kind of went away, I guess. I hate that."

She's still for a minute, then squirms up on the sofa and pulls the white cushion into her lap, turning to face me. "Are you sure? Maybe we ought to go find some, maybe it's still out there."

# At Heart

WHEN SHE SEES me at Carl Kobioski's New Year's party eight months after our separation, Jennifer throws herself into the swimming pool. I guess it looks pretty funny to the guests. Jennifer's dressed and she can't swim, never could, so as soon as she hits the water she starts flailing. Three of us go in to get her—Carl, Simon Oster, and me. She likes Simon Oster because he saved some kid in an apartment fire once. She always said I ought to be more like him. I said she was a big help. Oster was our local pharmacist, with a degree from a place I'd never heard of called Piedmont College. Maybe he's not such a terrible guy. I mean, I don't like him. I think he's priggish, heartless, self-centered, anal, and living in a dream world, but I may be wrong.

Jennifer's done this before. On our third wedding anniversary at the Sea Inn in Florida she did a belly flop in the lobby fountain wearing a four-hundred-dollar silk jacket I'd just given her. The jacket was crimson. I don't remember why she was upset. Last year, the night we agreed to separate, she went into a mudhole at a construction site and I had to drag her out with a two-by-four. I swung the two-by down in the hole and told her to grab on, then I pulled her out hand over hand. With Jennifer, things just go along until you reach a certain point and then bam!—she takes the dive.

Four of us are in Kobioski's pool with all our clothes on. Nobody's a champion swimmer, so we're splashing around like Red Cross lifesaving victims. The three of us who are doing the sav-

149

ing are yelling instructions back and forth. People come out of the house to cheer us on.

Somebody shouts, "Attaboy. Go get 'em, Tarzan."

Carl gets Jennifer's legs and he wants to shove her up over the edge of the pool, but by the time he's ready for the big push, Oster's got her flipped over on her back and he's doing a neck-and-shoulder pull, trying to get her down to the shallow end. She's throwing her arms around and she hits Oster on the side of the face, cocking his clear aviator glasses up over his forehead. He has to stop what he's doing to fix the glasses, and, in that minute, Carl heaves from below and gets Jennifer over the pool edge and onto the concrete apron, her legs still dangling in the water.

I notice the legs—thin and smooth and taut like a young girl's legs. She always used to talk about her skin, how it was hers and she had to take care of it. She did. Lots of protein and exercise, glass after glass of water, six kinds of vitamins, and a bone-white powder that came in a dark jar from the Health Hut. The skin stuff always annoyed me, I don't know why. I complained. I told her her skin was fine. She didn't listen. Now I think maybe she was right. There's something magic about it.

"Great job, Carl," Oster yells.

I go up the chrome ladder and then come around and catch Jennifer under the arms, lifting her away from the water. Oster hoists himself out, and he and I put her on her back in the chaise that she was in before she went into the pool. Right away Oster starts thumping on her chest like he's a Catalina lifeguard.

"You want the other side, don't you?" I say, getting a folded beach towel off the low wire table by the chaise.

"That's the old way," he says between thumps. "We don't do it that way anymore."

"Oh," I say.

We're all soaked, of course. I'm standing there rubbing my

shirt with the towel. Oster stops pumping on Jennifer, one of his palms still flat on her breastbone, and stares at me. He's meaty and silly looking, a Clark Kent type. People call him a hunk and he likes it. "You want to do this? She's your wife."

"She's not his wife," Carl says. He's gotten out of the pool and he's busy pinching his shirt and his pants with his fingertips, pulling his clothes off his skin. Carl is Jennifer's lawyer. "Technically, yes. But that's it."

I look at Sylvia, Carl's girlfriend, who is twenty-eight, a divorcée with two children and skintight Gloria Vanderbilt jeans. She's ushered the other guests inside and shut the sliding door, isolating the crisis. She's standing well back from the pool with her arms folded across her chest. Sylvia gives me a quick look that might mean she feels sorry for me and might mean she thinks I'm a fool, then she does an "Oh, well—" shrug and tosses her blond hair. "True, Simon," she says. "Jennifer's ready for harvest."

"I'll give you a big amen on that," Oster says, going for some kind of joke, a CB radio joke, I think. All this time he's poised over Jennifer, hitting her chest, pinching her nose, and occasionally kneading her shoulders for good measure. He's also counting under his breath. The chaise, one of those aluminum-framed things with green plastic webbing for the seat, is twisting out of shape and ratcheting back and forth on the pea-gravel concrete.

I must look glum. Sylvia slinks up beside me and says, "Why so forlorn?"

"It's worse when you're forty," I say. "It's really ridiculous."

She pats my wet bottom and says everything will be all right. It doesn't help. I shouldn't have noticed Oster's groping, and I sure shouldn't have said anything. There's a line of people standing inside the sliding door to the beach house, watching. Jennifer is glistening on the chaise. Whatever I didn't like about the way she looks is gone now. She's familiar, but changed. Her hair's shorter and breezy looking, and she's lost some weight. Her makeup is different, more elegant and yet almost painted, doll-like. She looks gorgeous, like she's from a foreign country.

Oster gets off of her and says, "Sexy like lacquer, isn't she?" He taps my arm. "I can hear you thinking, friend." A zipper of lightning crosses the sky, then comes thunder. He takes a towel from Carl, removes the Batman glasses and drops them in his shirt pocket, then wipes at his face and his hair. "Storm," he says.

"I'll get a blanket," Sylvia says. "You dopes take her inside."

"Probably suffering low-grade depression," Oster says, looking down at Jennifer. "Resultant upon termination of wedded bliss." He gets one knee on the aluminum rail of the chaise and starts playing with Jennifer's shoulders again, massaging them this time. He's finished with the tough stuff. She opens her eyes, but he doesn't notice.

Carl steps up to the pool and stares at the water, which is sparkling blue. "Lucky she didn't mash her potato going in here," he says.

Jennifer's grinning at me, sheepishly, wagging her head as Simon works her over.


I came to the party with Clare. She teaches physical fitness at the university. She's twenty-three, tall, with eyes the color of oysters, strong cheekbones, and too-large front teeth. She's an acquaintance, not a romance. "Enjoy your dip?" she says, when she finds me in the kitchen.

"We're taking Jennifer," I say. "Is that all right with you?"

"Sure," she says. "She O.K.?"

Carl comes in and says, "Listen, if you need something dry, there're clothes in the bedroom."

"I think we're going," I say. "Who'd Jennifer come with? Where is she?"

"I don't know and on the porch with Sylvia. You want me to
fetch her?"

"I'll do it," I say. I go through the small house and find Jennifer wrapped in a bright yellow comforter on the glassed-in
porch. Sylvia sees me coming and says, "She doesn't feel so
good. Are you driving?"

"Yep," I say. "You feel better, Jennifer?"

"Where's the statuesque and marvelous Clare?" she says.

We say two minutes worth of goodbye and get to the car
without running into Oster, but the car turns out to be stuck in
the sand.

"Hey. An adventure," Clare says, twisting in the back seat of
the Subaru. "We can camp out all night. I can even straighten
my legs back here."

"I hate sand," Jennifer says. She squints out her window at
the beach. "It's so tiny."

"Me too," Clare says. "It gets in your pants and everything."

Jennifer rubs her eyes with her knuckles and says, "Right.
That's exactly what I was thinking, Clare. How it gets in your
pants. I wonder where Simon is. I should tell him I'm leaving."

"Strapping on his emergency gear," I say. "Water wings,
merit badges—that stuff."

"Oh, fine," Jennifer says. "The man likes me so he's automatically pudding, right?"

"O.K.," Clare says, pulling herself forward. She runs her hand
straight back through her hair a couple of times. "What I'm
hearing here is a lot of anger and hostility. Stuff I know about
from radio, TV, and film—we call it RTF in the trade. Do you
think we ought to talk about that, just the three of us?"

I look at the Subaru's headliner.

"It's raining," Jennifer says.

Clare drapes her arms over the back of the front seat. Maybe
it is romance. Everybody's in love with Clare. She's big and
pretty and in November she still smells like Sea & Ski. "Or

should we take it easy, have a wonderful time?" she says. "With the rain and everything?"

"Are you irrepressible or what?" Jennifer says. She reaches around and touches Clare's wrist.

"I'd better get out there and push," I say.

"Take it away, Bosco," Jennifer says. She's been calling me Bosco since the divorce business started. "Whatever you do don't go back up to the house and get help."

"I can push," Clare says. "I like pushing."

"Don't we all," Jennifer says.

I get out and Clare follows and then Jennifer slips over behind the wheel. "Let's try backwards," I say. "The sand's better back there. Maybe it'll be easy."

"You got it," Jennifer says, peering at the floor-mounted shift.

"Backwards is the only way to go," Clare says.

We push on the front of the car, Clare on one fender and me on the other, and Jennifer hits the gas pedal too hard and then not hard enough. I wave her off and go around to the window.

Jennifer bounces in the seat. "Backwards is the only way to go," she says. She wiggles in the seat.

"How about a nice steady pedal?" I say. "Nothing fancy. We're just trying to get out of a hole."

"I'm sorry," Jennifer says. "You're really doing O.K." She slumps forward over the wheel and stares at my hands, then at Clare who's crouched in front of the car. "You look good out there. Both of you." She traces an outline of my hand on the car door.

Clare is picking at her fingernail in the glow of the parking light.

"What happened?" I ask.

"I chipped it playing Whack-A-Mole," she says. "I was at the mall playing Whack-A-Mole with some guy from the biology department and I banged it on this mole's head. Have you ever played Whack-A-Mole?"

"Never," I say. I signal Jennifer and then lean on the headlight on the driver's side. Jennifer starts revving the engine, but the car just rocks a little. Out of the corner of my eye I see the porch door open. "Let's take a rest," I say, and I drop on my knees in the sand. Jennifer is determined to get the car out, so she guns the engine, and the front end of the Subaru digs in deeper, then settles. She gets off the gas and the car rolls forward, lightly bumping me. I fall over onto my back.

"What's the story out here? You people can't bear to leave?" It's Carl. He's carrying a huge tricolored umbrella and a pair of yellow waders. "Car stuck?"

"Maybe we can stay all night?" Clare says.

Jennifer bends out the passenger-side window holding a magazine over her head. "Clare's loony for you, Carl. Where's Simon?"

"He was eating," Carl says. "I told him you were indisposed."

"Am I ever," Jennifer says. She shakes the wet magazine, then tosses it into the back seat and fiddles with her hair, which is soaked and black and pushed away from her forehead.

Carl hands me the waders. I'm covered with mud and sand and my clothes are sticking to me. I give the waders to Clare. She grins and starts climbing into them. "I've got a chain in the Blazer," Carl says. "I'll bring it around and pull you out before you can say Jack Robinson. You wait inside."

Jennifer jumps out of the car and runs for the porch, and Carl heads for the garage, which is around the other side of the house. Clare drapes her arm over my shoulder. She's swamped by the waders. "All right," she says. "Who's this Jack Robinson?"

"I've been watching you people," Simon says when we get to the porch. "Not having much luck, are you?"

"Not much, thanks," I say.

"Could be worse," he says. "You could be stuck somewhere else. I mean, out in the sticks someplace. At least here you've got friends."

"He was trying to give me a ride," Jennifer says. "But he isn't functioning properly tonight."

"No news there," Oster says. He grins at me and I watch the lights bounce off his glasses. He puts a thick arm around Jennifer's waist. "You tired? You want to go or you want to boogie some first?"

"I figure she wants to boogie," I say.

"I'm for that," Clare says. She does a couple of bearlike dance steps.

"You two ought to get together," Jennifer says.

"I want dry pants," I say, heading for the bedroom. Clare follows, leaving Jennifer and Oster by the door.

"I really love your hair," I hear Oster say. "It looks like Richard Gere's."

In the bedroom Clare pushes some coats off the side of the bed and flops onto her back. There's a wicker elephant on the bedside table. She picks up the elephant and swings it around by its trunk. "It's really great being here with your whole family," she says.

All the pants in Carl's closet are bright colors—lemon, persimmon, royal blue, purple. I hold up the persimmon pants for Clare to see. "How about these?"

"Great. Slam 'em on," she says. She puts the elephant away and opens the drawer in the bed stand. "Wonder if Carl keeps a Bible?"

There's a light knock and then the door opens. Jennifer peers around the edge, just above the door handle. "Are we decent?"

"Just about," I say.

"Are we going on the PGA?" she asks, pointing at the pants I'm holding.

"Who's going on the PGA?" Simon says. He pushes into the room behind her.

"PGA?" Clare says. "PGA?"

"Professional Golfers Association," Jennifer says. "He always wanted to be a sports personality."

I put the persimmon pants back in the closet. "Maybe I can find something in the way of a pink."

"I almost went on the Pro Bowlers Tour one year," Simon says. "I roll a two-twenty, two-thirty, somewhere in that area."

"The two of you ought get together," Clare says. "Big roll-off. Winner take all."

"All what?" Simon says. He gives her a curved-lip grin.

I flip a pair of pants over my shoulder and turn toward the bathroom. "I'm getting into these. Did Carl move the car?"

"Purple," Jennifer says, indicating the pants. "Standard equipment at a time like this."

Clare bounces off the bed and makes as if she's going to follow me into the bathroom, but stops at the door. "You just take your time," she says. "Lots of wonderful things are purple. I'm going to the kitchen and get a pig-in-a-blanket or whatever they are."

"That's exactly what they are," Simon says. "I've eaten about a hundred so far. Let's go together, all three of us."

"I do like purple," Jennifer says. "If anybody cares."

"I care," Clare says. She puts an arm around Jennifer and gives Oster a little push out the door. "Come on. Let's help Simon eat."


When I come out I shut the hall door and then sit on the floor by the bed. There's a round rug there, very small and fluffy, like a bathroom rug. Cinnamon colored. There's a Panasonic pop-up television, one of those with a three-inch screen, under the bedside table. I've never seen one except in a store, so I turn it on and put it in my lap. It isn't hooked up to the cable. Even with the rabbit ear fully extended I can tune only one channel. The people on the set look much more like toys than the people on regular TV sets. I watch a guy do the weather forecast and that's real interesting because he's got this little tiny map he keeps pointing to. The guy's the size of my thumb.

I like this television set and I don't want to quit watching when the news is over, but I figure I should. I get up and look out the window. The Subaru isn't there. I pull my wet pants off the shower rod in the bathroom and go down the hall looking for Clare.

She's in the oak-panelled kitchen talking to a thin kid who's wearing cutoffs and a black T-shirt with the sleeves rolled up. The kid is a student. I've seen him around the gym where the swim team practices. Sometimes he tries to talk to one or another of the girls, but they don't usually give him much.

"This is Teller," Clare says when she sees me. "He's at the pool all the time. He was a swimmer once."

"Howdy," I say, shaking the kid's soft hand. He's got bad skin and some kind of problem with his mouth—it seems to want to hang open all by itself. He's got his cigarettes rolled up in his shirt sleeve.

"Bad circulation," he says, waving the hand I just shook in my face. "That's why I gave it up. It was back in high school, anyway."

I nod at him and look across the kitchen at Simon and Jennifer who are in the corner by the table of snacks. She's feeding him a small pastry. He's chewing and laughing, and she's trying to push the remaining twist of dough into his mouth. "You've got to keep after it," I say to Teller. "Can't lay off."

"Yeah," he says. "The lungs go. Like horn players."

"The lips go on horn players," Clare says.

"Lips, lungs," Teller says. "Whatever."

"Yeah," I say.

Jennifer sees me and waves at my pants with a piece of meat on the end of a toothpick. "Snappy, Bosco," she says.

"Bosco?" Teller says. "Your name is Bosco? Did you know there used to be this drink called Bosco? Wow. That's neat."

"Thank you," I say.

"Carl's on the porch," Clare says. "He got the car out but I think he creamed the bumper or something."

"Look," Teller says, talking to Clare. "You people want to come over to my place? I've got a little stash, you know—"

"A time warp," Clare says, patting Teller's shoulder.

"Yeah, I'm having some kind of resolution problem tonight," he says. "I mean, it's a little slow, you know? Not fully formed. But I like things just hung out, see what I'm saying?" The kid has the tail of his T-shirt wrapped around two fingers, and he's pulling down on the shirt, stretching the neck opening and showing a chest with no hair.

"I'd prefer you go ahead and keep your shirt on," Clare says.

"I'm kind of dumb," Teller says, still pulling the shirt. "I don't know why. I've always been that way. People pick on me. I'm always getting pounded by loaders at all-night gas stations." He gives the shirt a vicious tug. "But, hey, I do all right with women."

"You're blowing me down," Clare says, gripping his shoulder. "Maybe another time, huh?" She releases Teller and steers me toward the porch. "Let's get Carl and get out of here," she whispers. "Did you see his skin? What is he, a hairless?"

We go through the living room, which is cramped, full of homemade furniture. Some people I've met once are gathered around a small coffee table looking at and talking about a large frozen fish Carl has brought out. He's been saving the fish in his freezer for two years. I've seen it before. There's a guy in front of the TV playing a video game and arguing with himself. Carl is standing by the door to the porch wearing the waders Clare had on earlier.

"I dented your fender," he says, handing me one of the door mirrors off the Subaru. "This fell off."

"Doesn't matter," I say. I give the mirror to Clare. "I took a pair of your pants. That O.K.?"

"Those are my purples," Carl says. "I like them pretty much."

"You've got the yellows as a fallback," Clare says. She picks a thread off the pocket seam of the pants.

"Right," he says. "What about Jennifer?"

"She's in the kitchen with Oster."

"Not anymore," Clare says, looking in the car mirror.

Jennifer and Simon and Teller come out of the kitchen together. Jennifer's between the other two, with her arms around both of them. "Teller's got us," Jennifer says as the three of them brush past. "Don't you worry."

"So long," I say.

"Later," Teller says.

We step outside and watch them get into Oster's Mercedes and drive away, the car lights sweeping over the Subaru, which Carl has dragged all the way back to the scrub line. Clare holds up the mirror, flicks a finger at the hair above her forehead, then looks at her eyes. "Me, I'm a young person," she says, and then she sticks the mounting stem of the mirror in my back pocket.

I grab the mirror before it falls out of my pocket and then wave toward the car. "Ready?" I say.

Clare does a shallow curtsy and then jumps the five steps to the beach. "Yes, sir," she says. She squats and duck-walks across the sand. "I'm just a girl at heart. I don't want to hear anything about adults." I look at Carl and he looks at me and then both of us look toward Clare, who's halfway to the Subaru already and almost invisible in the darkness. I give him the mirror and jump the steps just the way Clare did, nearly landing on my face in the sand, then I duck-walk a couple of feet, but it's hard and I hear my knees cracking, so I straighten up and stroll the rest of the way.

# Lumber

THE WINDOWS of Cherry's station wagon are open, and bits of her furniture—a rolled-up rug, the legs of a chair, a lamp with the light bulb still in it—stick out on three sides. The engine is running, and there's white smoke shooting out the exhaust pipe. She's stopped to talk to me in the parking lot, turning in the seat so she can fold her arms on the car door.

"I never wanted to leave in the first place," she says.

"Sure you did." Then I remember she doesn't like being told what she thinks. "Or maybe you didn't. It's not that far, anyway."

She's moving from Palm Shadows to another, newer apartment group, Courtland, three blocks away, because some kids broke into her apartment a week ago, terrorized her, threatened rape, then took her stereo and TV and a hundred dollars in grocery money.

"You think I should stay?"

"No. I think you're lucky it wasn't worse."

Cherry is forty; she looks like an out-of-date teen-ager. "Don't be silly," she says. The engine is loping now, faltering and catching up again. She hits the gas pedal once and a fresh pillow of smoke gathers behind the wagon. "You could move too, you know. That might be fun."

I like the way we both stop and wait for the remark to get sexy; in eight months as neighbors, this has become a routine.

"I've got to go now," she says. "But you're going to call me, right?" She straightens up behind the wheel, then reaches into her purse and pulls out a felt-tipped pen. "You got paper? I'll give you my new number."

I don't have paper, so she prints her telephone number on my wrist in big square letters. I crook my hand around, trying to read it. "What's that?" I say, pointing to something she's drawn at the end of the number.

"That's a picture of you and me. Sitting pretty."

Later, in the Handy Andy annex, I'm looking at the half-inch plywood sheets when Cherry comes up behind me and pats my backside. I yelp and jump about two feet. Cherry laughs. "What, you gonna board up the place now that I'm gone?"

"I'm just here being lonely."

"Not me. I'm having a great time. This looks like bad plywood." She fingers the topmost in a stack of precut four-by-four sheets. "What is this, A.D.?" She looks at me. "That's plywood talk. Do you want to do something?"

"Yes. Anything."

She moves away toward the full-size plywood and says, over her shoulder, "I could take you to my new place. It's got great locks. We could arrange my furniture." She squints and twists her head like a puzzled dog. "Or we could not arrange my furniture, and eat something instead. I've got peaches."

The guy who works the annex comes up and says, "So you're looking for some first-rate plywood?" He's about forty-five and so thin he looks sick, wearing checked pants, a short-sleeved white shirt, and a purple tie about eight inches long.

"This is the ugliest plywood I ever saw," Cherry says. "What kind is it?"

"Just plywood," he says. "Plywood."

"I guess you're right," Cherry says. "I'm thinking about building a bed—a frame, you know."

"Yeah, well," he says, banging his knuckles on the stack, "this is the stuff, all right. We get a lot of people want to build beds, and this is what they use right here. Fifty cents a cut, but my saw man is gone."

"I'm just shopping, anyway," Cherry says. "I'm not ready to buy."

The salesman frowns and rubs a hand back over his scalp, looking toward the front of the huge store. His tie has a polo player on it. When he turns back to us, I say, "Maybe we'll come back tomorrow. Your saw man be in tomorrow?"

"Sure will." He shakes his head and starts to walk away. "I don't know why you types come in here."

When he's out of earshot, Cherry whispers, "How rude."

"I don't think you build beds out of plywood, usually."

"No? Well, no wonder."

We go to her new apartment. Courtland is a small complex, only twenty units, and it looks like a Motel 6. I have to park my car behind hers in the parking lot, because all the spaces are assigned. It's a cool night and it smells as if it's going to rain. Cherry stands by my car door as I get out. "You'd better lock it," she says.


It's raining hard when I wake up. Cherry's asleep. The telephone is ringing, but I can barely hear it for the rain. I don't know what time it is. I shake Cherry, but she groans and rolls over. She's not going to wake up in time to get the phone, so I go out into the cluttered living room. It's dark, and I accidentally kick the wooden crate the telephone is on, knocking the receiver off its hook. When I finally get the phone to my ear, a woman's voice is saying hello.

"Hi," I say. "Cherry's asleep. I kicked the phone over."

"Mark?"

"No. I'm Frank. Mark's not here. Who is this?"

There's a pause; then the woman says, "Lois. This is Lois. I've got to talk to Cherry—could you wake her?"

I tell the woman to hold on, and I go back into the bedroom and snap on the desk lamp; Cherry's already up, sitting on the edge of the bed with my shirt on. "That's Lois, I guess," she says. "What time is it?"

I hand her the travel clock from the desk and go over to the window. There's a yellow light on a pole in the alley that runs behind Courtland, and below it the bushes are whipping around in the wind. "Good storm," I say.

Cherry tosses me the clock and heads for the living room. It's four-ten. I put the clock on the desk and follow her.

She's sitting on the floor by the crate, her legs crossed under her, waving a pack of cigarettes at me and pointing across the room. The only light is from the lamp in the bedroom, so I can't see what she's pointing at. I step over a couple of cardboard boxes full of phonograph records and open the drapes in front of the sliding doors which gives me enough grayish light to find the matches. Cherry's saying into the phone, "Now, just start over, real slow, O.K.? Take it easy." I hand her the matches and watch her light a cigarette and push the hair away from her face with her palm.

There's a beach towel on the arm of the couch; I wrap the towel around me and look out across the street, where there's another apartment group, all lit up with thin green light that's distorted by the water on the sliding door. The rain is banging up into spirals where it hits, slapping the glass and blowing off the overhang at forty-five degrees. In the parking lot across the street there are two cars with their lights on; somebody in a yellow rain slicker with a Day-Glo pink stripe across the shoulders is running back and forth between the cars. One of the cars has its emergency lights on, so the taillights blink together; the red-orange flashes are magnified and splintered by the rain. I keep switching my focus between the cars and the glass in the door.

Cherry rocks awkwardly as she talks softly into the phone, coaxing the woman on the other end of the line. I go into the kitchen and open the refrigerator. It looks peculiarly bright and precise inside. I'm trying to decide if I want the half cantaloupe on the top shelf next to the milk when Cherry starts snapping her fingers at me from the other room. When I look, she makes a drinking motion with her hand and then points at me. I pull things to drink out of the refrigerator—beer, orange juice, apple juice, tomato juice, milk. Coke. It turns out she wants apple juice, which was the third thing I showed her; I give her the bottle and a glass. She gives the glass back, then twists the top off the juice and takes a drink.

She's twenty minutes on the phone. I sit on the couch and talk to the cantaloupe, listening to the rain and to her end of the conversation. She's lovely to watch, all folded up on the floor—sloppy but businesslike, deft somehow. I think of the nights I've spent wondering if she was alone in her apartment; even if she had been, she probably wouldn't have been alone in the same way—she'd have had something to do, some project, some work.

"Lois is coming up," Cherry says when she gets off the phone. She hangs her head and fiddles with the juice bottle, which is on the floor between her legs. "I'm real tired. Are you? That's a stupid question, I guess."


Lois comes in wearing a turban and light-blue pin-cord Bermuda shorts. She's got dark skin and a pear-size red birthmark on one side of her mouth and under her chin. She seems cheerful and wide awake. "You must be Frank, right? I'm Lois." We shake hands and I see another birthmark, this one smaller and cloud-shaped, running up the back of her thumb.

"Good morning," I say. I've got my jeans on and the towel draped over my shoulders; Cherry still has my shirt.

"So," Lois says. "What's for breakfast?"

Cherry comes out of the bedroom zipping her pants. "Hiya, baby," she says, opening her arms to hug Lois. I back up a little, trying to get out of the way, trip over one of the record boxes, and then, to avoid falling, do a kind of somersault onto the couch. The women pause in their embrace to look.

"He an acrobat of some kind?" Lois says.

Cherry gives Lois a slap on the rump.

"I could eat a hundred something right about now," Lois says. "First I gotta get rid of this." She hooks her fingers under the turban, pulls it off her head, flips it toward me.

"Frank needs attention," Cherry says. "Why don't you amuse him while I check the food."

Cherry goes into the kitchen, and Lois sits splay-legged on the arm of the couch. "So, Frank," she says, scratching her scalp with her fingernails. "How are you?"

Lois has a burr haircut and pretty eyes, but because of her size and the haircut she looks like a man. I say I'm O.K., and ask her how she is.

"I'm a mess—oh, maybe you guessed that. I'm having a crisis. I always have my crises at four in the morning, usually. That way they seem more crisislike, know what I mean? What's that on your stomach?" She points at a crescent-shaped scar on my left side where my sister caught me with the broken neck of a Coke bottle when I was fourteen.

"Scar," I say.

She nods and chews on the side of her lip. "So I'm having this crisis and I call Cherry and here you are answering the phone. It surprised me."

"Me too. What's the crisis? Or is that not my business?"

"Well, no—I'm just having this crisis." She looks at the window. "I mean, I could tell you, but you probably wouldn't understand, because—oh, this is going to sound so stupid."

"What?"

"Oh—because you're a man.

"You're right—it sounds stupid."

"That's clever. Who are you—Sheriff Lobo? What happened was, my boyfriend hit me." She points to her ear. "Here. He smacked me in the head. I didn't like it."

"What did you do?"

"What do you mean what did I do? I didn't do anything—he just hit me because he was mad."

"No, I meant what did you do then, after he hit you."

"Oh. I ran like hell. I don't want people hitting me all the time." She tugs at her crotch. "Doesn't matter. He's just some new thing I picked up. I probably should've known better."

"How many eggs out there?" Cherry calls from the kitchen.

"I wish I'd had some eggs before," Lois says. "I'd have given him a scrambled face." She slaps her palm into her forehead as if she's smacking somebody with an egg. "Take that!"

"Hello?" Cherry says, leaning around the kitchen doorframe and waving a white spatula in her hand.

"Two for me," I say. "Want some help?"

"I don't think I want any," Lois says. She sticks her hands in the pockets of her shorts and leans back, crossing her feet on a box by the couch. "So, you ever hit a woman, Frank? I mean, you know, really hit her?"

"I don't think so."

"What's that mean? Either you did or you didn't. Are you prissy?"

"No."

"Ah." She nods vigorously and loses her balance so that she has to drop her feet to the floor to steady herself. "Yeah, well— some men don't. That's true, I guess. Maybe you're one of those. Anyway, this guy was a jerk, a real bohunk—what's a bo-hunk?"

"A bad guy, rat."

"Cherry? You got a dictionary around here somewhere? I want to look up 'bohunk.' "

"It's not in the dictionary," Cherry says from the kitchen. "I already looked."

"When did you look?" Lois says.

"So maybe it is," Cherry says. "The dictionary's packed and the eggs are ready."

We eat in the living room. Lois goes over the details of the fight with her boyfriend, Milby. They were in the car, sitting out in front of her apartment downstairs; they were arguing. Milby slugged her when she yelled at him about leaving his junk all over her apartment. Then she got out of the car and ran inside, gathered up everything that belonged to him, and threw it out on the sidewalk. He sat in the car and watched her do this. He looked pretty sitting there in the car in the rain. She stood in the doorway for a long time, staring at him. He was so gorgeous she wanted to get back into the car with him, but was afraid to; as a conciliatory gesture, Lois went out into the rain and got all of his stuff and took it back into the apartment. Then she stood on the doorstep and watched him for another five minutes before he started the car and drove off. He didn't say a word, didn't even wave, just started up and left. This all happened at about two-thirty. She tried to call him, but either he wasn't home or he wasn't answering the phone. She put all his stuff in the bathtub, except the boots; those she put on the top of the stove the way her father used to do with his boots. She tried to call Milby again, then changed her clothes and tried again. No answer. That's when she called Cherry. "And got you," she says, pointing her fork at me. "You guys were probably sleeping, right?"

"Milby's an ape," Cherry says.

"He's a nice ape," Lois says. She looks at me. "O.K., let's have the man's point of view on this."

"Love conquers all?"

"It's the first time he's ever done anything like this."

"Maybe it's a freak thing," Cherry says.

"If you're lucky," I say.

"You're the one who's lucky," Lois says. "You don't get hit in the face if you don't do what we want."


When I wake up on Saturday morning, Cherry's on her back on the bedroom floor, grunting softly as she does stretching exercises for her legs. The bedroom isn't large, so all I can see is her feet—which have thick half socks on them—coming together and separating suddenly. I watch the feet for a few minutes and then say, "Good morning."

"Oh, hi," she says, sitting up beyond the end of the bed. "Did I wake you?"

There's not much light in the room and I have a hard time making out Cherry's features; her face looks bloated and too white. "No. I just woke up. What are you doing?"

"Working on the legs. I probably shouldn't worry about it, but I do."

"They're very pretty—kind of leglike and pretty."

She turns and talks to the chair that's tipped against the wall. "What does he mean by that? Is he talking to me?"

"Where's Lois? She not here yet?"

"Don't be nasty about Lois," Cherry says. She struggles to her feet and stretches, reaching straight above her head with both hands. I hear things in her back popping. "I suppose you're going to want coffee?"

I roll out of bed and stand there looking around the room for my pants.

We have coffee on the couch. She has on chrome-green running shorts and a white T-shirt with "Spider" stitched in a shallow arc over the small pocket. The shirt is tucked into the waistband of the pants. Outside, the cars I saw last night are still in the parking lot across the street; the hood on one of the cars is raised, and there's somebody bent into the engine compartment. The coffee is bitter.

"This is the part I don't like," Cherry says after we've been silent for a while. "Waiting for the guy to leave." She touches my leg. "I shouldn't have said that, huh? That was a lousy thing to say."

"It's all right. I know what you mean. Maybe I'll go and then call you later."

"We could eat or something." She props up a knee and balances her cup on it. "Maybe we could go to the coast? I just hate this part. It doesn't have anything to do with you." She sighs and gets up quickly, almost losing the coffee, and stands at the glass door. "No, that's worse, isn't it?"

"It's really O.K. Just let me get set and I'll move along." Her shorts bag a little in the seat. "The coast sounds like a terrific idea."

"That's the most insincere thing you ever said to me."

"I know. It wasn't very good, was it? But maybe the coast will sound terrific later."

"What a man," she says, picking up my jacket and brushing it with her hand.


Milby is about five eight, with curly black hair and a drooping mustache that almost covers his mouth. He's wearing a plaid cowboy shirt with pearl snap buttons, and he has spurs on his boots. He's leaning over the railing outside Cherry's door when I open it. "You Frank?" he says, combing the mustache with his forefinger. I nod, and he says, "I'm Milby. We need to have a little meet."

Cherry, standing just inside her apartment, holding on to the edge of the door, says, "You kind of screwed up last night, didn't you?"

"Hello, Cherry," he says. "I didn't want to wake you up, so I waited out here. I figured you'd have to come out sooner or later." He waves to show us where he waited. "Maybe I'd better just talk to Frank here."

"Maybe you'd better talk to Lois," she says.

"I did that already. I've been talking to her since five. I didn't get any sleep." Milby moves a lot when he talks, and the spurs make a noise like a cash register. "She told me I better talk to you all."

"It's you and Lois," I say. "No reason to talk to us."

"I want to talk to you," Milby says. He reaches up, grabs me by the shoulder, and squeezes gently. "I really need to."

"Jesus Christ," Cherry says. "What kind of jerk are you?" She shakes her head. "I'd have your ass in jail."

"I should be in jail," he says. "That's where I should be. I'm really sorry I'm not, but I'm not." He backs up when Cherry steps out of her apartment onto the balcony. "I was thinking maybe I could buy you a steak, Frank. We could talk things over."

I look back at Cherry, and she shrugs and looks away. "I don't care," she says. "He just wants somebody to tell him it's O.K."

"It's not," Milby says. "I know that much."

"Then you want somebody to listen to all the reasons, and there aren't any reasons worth talking about."

"No, really," he says. "I just want to talk to Frank a bit. It's nothing like that, Cherry."

"So talk, already. Go get a steak and talk. Be men all over the place. Practice spitting."

He cocks up his boot and kicks at the concrete balcony with the spur, spinning it and holding it up until it stops. Cherry says, "Oh, go on," kisses my cheek, and gives me a push.

When we get downstairs, Milby points at his black Camaro and says, "Let's take mine, O.K.?"

We go to a place called Western Sizzlin, a franchise with fifteen kinds of beef and a sad-looking salad bar. He tells me to get whatever I want, so I order the eight-dollar rib eye. We take a booth by the window and look at the cars going by in the street. Finally Milby says, "It wasn't that hard. I mean, I know it's stupid, but it wasn't real hard, you know? I just kind of popped her to shut her up."

"Like they used to do in movies."

"Yeah. Hey, there's no bruise. I'm telling you it wasn't that bad." He fiddles with the A.1. sauce, unscrewing the cap and turning the bottle upside down on his thumb, then sucking off the brown sauce. He sighs. "Yeah, O.K. I don't know what happened. I knew enough to pull it, though. While it was happening."

"That's a start."

"You damn right it is," he says. "She deserved it, you know what I'm saying? I mean, bitch, bitch, bitch—you got to do something."

He looks tired and short-tempered, and I wonder what I can get away with. "Try a wall."

"You don't think fast enough. The thing is, they take advantage of everything—all the differences—but you can't. You get pissed after a while."

"Everybody gets pissed." I wonder why I don't tell him what I want to tell him, why he scares me. "Who's this 'they,' anyway?"

"The bitches—what are you, some Holy Ghost or something? I don't need catechism lessons, brother. It's jerks like you screw it up for the rest of us. I'm telling you it just happens, and you're telling me Hail Mary, full of grace. That's a big help."

"Yeah, O.K.," I say, cutting through my steak. "You're probably right."

That does it. He doesn't want to talk about last night anymore, he wants to talk football—what do I think about the Bears? I tell him what I think, something I read in the paper about Payton's legs. When we're finished eating, he pays with a credit card and I thank him for the lunch.

In the car on the way back to the Courtland he tells me there's nothing wrong with Payton's legs, the legs are O.K., and then skids into a place in front of Lois's first-floor apartment.

Somehow Cherry has gotten her station wagon out from in front of my car. I thank Milby again and leave him sitting in the flashy black interior of the Camaro, the radio pumping out news. At Palm Shadows I get my mail, say hello to the robust landlord who's digging around in some bushes near my door, and go upstairs. The phone is ringing, so I have to hustle to get through both locks. It's Cherry, calling to tell me she's busy and maybe she'll give me a call tomorrow. I tell her I'm going to take a bath, and she says it's high time.

# Exotic Nile

THE WATER was running in the tub and I had Theo on the telephone when Dewey Nassar appeared outside my door waving a plastic bag with a four-inch goldfish in it. This was a blue goldfish. Nassar was my landlord at the Nile, a thin fellow with no black hair on top of his head but plenty around the sides. I told Theo I'd call her back and turned off the water in the bath.

"Let's get him into something where he can breathe," Nassar said, jiggling the fish at me. We dug through the boxes of kitchen equipment. "How about this?" He peeled newspaper off a white mixing bowl. "This is Theo's, right?"

Nassar liked her because she used to clip Egypt stories out of newspapers and magazines for him. He was crazy about Egypt. When she and I separated, he was upset, and he never missed a chance to remind me that his life too had been impoverished by her departure.

The day after she left, she sent some people to take the furniture. All of it. Left me with a studio apartment, the crockery, and four table legs that belonged to my father. They were wonderful legs—Aalto, I think—but that hadn't been our arrangement. I liked Theo and I didn't care much about furniture, so I bought a bed and two lawn chairs, and a tripod lamp, and made do.

"No more cakes, huh?" Nassar flattened his hand and swam it around inside the bowl. "Plenty of room."

"Keep looking," I said.

We finally settled on a quart orange juice bottle, but the fish didn't quite fit. It had to swim at a sixty-degree angle to keep from hitting the glass. "Looks a little cramped in there," Nassar said. "I'll get you an aquarium tomorrow." He tilted the bottle so the fish could straighten out. "Make this a happy fish."

The fish was gulping and staring at us through the bottle.

The Nile was thirty apartments bunched around a small courtyard. Nassar had built the complex in 1953 after a trip to Cairo with his mother—designed it all himself, right down to the camels in the peach stucco and the carnival-striped awnings. The courtyard featured rock flower beds, a kidney-style pool, three pyramid doghouses, one each in red, blue, and yellow, and palms—skinny, wretched-looking things nine feet tall, with bits of growth at their tops. At one end he'd put a fountain shaped like a crescent moon. The water shot out of a green boat that was supposed to look as if it was flying out of this fountain. He'd put a life-size papier-mâché steer next to the pool and hand-lettered O-F-F-I-C-E on its side, with an arrow pointing toward his door. And at night, every night, colored flood lamps lit the buildings of the Nile.

He stood at one of my two sliding-glass doors, looking out into the court. "I wanted a real cow," he said. "Wouldn't that have been something? Theo would've loved that."

"Thanks for the fish," I said.


The next afternoon I went to the university library and got the new Dick Francis book. I'd been reading more since Theo left. On the steps outside the library I bumped into Nassar's wife, Mariana. She was using the pay telephone. She was wearing a short-sleeved shirt with pink and blue triangles all over it—the kind of shirt young girls find in thrift shops—and it looked good on her.

"My fault," I said. "Pardon me."

She put her palm over the mouthpiece. "Thanks for the rub-down, Buster."

"Absolutely an accident," I said.

"I believe you," she said. She was smiling, laughing a little. "Really. So get lost, O.K.?"

Nassar was parked three cars down from mine, sitting in his Toyota truck with his windows up. He had on clear-rimmed dark glasses, and he was toying with his newly grown pencil mustache. He too was talking on a telephone, a white one with a curled cord stretching toward his dashboard.

I started my car and then sat for a minute watching his wife. I didn't know her well at all. She and Theo had gone running a few times, and when they finished they'd come into the apart-ment for water. Sometimes in summer they sat by the pool to-gether. I'd gotten the impression that Mariana thought I was silly, but there wasn't any evidence that that's what she thought.

Nassar rapped on my passenger-side window. He did it with his ring, so the noise was annoyingly sharp. "Hey," he said, twirling his forefinger next to his ear and then pointing toward his wife. "She's nuts. She made her hair red."

"It's very pretty," I said, turning the window crank.

He wore a yellow-and-black plaid shirt, and his face was an al-most perfect oval, the wrong shape for the mustache. He tucked his head in the window and glanced around at my car. "Clean," he said. His wife had hung up and was walking toward the li-brary entrance.

"Thanks."

"You busy? Want to take a ride?" He popped up my door lock with a thick finger. "I gotta get back before dark, though."

"I don't know," I said. I let the car roll back a little, but he opened the door, so I braked.

"Sure you do," he said. He grinned and stepped into the front seat. His boots were too big, laced up in front almost to the knee, with his pant legs pushed inside. He drummed on the glove-compartment door with the nails of his fingers. "You looking for Theo?"

"Hunting a book," I said. Theo worked at the university, but I hadn't seen her, hadn't gone looking for her. She was living with her new boyfriend at another of Nassar's properties. I'd been to her apartment a couple of times, but I hadn't met the boyfriend. In fact, I'd only seen Theo a few times, maybe half a dozen, since we split.

At the highway intersection we stopped behind a Cadillac. "A book," Nassar said. "A book. That's what I figured. I just got this new phone in my truck. I was trying it out."

"So I saw," I said. "You were talking to Mariana."

"Right. But she didn't say anything. She said you bumped into her." We got caught at the light again and then watched a fire engine go by. He said, "How about that? Must be a fire. Let's take a look, huh?" He banged me on the arm with the back of his hand, then pointed after the truck.

"Chase the truck," I said. I swung into the turn lane.

"Might be headed for one of mine," he said. "Blue Gardens, out beyond the loop."

I made the turn and then got sandwiched between a rental van and a four-door Mercury on the highway.

"Hit this dude with your horn," he said.

I poked the horn stalk a couple of times and watched the Mercury's turn signal come on, blinking slowly as if the car had some electrical problem. The fire truck was gone when we got past.

"Doesn't matter," he said. "Let's go to Howard Johnson's. Unless you've got a major date."

The road was new, smooth blacktop. A bright-green gully separated the in and out lanes, and the amber lights must have just come on. Damp air swirled through the car, tossing some papers around in the back. I let up on the accelerator. Nassar twisted around and reached over the seat.

"I'll handle it. You drive," he said. "Past the light and make a U." He sat up and hit me on the shoulder. "Get you a waffle. You've got waffle written all over you. How's my fish doing?"

"Great," I said.

The motel was on top of a small cliff overlooking the freeway. Nassar pointed to a blue-lined handicapped-parking zone by the front door. "Take that one."

The lobby smelled bad. A kid in a white short-sleeved shirt and a solid-black tie asked us if we had reservations.

"This is Ramone," Nassar said, pointing to the kid. "Ramone, this is my favorite tenant, Mr. Leaf."

"Sure," the kid said, tipping an imaginary hat.

The restaurant was large and empty. The chairs were studded with big black-headed furniture tacks. Nassar took a booth by the window, but a pretty teen-ager came out of the kitchen and told him to move because she wasn't serving that station. The girl had rough skin, blue eyes, and freckles. Her hair, which fell to her waist in back, was the color of boot leather. "Didn't you see the sign?" she said. Then she realized there wasn't any sign. "There's supposed to be a sign over here." She walked toward the table. "Says 'Section Closed' or something. You know the sign I'm talking about?"

"We missed it," Nassar said. He got out of the booth. "Which section's open?"

"Depends what you want," the girl said. "I mean, you want a meal, you're out of luck. Coffee, maybe a piece of pie. I guess you could sit anywhere. Except here—this is closed." She stuck a knee on the seat of a booth two down from ours and leaned close to the window for a look outside. "This must be the winter," she said.

"My wife's baby sister Lorraine," he said, gesturing toward

the waitress. She turned around and smiled, and he said, "Two coffees, and a waffle for Mr. Leaf."

"Got no waffles," she said, smiling at me.

I smiled back at her. She looked a lot like Mariana, only younger, fresher. "Hi," I said. "How about pie?"

Nassar pointed across the room. "We're going to sit over here at the counter."

"Takeouts," she said. She wiped at the tabletop with a brown rag she was carrying, and then straightened and came back toward our booth. "Hey," she said. "What the heck. Go on in the booth. Just don't make a mess."

"O.K.," Nassar said, sitting again.

She did our table with the rag, bumping the sugar bowl and the salt-and-pepper shakers out of the way. "Now, on the pie"—she turned to look at the glass-fronted cooler behind the takeout counter—"I know I've got lemon, and there's a new thing, raisin delight or something. Does that make sense?"

"Well, pie's pretty messy," Nassar said.

"Naw, pie's fine. But these two aren't real good. Even the showboats won't eat 'em." She sighed and slapped the rag at the back of my seat. "We get these guys, you know? Black hair and all that, pointy shoes in ice-cream colors, and they're real polite for about ten minutes, and then bang, they're on you like some kind of squid." She started for the kitchen but stopped halfway across the room to get a ketchup packet off the floor. "See what I mean?" she said, waving the packet at us.

Outside, the motel's sign was blinking, and the sky behind it was the color of pewter. Lorraine's radio was playing "Hotel California," and through the slit into the kitchen I saw her dancing. A fat fellow in red checkered pants peered into the restaurant. He was bald, with a black beard trimmed very close to his skin.

"I sure don't like the look of that moose," Nassar said.

Lorraine brought the coffee. "Ardith's late," she said. "I guess that's why you came, huh? She may not even be on tonight. I'll have to check the schedule. Actually, I'm not on, either. I was on this afternoon."

"She thinks I'm in love with her friend Ardith," Nassar said. He got out of the booth and took Lorraine's arm, and they went across the room. I heard them talking, but I couldn't make out what was being said. Then Lorraine disappeared into the kitchen, and he came back to the table grinning. "Well, Mr. Leaf, we're going to the bay."

"We are?"

"Yeah. The Wet Club—you know that place?"

When I shook my head, he said, "It's terrific, really. Lorraine wants to eat. It's only twenty minutes." He smacked me on the biceps and wagged his head toward the kitchen. "She's driving. Don't worry. We can get your car on the way back. She's got a convertible."

"I don't think so," I said. I yawned and stretched. Then I yawned again. "I think I'll go home, take a rest. Thanks anyway."

"Aw, come on. You've got to eat, don't you?" He raised an eyebrow and pointed toward the kitchen with his head. "She's young, but she's not that young. And she likes you."

"She does?" I said. I punched him in the arm. "That makes all the difference in the world, doesn't it? Tell me how you manage to be so charming."

"Breeding," he said.

Lorraine came through the kitchen doors smoothing the skirt of her black uniform. She stopped for a minute at the cash register, then came across the room and dropped a set of car keys into Nassar's hand. "You get him?"

"Hard to say," Nassar said. "I think he wants to go home."

"Oh, don't be such a bozo," she said, linking her arm through mine. "It isn't that far. I want you to come."

"Tell him please," Nassar said.

*       *       *

We went back through town in Lorraine's convertible with the
radio too loud and the top down. We had to shout to talk.
"Dewey says I look like a hippie," Lorraine said. "Do you think
so?"

"You aren't old enough," I said.

"I know. I've seen pictures, you know—magazine articles."

I nodded and tried to keep her hair out of my face.

"He just says it because I wear a lot of tank tops in the summer."

Nassar was low behind the wheel, playing with his mustache.
He caught me looking and winked. Lorraine turned around and
yelled something into his ear, and he grinned and gave her a
hard squeeze on the thigh. Then she was back at me, her breath
warm on my ear. She made me nervous, and I think she knew it.
I liked that about her.

Nassar was doing seventy-five and Lorraine's hair kept slapping around. Finally she pulled both hands back over her forehead and twisted the hair into a roll that she brought over her
shoulder and held up in front of her to look at. "I probably
ought to get rid of this," she yelled.

We went through a little town with shiny dark bushes and
soft-looking lawns. Even the buildings looked good, because of
the copper light. Then we were back on the highway, which was
lined with billboards, property-sale signs, barbed-wire fences. No
trees. At intervals along the road there were brick houses that
looked as if they ought to be in subdivisions. I wondered how it
would feel to live out there, with the highway and the big electrical towers.

"I love it," Lorraine yelled into my ear. She pointed her hair
toward the scenery. "Makes me feel romantic." She put an arm
around my shoulder and pulled me toward her. "Are you married?"

"I was. Not anymore."

"You probably liked it."

I smiled at her and at Nassar, who was just then looking in our direction. "I'm afraid so," I said.

We passed a shopping plaza—a mall and a dozen smaller buildings scattered across acres of new black parking lot. A theatre marquee in one corner of the lot read BRING 'EM BACK ALIVE FILM FESTIVAL.

"That's really wonderful," she said. "To say that. About being married, I mean." She looked toward the shopping center and at me again, then wiped a thin curve of hair off the side of her face and started playing with the radio.

By the time we reached the bay exit, the sun was gone and the juke joints had their signs on—the Hi Hat Club, the Green Parrot, Topper's, Redfish & Candy's, the Surf Café. The oystershell parking lots were jammed with trucks. The air was salty. There was the smell of rotting fish around. As we got closer to the bay, there were more joints, bars, fish camps. The gas stations were selling live bait and cane poles. Horns honked and cars whistled by with riders sticking out windows waving beer cars and shouting obscenities at people in front and back. There was radio music all around us—a couple of the cars had loudspeakers mounted in their grilles. A place called the Heron had a covey of white neon birds flapping across its roof.

We were moving very slowly, stopping and starting in the traffic. "So, do you like me?" Lorraine said.

Nassar bent forward over the steering wheel and nodded at me. In the open bed of the truck in front of us a huge spotted dog licked at some kind of bone between its crossed paws.

"I do," I said.

We followed the truck over a wood-planked bridge, then turned onto a gravel road. For two or three blocks we plowed through gravel that felt a foot deep. There was thunder off in the distance. The sides of the narrow road were lined with boxy houses built on top of telephone poles. It was very dark. Behind us the hump of the bridge was silhouetted by tavern lights. In front, the car lights hit chrome bumpers, bike reflectors, and the gold eyes of a cat that looked and then vanished.

Nassar put up the top. It made a whirring noise. The car's engine barely idled as we crunched forward. He latched the top and then pushed buttons on the armrest to raise the windows, and we were sealed in.

"I'm real glad you like me," Lorraine said.

I threaded my hair with my fingers and then pressed my palms over my ears. "I can't hear anything."

"Don't be silly," she said.

"You're dead, pal," Nassar said.

Lorraine frowned at him. "Be quiet, Dewey." She rubbed my shoulder where she'd stuck her finger earlier, when she was telling me about the tank tops. "We're almost there." There was a line of what looked like Christmas decorations a couple of hundred yards ahead. We crossed a narrow bridge with no railing.

"What's over here?" I asked, waving to our left where it was pitch black except for one blue bulb dangling under a corrugated-tin shed.

"Inlet," Nassar said.

Lorraine looked. "You can't even see it." She tried the radio buttons one after the other and got static and an ad for True Value Hardware. She clicked off the radio. "I love new guys. I mean, look at how nice you're being."

"I am being nice," I said. I looked out my window at a man in leather shorts who was washing his underarms using a spigot next to the road. "But I'm having a good time. You're really strange."

"Me?" she said.

The Christmas lights were Japanese lanterns hung over a

makeshift walk running from a building down to a pier. There were a lot of bugs.

Nassar twirled the steering wheel, and the car bucked up an embankment that served as a parking lot for the restaurant. We got out. There was a wind coming off the Gulf, and there were metal things banging, a boat motor, the sound of ropes straining.

From the boardwalk the restaurant looked like a milk plant or some other factory built in the forties. It had a fresh coat of whitewash. The walls facing the bay were clear glass block.

"Are you hungry yet?" Lorraine said. She wrapped both arms around my waist and steered me toward the building.

"Not a bad joint," Nassar said.

"Lemme take a look at you," she said, squeezing my waist. She stopped on the boardwalk, then stepped in front of me, fingering my shirt but talking to Nassar. "You know, Mariana's crazy," she said. "He's just a regular guy." She started walking again, bouncing down the boardwalk toward the restaurant. The paper lanterns were jerking in the wind, making a rattling noise. I held the door and Lorraine ducked under my arm.

Nassar said, "There's this piece of furniture in here I want to show you. A highboy. Red lacquer, and paws for drawer handles, animal paws, bells all over it. Has a hydraulic system, so if you even touch it the thing floats away, tinkling."

"Sounds terrific," I said.

We got a round table next to the window, and Lorraine started reading the menu out loud.

"It's a fantastic deal," Nassar said. He looked toward the rear of the restaurant. "Used to be right back there." He shook out his white cotton napkin and tucked it into the neck of his lumberjack shirt.

I looked over my shoulder. "I don't see it. Is this the Wet Club?"

"The what club?" Lorraine said. "This is Red Head Boats." She flapped her menu at me so I could read the name.

"There ain't no Wet Club," Nassar said. "I made that up."

"That's the kind of guy he is," Lorraine said. She didn't look out from behind her menu. "Just makes up stuff all the time. What's a wet club?"

"Boy, what a low-brain," Nassar said, pointing at her. "Where'd we get this low-brain, anyway?"

"Mariana's got school tonight is where you got me," she said. "That's how come we can do all this."

Nassar stretched across the table and clapped a hand over my wrist. "We're taking you out to dinner, O.K.? Because we honestly like you. Mariana would be with us but she's at school, she's not here. You following this? The only people here are the three of us. You and me and Lorraine."

"I've got it," I said.

"See," Nassar said to Lorraine. He opened his hand toward me. "Angel of mercy."

"Pleased to meet you," I said. I swept my menu off the table, opening it with a flourish that rocked my empty wineglass. Lorraine caught the glass before it hit the table. "Thank you," I said.

"We'll just get the girl a snack," Nassar said. "Then speed by the blimp ruins on the way home. You know about the blimp ruins? Out past the Air Force base? It's crazy out there at night."

# Monster Deal

TEN O'CLOCK Friday morning I'm on the porch in the landlord's burgundy robe, smiling at a tall woman who has clear blue eyes and slightly curly light brown hair—she looks like an athlete. She might be thirty-five. Her fingernails are glistening and perfect in the morning light. "I'm a friend of Elliot's. Tina Graham—he didn't mention me?"

Elliot is the landlord. I tell her Elliot's out of the country until August, which is true.

"You must be Bergen, am I right?" She flaps open a legal-size suede-covered clipboard and reads, "B-E-R-G-E-N," sliding a forefinger along under the letters as she spells my name.

"That's me," I say.

"Sorry to bust in on you like this," she says, closing the folder and stepping past me into the dark foyer. "Elliot was supposed to tell you about me." She smiles as if we've settled something. "Maybe if we have some coffee I can explain—that's a pretty robe you've got." She picks up the day-old newspaper.

"I just rent," I say. "The house, I mean." Elliot's spending a year in Singapore on a cultural exchange. I leased the house—a forties' bungalow done in lobster-pink stucco and trimmed with black wood and culvert tile—for the year. The neighborhood is steep driveways and cars parked in yards, wood-frame houses, dirty white paint. Kids in striped shirts go by in groups of three or four, one of them always dragging a stick he uses to ward off dogs. Elliot told me he didn't care about the money.

Tina leads me into the kitchen. "Listen, do you play squash? Maybe we could play later." She drops the paper on the table and points at several different cabinets. "Coffee?"

"Sure," I say, showing her the coffee.

She takes off her jacket, rolls up her shirt sleeves, washes her hands with the Ivory. "No beans?"

I shake my head. "Sorry."

"Doesn't matter," she says. "The grinder didn't work last time anyway." She finds the filters in the cabinet above the coffee maker and glances at me while she puts eight or nine measures of coffee into the machine.

I rub my face. I start to say I'll make the coffee, but she playfully elbows me aside and takes the pot to the sink for water.

"Elliot should have explained this deal." She gestures toward the coffee maker. "I don't like to drink things I can't see through. How about yourself?"

The kitchen is small. I have to get out of the way as she moves from counter to cabinet, getting cups, starting the toast, collecting the silverware from the dishwasher. I sit at the breakfast table and play with the newspaper, spinning it absent-mindedly, thinking about the girl who delivers it. She's rough, young, and sexy—I've only seen her up close once. Yesterday. After picking up the paper, I tripped on the front step trying to wave to her. She stopped to see if I was hurt. I invited her to dinner, but she told me she couldn't because she wasn't really a paper girl and she had to go to class. So I said what about Friday, and she said O.K.

That awkward stuff has been happening to me. I bump into doorframes, hit my head on cabinet doors, trip on the legs of the bed—one morning last week I fell down trying to put the orange juice back into the refrigerator.

"They call you Jerry, right?" Tina says from the kitchen. "O.K. if I call you Jerry?"

"Sure." Through the French doors there's a courtyard filled with big-leafed plants and twisted vines that hang from a large tree. The court is paved with Mexican tile—blue, white, rose, yellow—and built around a bird fountain. The sun is bright but thin—a winter sun, even though it's May—and the courtyard is still shadowy and wet looking. There's a foot-high crucifix made of colored glass embedded in the part of the garage wall I can see from the breakfast room.

Tina comes around the counter balancing two cups of coffee, one on top of the other, the way waitresses do at diners. In the other hand she's got a plate stacked with toast, and, on top of the toast, the butter dish out of the refrigerator. "Sloppy," she says, raising both hands slightly. "But it gets the job done. You like toast?" She puts the cups and the toast on the table, then returns to the kitchen.

"Looks good," I say, unstacking the coffees. "What's this deal with Elliot?"

She comes back carrying my peach preserves and a big jar of Welch's grape jelly. "Well, I'm here three, maybe four times a year, last couple of years, anyway. Always stay with Elliot. We were in school together—St. Dominic's in Mobile. Same class with Snake Stabler, you know? The quarterback? Here, try this peach. It's really delicious."

She spoons peach preserves on a slice of toast and pushes it across the linoleum tabletop on a napkin.

"I handle specialties, stuff you can't find ordinarily, stuff I pick up here and there. Right now it's housewares—Tupperware quality but no name, so it's cheap. Or I can go the other way, get you a thousand-dollar vacuum cleaner. Best damn vacuum cleaner you ever saw." She shakes her head and stares over her raised coffee cup out into the courtyard. "Absolutely vacuum you out of your socks—I demo'd it in Virginia and sucked up a cocker spaniel. Not the whole thing, just the tail. I got it out right away. I thought it'd be broken or something. It was cut up pretty good and didn't have much hair, but it was O.K. I was scared to death. The woman took the demonstrator and gave me a check."

She backs away from the table and takes off her shoes, using the toe of one foot on the heel of the other. "Look," she says. "It's a terrible imposition, but do you mind if I stay? That's my deal with Elliot—I stay and buy the dinner." She picks up her shoes, putting a finger in the heel of each. "Tell you what, you check me out. Meanwhile, I'll catch some sleep." She hooks the heels of her shoes on the table edge, folds a slice of toast in half, then dishes grape jelly into it. "Sandwich," she says, picking up the shoes again. "Fair enough? Which bedroom do you want me in?"


I go to the office and call Larry, a friend of Elliot's. I tell him what's happened, and he tells me it's fine, he knows Tina. "She's great," he says.

"Good looking," I say. "But she's a monster. Six feet if she's an inch."

"Six two," he says. "So wear boots and go to a monster movie."

"Funny," I say.

"I'm serious," he says. "She loves 'em. She'll make all the noises like the creatures, whatever noises they make—I saw an alligator movie with her once and she yawned menacingly all night."

"I'm busy tonight, Larry."

"So maybe I'll come over and take care of Tina. We can double up."

"You come over and we'll discuss that." When I hang up, Ruth, the woman who works for me, comes in and says we've got a report due Tuesday and she doesn't want to be typing all night Monday.

I yawn at her. It doesn't have any effect, so I tell her about Tina and she says, "You want me to handle it or is this two-for-one week?"

Ruth is thirty-five, an ex–collegiate wrestler, conference champion in her division three years running. She and her boyfriend and her three kids from a previous marriage live in a trailer on the East side. I've been talking about the girl who throws the paper for several weeks, and yesterday, when I said I had a date with with her, Ruth got annoyed.

"Tina's real pretty," I say.

Ruth pushes her hair away from her face. "So's Sylvester Stallone. So's a bazooka." She reaches for the phone. "Listen, I'll call her. You want me to call her?" She's wearing a blouse with a ruffle at the neck. The blouse is too sheer. She wiggles the telephone receiver in its cradle. "Well?"

"Don't worry about it. Larry's coming over. Larry knows her. Anyway, she's probably sleeping. She's got to rest up."

"Jesus, you're sick," Ruth says. "You know what I mean? You're so sick."


It's three-thirty when I get home. Larry and Tina are sitting on the front step. The door to the house is open and the hall phone is on a chair in the doorway. I swing around the blue Cadillac Seville in the driveway and park in the garage. Tina's wearing red espadrilles, the pants to one of Elliot's suits, and a lilac Polo shirt. Her arms are tan and she's wearing a big round watch with a black band. Her hair is freshly washed, the curls tighter and darker than they were this morning.

"Hiya," she says. "Get lots of work done? I slept like a sweetheart."

"Tina's got people she needs to see," Larry says. "She's got to be in Clifton tomorrow afternoon."

"Yep," Tina says. "I've got a priest over there wants three hundred chickens for a church bazaar. My distributor in New Orleans gets 'em and I bring 'em up myself, as soon as we nail the deal."

"That's a bunch of chickens," Larry says.

"I ought to get a refrigerator truck," Tina says. "But I might just load up the Caddy and save a few bucks. It depends on what I can do with Logan. He's the distributor. He gets these old fryers from A & P and shoots 'em to Hartz Mountain or somebody for fish food—maybe it's the wiener people, I don't know. If the chickens are bad I've got trouble. Even I can't sell bad chickens. We'll spray 'em, of course, but you can't be sure. Anyway, Logan takes a beating on the deal, so I come in and help him on the per pound, then turn around and save this priest in Clifton a bundle. Everybody's happy. The priest can't make this kind of a deal because Logan won't even talk to him."

"Poor church," Larry says. "Lucky I quit."

"Cinnamon rolls and chocolate milk," Tina says, stretching prettily. "That's what I liked. Some Sundays I buy a pack of rolls and a quart of chocolate milk and get crazy—maybe if this deal works I'll do that." She reaches to brush a gnat away from her forehead. "And if the chickens don't go maybe I'll do it anyway. Sell him some of these flamingos Elliot's got all over the place." She waves at the three plastic birds in the front garden and chuckles when Larry rolls his eyes back into his head. Tina has pretty teeth. "Hey, Jerry," she says. "What're you doing about supper?"

"You mean supper? Or dinner?"

"Hell, I don't care what you call it, friend, I just want to know what you're doing about it." Tina smiles and pokes Larry in the ribs. "Tell you what," she says, gesturing over her shoulder.

"I'm waiting on this call here, but soon as it comes in I'll take you out and buy you some food you'll never forget—how's that sound?"

"Sounds terrific," Larry says.

"Nobody's talking to you, Larry," she says. "You had your chance."

The paper girl pulls up in her Jeepster. She waves, then gets out of the car and comes across the lawn toward us. She's fooling with a receipt book and a sheaf of carbons, carrying the rolled-up newspaper in her mouth.

"Hi," I say.

She flips the paper end-over-end in my direction. "You mind if I collect, Jerry? My envelope's in there"—she points to the paper—"but it'd be easier if I just go ahead and collect now."

"Sure. That's O.K. What is it?"

"Twenty-one," she says. "Three months, including this one."

"Nice Jeep you got," Tina says.

"Thanks," Karen says. She twists to look at the car. "My brother had one when I was a kid."

"Who did the paint? Looks like pretty good paint from here."

"I did it myself, and some of the body work—Bondo, mostly. A friend of mine did the running gear." She has a husky voice that makes everything intimate, and the way she stands in my front yard, smiling just slightly, shifting her weight from one foot to the other, is very sexy.

"Sure is sharp," Tina says. She gets up and starts for the Jeepster. "Mind if I take a look?"

Karen does an "aw, shucks" turn in the grass, then says, "Help yourself."

"I'm going to give you a check," I say, making a writing motion in the air with my hand. "That all right?"

She gives me her ballpoint. "Who's the Amazon lady?" she says, gesturing toward Tina's back.

"You want to take her with you?" Larry says.

Karen grins and flicks her bangs away from her forehead. "I don't think I'm going that direction."

I finish filling out the stub in my checkbook and hand her the pen and the check together.

Larry says, "Are you the same person who delivers my paper? On Crestmont, about six blocks over this way?" He tilts his head in the direction he's talking about.

"Nope. That's Carly. I know her, though. You got a problem?"

"I guess not," he says.

Karen gives me a receipt and I walk with her back toward her car. "We still going out later?"

"Sure," she says. "I shouldn't have said Amazon, should I?"

"It's O.K. She's some friend of the landlord's."

Tina's making a production out of the paint job, squatting to sight along the quarter panel, opening the doors to look at the jambs, checking the insides of the wheel wells. Karen looks patient and pretty following her around.

"All the carriers are women now," Larry says when I get back to the porch. "You notice that?"

"I don't know. There was a woman at the apartments where I used to live and now there's Karen—that's two."

"And mine. I don't think I've missed a paper in a year. The phone installers and the cable people are women too. And the UPS people. I've got this one UPS girl who always brings stuff to the house, you know? All decked out in that brown—she looks great. And my exterminator is a woman, a teen-ager. She hates it when I'm there alone and she has to spray. I make a lot of jokes, but that doesn't seem to help." Larry rubs his eye socket with his palm. "She doesn't crack a smile."

Larry tells me he thinks it's fine to leave Tina in the house alone tonight, then he leaves. Inside, I leaf through a magazine and wait for her, wishing she'd let Karen get on with the paper route. I'm about ready to go see what's hapening when they come in, each of them carrying a flamingo from the front yard. They're squawking like imaginary birds, and laughing about it.

"I'm helping Elliot to be a better person," Tina says, standing the two birds in the corner of the living room. "We're going to get a couple of highballs and then finish up Karen's route. I'm going to throw for her. You want to ride along?"

"I think I won't, thanks," I say.

Karen asks about the bathroom and Tina points to the hall. "Go back there, third door. I'll make the drinks."

Karen smiles at me and heads off toward the bathroom. I follow Tina into the kitchen.

"Elliot still keep the booze up here?" she says, opening a cabinet above the dishwasher. She grabs a bottle of bourbon by its neck and puts it on the counter. "Now, what we need is plastic glasses—I don't see any." She looks at me. "What the hell. Just go ahead and use glass glasses, right? You feeling O.K., Jerry? Listen, you could do me a favor. You're going to be around, aren't you?"

"I think so." I get a hard-boiled egg out of the refrigerator and toss it from hand to hand to crack the shell.

"You can catch my calls. Tell anybody who wants me I'll be around later."

"I may go out. That's the only thing."

"Don't do anything special, but if you're here I'd really appreciate it." She stops what she's doing with the drinks and looks out the window. "I've got a Code-A-Phone in the car, we could put that on."

"I'll be here until you get back," I say. "Karen and I are going out later. Just for dinner."

Tina nods. "She told me that. Said you fell off the porch or something."

I go back to the living room. Karen's standing in the foyer doorway with her arms crossed over her chest. She's wearing a bright green crew-neck sweatshirt and jeans. Her skin has a little sheen to it, as if she's just washed her face. "Got a helper," I say.

"What? Oh, right. She doesn't want to take no for an answer." She frowns for a second, then swings her arms wide, palms open, and lifts her shoulders. "Sorry," she says. "We'll be out of the way in a minute."

"You're not in the way." There's another silence, then I say, "So, how's the paper business?"

She gives me a quick, odd stare and says, "Fabulous." Then she turns and scratches at the doorframe with a fingernail. "Really, it's O.K. It's not terrible. I used to be a night watchman at Clover Chemical—did I tell you this already? That was the pits. Now I party at night, sleep in the morning, deliver in the afternoon—it works out pretty good.

"Doesn't sound bad," I say.

"No. It's all right." She waves a hand at the living room. "It's nice in here."

"What time do you think you'll be finished?"

"I don't know," she says. "I'm running late. We can make the arrangements when I bring Tina back."

I nod and watch Tina come out of the kitchen carrying two drinks, one in each hand. She's got the bourbon bottle under her arm and an ice-filled Baggie clamped in her teeth.

Karen grabs the Baggie and says, "Open," then takes one of the drinks.

"Thought we might need a refill somewhere along the way," Tina says, putting the bottle down on the floor. "Let me get some real shoes and I'm ready to bomb out of here. Jerry's going to handle my calls."

Karen nods at me. "That's nice of him," she says.

*    *    *

When they're gone I go to the back bathroom for a sinus tablet, then walk around the house, making a complete circuit of all the rooms. In the kitchen I sit down and read an article in *News-week* about video cassette recorders. When I've finished that, I make a Canadian bacon sandwich. I vacuum the living room, then go out to the back porch and get a six-foot piece of one-by-eight pine and bring that inside. I use it as a comb for the carpet, holding the pine lengthwise, dragging it across the room. I do that a couple of times to get the pile even, and it works pretty well. I put the board back outside, then go around the house and come in the front door so I won't have to walk on the living room carpet.

Ruth calls to see how it's going, and I tell her Karen and Tina left to finish Karen's route.

"You're doing a great job, tiger. You've got 'em right where you want 'em."

"Larry said it was O.K. to leave Tina here," I say.

"Great," she says. "Good stuff."

"I'll just wait and then go to dinner with Karen later—what's wrong with that?"

"That's a good plan," she says. "You stick with it. See you Monday."


Saturday morning at nine-thirty I'm sitting in the kitchen in El-liot's robe when Tina starts banging on the front door. "Hey. Open up in there. What in the goddamn hell is this, anyway?"

Going to the door I can hear Tina giggling and Karen trying to hush her up.

"Sleep," Tina says, when I open the door. She thrusts a fore-finger ceremonially into her chest. Then she starts giggling. Both of them are slumped against the wall by the door, giggling.

"We've been in the woods all night," Karen says, making a straight face and handing me a newspaper. "I'm early today."

"How's that for service?" Tina says. She stumbles over the doorsill and I reach out to steady her. "Camping is"—she turns to Karen—"what is camping? I forgot."

"Not your style," Karen says. And they break up again.

"The woods have not been good to us," Tina says, holding the lapel of my robe. "Now, if you'll excuse us"—she sweeps an arm toward the bedrooms—"Smokey the Bear and myself will retire."

They stagger down the hallway together, arm in arm, and, after a lot of maneuvering and laughing, get into the bedroom and shut the door.

At noon I put a frozen strip steak in a frying pan and open the kitchen window to let out the smoke. I'm standing next to the sink buttering raisin toast when Tina leans on the counter between the kitchen and the breakfast area. She looks all brushed and groomed.

"Hey, Jerry," she says. "Listen, I'm really sorry we didn't get back last night. Karen's sorry too. We got drunk and threw papers all over the place. Then we went to a cowboy bar and teased the locals, but we got lost after. I get any calls? I've got to get moving here."

"There weren't any calls," I say.

"Damn that looks good," she says, eyeing the toast. "Nobody called? You sure?"

"I was here all night. No calls."

I offer her a piece of toast. She gets the grape jelly out of the refrigerator and spreads a half-inch layer on one slice, then closes a second slice on top. "Got a paper towel?" she asks, taking a bite out of the sandwich.

I pull two towels off the roll attached to the underside of the cabinet.

"She's still asleep," Tina says. "I didn't want to bother her. She feels really bad about your date and everything. She tried to call you, I think." Tina puts the last quarter of the sandwich in her mouth. "Anyway, I'm overdue in Clifton, you know? Got to power on."

"Chickens," I say.

"Yep. Sounds bad, doesn't it? A grown woman selling chickens." She chews and looks at the frying pan. "What've you got going here? What's this, steak?"

"Breakfast," I say.

She nods at me, wiping her mouth with the towels. "Gotcha. That rug sure looks good in the living room—how'd you do that? You going to paint or something? I can get you a monster deal on thirty gallons of gray—good quality stuff. First-rate. How about spray equipment? Compressors—the whole business. Knock that room off quick."

"I don't think so. Thanks anyway."

She shrugs, balls the towels, and throws them toward the trash can. "I guess gray's a bad idea. Who wants a gray house? Listen, I've got to go." She reaches behind the counter and picks up her bag and the two flamingos they brought in yesterday. "I'll just swing out the back here."

I follow her through the garage to her car. Karen's Jeepster is parked behind the Cadillac. There's a lot of pumpkin-colored mud on the tires and splattered up on the side panels.

Tina holds the car door open and tosses the birds and her bag into the back seat. She crosses the yard and pulls the third flamingo out of the ground, and puts that in the car too. Then she pulls me into a quick, awkward hug. "You're O.K., Jerry. Thank Karen for me, will you? And look, let me give you a tip—take her someplace dancing, O.K.? Last night she would've killed to dance."

After Tina leaves, I stand around in the drive for a few minutes, then go back inside through the front door, through the living room, into the kitchen. My steak is still cooking. I pour a fresh cup of coffee and start to read the newspaper, but then I don't want to read, I just want to look at the headlines.

# Safeway

FIRST YOU SEE the woman's beautiful hair, steel gray and cut to brush the shoulders of her vanilla silk blouse. She is thin and too elegantly dressed for the supermarket. Her coat is folded neatly over the center of the shopping cart handle. You pass behind her and stop thirty feet away, facing the low-fat milk, for a second look. You shove the half gallons around, reading the dates on the cartons without registering them. She is standing on one foot, leaning on the yellow handle of her basket, studying some generic-brand product.

She skips the next aisle, leaving you there to read the labels on two spaghetti sauces.

You go to the front of the store, see where she is, keep your distance—skip aisles, slip by her with a preoccupied expression on your face, compare products—until the two of you have made one complete turn through the market. When she stops in the far corner to look at the whole fryers, her basket is still relatively empty; yours contains only two quart bottles of Tab. You pull a folded envelope from your shirt pocket to check your list.

The first aisle in from that side of the store is bread and cookies. There you stop near the back, staring at the Oreos. From that position you can watch her when she leaves the chickens.

Up front, you can see two checkout counters, and beyond them, through the plate-glass windows, the late-winter afternoon. It has been raining all day; you are wet, your coat is spotted, your hair is slick and dark. A college-age couple comes down your aisle very fast; he is wearing an ankle-length raincoat, she a gray hooded sweatshirt and a pair of faded khakis, soaked at the cuffs. She starts to put a loaf of wheat bread into their cart; he stops her, pointing at the white bread.

"Get the Colonial," you hear him say.

"This is natural," she says.

"I don't care," he says. He tries to snatch the bread out of her hands.

"I don't ask much," she says, pulling away.

The young man sighs melodramatically. "O.K.—you get yours, I get mine."

She looks past her boyfriend's shoulder at you, raising her eyebrows. The couple passes you, two loaves in the basket, still arguing breads. They are playing, having a good time.

The woman leaves the poultry cooler and comes down your aisle, looking directly at you. She is tan. Without thinking, you reach out, grab a box of cookies, pull it off the shelf, and drop it into your basket: Nabisco gingersnaps. The woman smiles prettily. Her hair, which is darker than you'd first thought, with many thin streaks of gray, moves so gently as she moves, and so regularly, that when she stops her cart and, with the long fingers of her left hand, lifts the hair slightly and draws it back, it falls strand by strand until it comes to rest again, in perfect order.

You look at her shoes. They are high-heeled, buff colored. "Hi," you say.

She doesn't stop, only pushes on toward the front of the store.

You race in the opposite direction, trying to get the waffles and the *TV Guide* and find her checkout line for a last look, but the store is out of the waffles you want, Kellogg's, so you take the house brand—small squares in a clear plastic bag.

Only three checkers are working; the woman is not in any of the lines. You linger at the magazine mini-rack on the end of one of the unused counters, thumb through a current *People*, waiting, feeling foolish.

She arrives unexpectedly out of the aisle behind you—soaps and toiletries—and as she gets in line behind two men, you catch a trace of her scent, delicate and flowerlike, almost jasmine.

You drop *People* into its wire slot and pick up *TV Guide*, then push your basket into line behind hers. You stare at the back of her head, the glistening hair, and at her shoulders, noticing, where the fabric is tight to her skin, the precise, shallow relief of straps.

She looks into her basket, then turns suddenly to you. "Will you go ahead of me? I forgot something. I'll just be a second."

You move forward, taking her place. The two men, wearing Wranglers and colorful nylon jackets over T-shirts, glance at you. With your left hand you pull the woman's basket in behind you until it's touching your leg. The taller of the two men drops his checkbook onto the counter and waits for the checker to ring a pack of cigarettes and several quart bottles of Miller beer; the checker moves the bottles, punching the repeat button on her cash terminal with a fingertip, her pink lips counting the repetitions.

The glass in the store windows is covered with transparent tinted Mylar—blue; waiting for the woman to return, you look at your reflection. You tug on your collar and straighten your tie, then look at the reflections of the two men. One of them is short, heavy, tough looking, with a jowly face and a couple of days of beard. He looks unclean in the blue glass. His stringy blond hair hangs in chunks from under a straw cowboy hat creased into a tight wedge. The second man is taller, better looking. You look from the window to the man—his face is smooth, but still there is a shadow; his teeth are perfect. The ugly man is talking.

"I don't know why I came in the first place," he says. He squeezes the brim of his hat, pushes it back from his forehead.

"Fletcher," the second man says, "calm down. I didn't promise anything."

"Of course not," Fletcher says. "Of course you didn't promise
anything. Why should you? You can't deliver."

The checker takes the tall man's check, looks at it closely,
turns it upside down on the top of her terminal, stamps it with a
rubber stamp, carefully fills in the new blanks. You push your
basket forward, bumping into the counter, then unload your few
purchases—the bottles of Tab, the waffles, the *TV Guide,* and
the gingersnaps. You arrange these in a neat row at the end of
the rubber conveyor belt. Then you see a small, peculiarly
shaped bottle of maraschino cherries in your basket. You don't
remember taking the cherries, and you don't remember the
cherries' having been in the basket before you started shopping.
You pick up the jar and examine the label, noting that these are
cherry halves, stemless, "packed in natural juices." You stare at
a high stack of toilet tissue cartons, feeling the weight of the jar
in your hand.

You are standing in the line like that, thinking, trying to remember, when the woman returns.

"We match," she says, showing you a jar identical with the
one you are holding.

"Are these yours?" you ask. "They aren't mine. I found them
in my basket, but I'm sure I didn't buy them." For a minute you
wonder if you took the jar out of her basket, but then you realize
that you could not have—her basket is behind you.

"Thank you," she says, and she takes your jar. Then, waving
her hand toward her basket, she says, "Was there anything else
you wanted?" Both of you laugh at this small joke, and you
point at her food, saying, "That, and that, and that looks pretty
good," but as you point, and as you laugh nervously, you are
thinking of her lips, her startling rust-colored lipstick, her fair
skin, her severe cheekbones, and the light white down on her

cheeks; you are thinking about the lovely hair, perfectly proper, perfectly behaved, waving softly around her head and shoulders as she laughs; you are thinking about her slim waist and about her ankles in their ultra-thin straps.

The moment passes. The woman opens her purse and begins fiddling with something inside it; you turn back to the counter and rearrange your purchases, thinking how foolish your Tab and gingersnaps and *TV Guide* must look.

The man in front of you is staring at your frozen waffles. He smiles. It is not a pleasant smile meaning "Yes, the flesh is weak" but a smile more on the order of "This poor bastard is buying frozen waffles": his opinion of your entire life is instantly communicated. He is waiting for the checker to finish with his check, and the checker is on her tiptoes, scanning the store for the manager.

The one called Fletcher picks at his teeth with a green toothpick, hissing occasionally to determine whether or not he has cleared the gaps; he nudges his friend with an elbow, jerks his head toward you, then whispers something. The taller man pivots, looks past you at the woman.

This makes you angry; you move forward, toward the counter, hoping to block his view of her. Then, to see how she reacts to the man's glance, you turn to her, but she is looking away toward the special racks of Pepperidge Farm products.

Then Fletcher taps your shoulder and whispers, through a twisted little smile, "Roy told me before we came that it'd happen here, but I didn't believe him. I told him you don't want to let 'em dig those flashy brown nails into your rump—you want to get one that speaks Japanese or something, else you end up singing Disney disco tunes off the TV the rest of your life." He lowers his voice more and says, "His woman's got juice for brains is the problem; you got to squeeze her chin to make her grin, and if you don't look out, she won't wash herself all over—

she'll end up with little scabs of chocolate pudding on her chest, here," and he pops himself on the chest.

Roy turns around at this point, shrugs at you, and says to his short friend, "Listen, Fletcher, why don't you go sit in the truck?"

"What?" Fletcher says. "I was just telling this fellow about the best day of your marriage; I mean, he needs to know, Roy. You can see he's on a need-to-know basis, can't you?" Then Fletcher looks at you. "Roy put a cast on her leg up to here"— he draws his hand like a blade across his upper thigh—"told her to look sexy, and shot her with his OneStep. Ain't that right, Roy?"

"That's right," Roy says to you.

"She's there with this cane his grandfather or somebody brought back from Europe after the Great War, and she's leaning on the cane with both hands, you see what I mean?" Fletcher says, suggesting the posture with his own. "And she's in front of a big Confederate painting with this look on her face, but Roy here don't show the picture to just anybody. I mean, he shows it to me, but we're friends maybe twenty years now— right, Roy?"

"Sure, sure," Roy says, and he's looking past you again, at the woman.

You're thinking of her, too, but you've got the idea that Fletcher is going to tell his story no matter what, that if you try to shut him up he's going to grab your shoulder, spin you around, and tell you, so you're trying to let it go.

"Listen," Roy says to Fletcher, dropping an arm around the thick man's shoulder and turning him back to the counter. "Maybe we ought to mind our own business, huh?"

"I feel bad," you hear Fletcher say. "I don't feel so hot."

The woman is still digging in her purse, pulling papers out and wadding them into a tight ball in her hand. The papers are mostly white, a few are yellow; they look like charge receipts. You grab your frozen waffles and wave them at her, hoping to lighten the moment, turn it into a mutual appreciation of some kind. "Not for me, of course," you say. "The kids—the kids demand them."

You put enough sarcasm into your voice so that the woman will understand what you are after: a little conspiratorial recognition, a small pleasure; but she seems to take you seriously. Looking up from her purse, letting her pretty smile open across her face, she shakes her head and shrugs, as if agreeing with you about the childishness of children. This is not the response you had hoped for, but it will do. You slide your basket away from the counter so that she can move forward, and when she does, you think about resting your hand on the uppermost chrome bar of her shopping cart, looping your fingers through the wire mesh—but you decide against it.

Fletcher has gotten impatient. Unzipping his yellow nylon jacket with one hand, he points the other, fingers folded to make a gun, at the checkout girl. "Listen, honey, I don't feel good at all," he says. "What is this crap? I'm taking this to the truck."

The girl is very young, maybe sixteen or eighteen, very tall and very skinny, wearing an ill-fitting rust-orange-and-brown smock; her makeup is smeared at the outside of one eye, but the cheap look of her face is strangely attractive to you. She is afraid of Fletcher and nervously fingers the midget gold pen attached by a retractable cord to a disc on her lapel.

"We're not supposed to let things—" she begins, looking frantically at the kid in the checkout enclosure two down. "The manager was here a minute ago. If you can wait, I'll go find him."

"We'll wait," Roy says.

The girl almost jumps out from behind her terminal, half running and half walking toward the manager's office.

Fletcher says, "I'll dance with that one, Roy. I'll have her wearing rubber pants in no time."

"Take it easy," Roy says.

"Those lips are so thick they got muscles you can't even imagine. Like crawling on oysters."

You stand there with your frozen waffles still in your hand, looking over the top of the chewing gum rack at a huge nurse in a crisp white uniform waddling along behind a basket stuffed with meats and paper towels.

The woman behind you bends over the handle of her basket and picks up a package of Sara Lee frozen cinnamon rolls, holds this up for you to see, looks quickly from you to your waffles and back to her rolls. "I know what you mean," she says. "My husband loves them." And she and you stand for a moment waving frozen pastries at one another, smiling, while you think about the mention of her husband.

Then Fletcher's voice, loud again, comes from behind you. "I wouldn't eat that crap for anybody."

"Excuse me?" you say, almost automatically stepping backward.

"I said that crap'll kill you." He points at the waffles.

"We know," the woman says. "That's what we were saying."

"They were saying that to each other," Fletcher says, pulling on Roy's jacket. "Get it?"

"Are you a nutritionist?" the woman asks, leaning to her left to look around you.

"He's a plumber, lady," Fletcher says. "We're both of us plumbers, but we know how to eat."

"So what's going on these days in plumbing?" she says. "What's all this PVC-pipe business?"

"Sorry," Roy says. "Forget it."

Fletcher tugs his hat over his eyes and pushes past you to get to the woman. "She's rich," he says, and he reaches up and runs a stiff finger along the woman's cheek.

She does not move, only stares at him.

"Jesus," you say to Roy. "Can't you control him?"

Fletcher says, "I like the checker better anyway. This one, you give her two weeks and she'll be wanting money for new panties. The other one, you wrap her ass around a thirty-dollar bicycle seat and you can stand her on her head in a mirror for life."

The checker is returning from across the store, walking slowly, pinching her smock, pulling it down in front.

"Here comes your friend," you say to Fletcher.

She slides into her booth, waves the check, and says, "It's O.K. I'm sorry it took so long. The manager was out on the loading dock talking to the architect about renovations. It'll just be a minute now." She sticks a button on her terminal with the point of her pen.

"Hey," Fletcher says, pulling on Roy's arm. "Hey, I think I'm going to take me a little walk—you take the beer, O.K.?"

"It's wet outside."

"I like wet," Fletcher says, walking out backward.

"It's the cash over," the checker says to Roy. "That's the problem, that's why I had to get the O.K." She counts twenty-five dollars into Roy's hand.

He folds the money over his thumb, then turns to the woman. "I'm sorry," he says. He squints at you and goes out the double door.

The checker begins with your cookies, pressing a button on the terminal and slipping the box to her left, calling out the price in a soft, childlike voice.

You start to say something to the woman behind you, but the conveyor belt suddenly lurches forward, knocking a bottle of Tab off the counter. It bursts when it hits the floor, spraying her thoroughly. Her blouse is soaked—the entire area beneath her breasts clings to her stomach. She takes two steps backward and stands there with her arms outstretched like a scarecrow, shaking her hands and looking down at her chest. All other activity

in the supermarket seems to stop; your aisle is stared at like a
traffic accident. Then you are surrounded by boys mopping and
being solicitous, and everyone is laughing. The woman is laughing. The manager, who appears from nowhere, is laughing and
trying to blot dry her blouse with a yellow sponge. The checker
is laughing and at the same time apologizing. The boys are
laughing as they fall to their knees in order to clean up the mess.
Someone goes to get another bottle of Tab, and while the lane is
still crowded with people, while everyone is still laughing, the
checker shoves your purchases to the foot of her counter, where
yet another tall, thickset, smiling teenager stuffs the goods into a
brown sack.

You stop by the ice machine just inside the door to let a small
boy in a silver costume of some kind run by you; he jumps with
both feet onto the rubber pad that controls the twin sliding-glass
doors. He runs out and back in twice, his Suzuki violin case
slung over his shoulder like a toy rifle, then attaches himself to
the leg of a middle-aged woman who is holding a transparent
shopping bag, standing on the covered walk outside the store
and gazing at the fine slate-gray rain. She is startled by the boy,
and turns quickly to scold him; but then, almost as quickly, she
stops scolding and smooths the child's hair as if unable to resist
his charm. In the far corner of the parking lot, just across the
street from the Pee Wee baseball diamond, you see Roy getting
into the cab of a three-quarter-ton gold pickup truck; the truck is
backed against the curb under a tall light, facing the store.
Shoppers are starting their cars, which suddenly steam at both
ends; the steam and the dark sky, the rain, and the water thrown
off by windshield wipers give the parking lot a close, magical
look.

"Well, we can't simply stay here," your woman says. She has

come up behind you, her smallish sack of groceries held against her chest.

"Oh, hello," you say. You turn too fast, hitting her shoulder with your forearm. "I'm sorry," you say.

"Two's a charm," she says, laughing softly. "Who's watching the store?"

Before you can reply, two nuns in brilliant blue habits start to walk out the door but, on seeing that it is still raining, stop suddenly. One of the nuns, quite a bit older than her companion, stands on the pad, and the doors slide open to the hiss of the outside. She turns to you and says, "Will it ever end?"

You look at the ceiling and say, "No," and the nun gathers her robes into a bundle at her knees and motions for the younger one to follow.

When they are out and the door is closed, the woman beside you says, "They make me nervous."

"All that beautiful blue," you say. "My name is Fred."

"Well, Fred, how do you do?" She frees one hand from her package and thrusts it at you. "I'm Sarah Garner."

"Hello, Sarah."

"Wet, isn't it? Still, I don't know why none of us has an umbrella."

"I was thinking that myself," you say, although you aren't thinking that at all. You're thinking about her perfect hair—for it to be so perfect, she has to *know* it's perfect. "Actually, I have one, but it's in the car."

"Ditto," she says. "I didn't remember until I was deep in peanut butter."

"Right," you say, laughing too abruptly, too loud.

People are coming into the store, shedding rain gear, stomping feet as they pull shopping baskets out of the rack and wheel off in the direction of the produce. Sarah Garner puts her groceries down on the brick ledge at the bottom of the huge blue

window you are both standing in front of, then lights a cigarette
from a gold case. She offers you a cigarette.

"I feel like John Garfield," you say.

"Maybe if you dirty up a little," she says. "Take one—see if
you can let it fall out of your mouth without using your hands."

"Some trick," you say, taking a cigarette.

"So—you're going to protect me all the way to the coffee
shop?" She points out the window, diagonally, across the parking lot. "We can take the long way around and never get wet,
although some of us are already wet." She sweeps a hand in
front of the stain on her blouse. "And sticky."

"Didn't I apologize for that already?"

Sarah Garner looks at you, then at her cigarette, then at the
dense haze of the parking lot. "Yes," she says.

You navigate the covered walk around the rim of the lot in silence, which makes you nervous. She's got a trench coat over her
shoulders, like a cape, and as you walk, you measure her—her
height, the length of her stride, the impact of her shoulder accidentally hitting yours, the sound of her heels on the slick pave-
ment; you register this random data too consciously, flicking in
imagination from one observation to the next, as if the moment
might soon be lost. When she gets a step ahead of you, her gray
hair catches the cold fluorescent light of the walkway and turns a
startling silver; you begin to imagine yourself in bed with Sarah
Garner, making slow and detailed love, touching her hair, and
her shoulders, and her skin in response to stern commands.


The coffee shop is a House of Pancakes. A tiny woman with her
hair in a wiry bun shows you to a window booth done in turquoise Naugahyde. You order coffee.

Sarah Garner drops her coat from her shoulders, and it sits up
against the blue seat-back like a shadow. She plays with her fin-

gers, interlacing their tips, then opening her hands like a kid playing here's the church and here's the steeple; you watch her eyes as she glances around the empty room.

"Do you go to New Orleans?" she finally asks, without looking at you.

"No," you say. "I hate it. I lived there a couple of years, went to school there. It's depressing."

"I love it. But I've only been once or twice."

"I guess it's O.K." You're not doing so well. She likes New Orleans. Where is the coffee? "I like the blouse," you say.

She looks down, then raises her eyebrows to look at you. "The wet look. Dangerous and seductive, but not so healthy." She sticks a finger between two buttons and pulls the blouse away from her chest.

"I'm sorry," you say.

The window beside the booth is bubbled with condensation; she starts to draw something on the window, something that looks like a rabbit, then quickly erases the drawing with the butt of her fist. "My husband's in New Orleans now. He's in contract law, oil law." She's still not looking at you—she's looking at the glossy window, at the distorted, flashing reflections of taillights and headlights.

"You always shop at the Safeway?"

"Night and day." She laughs. "I don't come over here very much. I used to live around here, by the park, but I don't now."

"I have an apartment on Richburg Hill," you say. "Forest Royale."

"Oh, yeah, those are nice."

You nod. "I work at the hospital."

"You play doctor?" she says, smiling.

The waitress arrives with two mugs and a steaming glass coffeepot. She grins at you, showing huge gums. She's wearing a black uniform with a slick lavender apron. "Coffee?" she says.

"Sorry I'm slow, but Mrs. Kelso forgot to tell me you were in my station, and from the counter you seemed to be in Janet's." She fills the mugs, then slides one to Sarah Garner and one to you. "Cream?"

"Yes, thank you," Sarah says.

The waitress reaches into her apron pocket and produces half a dozen cartons of cream, each the size and shape of a gumdrop. "These be enough?" she asks. "I don't know why they bother with these things. Here, I'll give you a few extras." She deposits another handful on the table, starts to leave, but then stops and returns to the booth. "The thing is that it wouldn't have mattered even if you were in Janet's station, because she's home sick today anyway."

"More work for you," you say. "That's too bad."

"Oh, I can handle it. With this rain, nobody's going to come in."

You and Sarah Garner watch the waitress walk away. "She walks like a man," Sarah says. "Do you think that's attractive in a woman?"

You pull all the cream cartons in front of you and begin arranging them. "Sometimes. I guess. I don't know."

"Peter says I walk like a man."

"Peter's your husband?"

"Yes. He plays racquetball a great deal, but he's not as good-looking as you."

"More distinguished, I imagine."

"Shorter," she says. "But we get along all right."

You look down at the tabletop and see that you have organized the cream cartons like players on a football team.

"He loves to go out of town," Sarah says. "And I don't mind; I like to be alone sometimes, at night, late. It's quiet."

"Sure," you say. "I watch television all the time."

You find a small hole in the turquoise seat and stick your finger in it, then suddenly realize she might be able to see what you're doing. You glance at her sheepishly.

"What do you watch?" she asks. Then quickly adds, "Never mind—I don't want to know."

"Movies. Mostly."

"The tall one wasn't scary," she says, wagging her mug at the window. "He seemed to know what he was doing."

"Do you have any more of these?" you ask, pointing to your team.

She picks two cartons out of the clean ashtray on her side of the booth, spins them onto the tabletop. Then she watches you carefully reseal the foil tops and place the containers with the others.

"I've got to freshen up," she says. She lifts her hair off her forehead, as if to illustrate the remark. "Did you see the restrooms?"

"They're by the door." You point behind her, toward the entrance, over a tray of very green vines that sits on top of a panelled, chest-high room divider. "See that little hallway?"

She slides out of the booth, carefully sidestepping a bubble-topped dolly loaded with pastries. She doesn't walk at all like a man. When she's out of sight, you pull a napkin from the dispenser and wipe the window, then peer out into the parking lot: Roy's truck is there, shining.


You push your mug to one side and move the cream cups around in an approximation of a football play—a sweep around right end, the quarterback pitching out to the tailback. But because you have too few cartons, and because you must move the cartons in sequence, one after another, and because you have no defensive team at all, the play isn't much fun. You start to arrange the players again but decide not to, and start stacking the cups into a kind of tower. You remember the frozen waffles in your grocery sack, which is tucked into the booth on the floor next to your feet, and you pull the sack out and put it on the seat. You look inside: the waffles are wet and limp, and there are spots on the bottom of the grocery sack.

You close the sack, then see Sarah Garner pressed up against the entrance door of the House of Pancakes, looking out, her hands cupped around her eyes. You push the cream cartons aside and pull the coffee back in front of you. You take a sip of coffee and watch Sarah come around the divider.

"I wanted to see if it was still raining," she says, slipping into the booth. "It is." The waitress is moving in your direction.

"Are you long waisted or short waisted?" you ask.

"What?" She is looking at the large, near-round spot where you wiped the window. "Long," she says. "I think. Long waisted. Listen, we'd better go or my stuff will spoil." She reaches under the table, and with one hand pulls up her groceries between the seat and the tabletop.

"My waffles," you say, pointing into the top of your sack.

She waves at the waitress, who is by now almost beside the booth. The waitress rips a green sheet from her pad and places it face down on the table.

"Something wrong with the coffee?" the waitress asks, pointing her pencil at your mug.

"Very good," you say.

Sarah Garner shoves a dollar bill toward you.

"I thought this was my treat," you say.

"Wrong." She starts to put on her coat, and in the bending and pulling you notice that she has opened the neck of her blouse.

On the walkway outside the House of Pancakes you say, "Do you want to follow me? My car's over here."

"You go ahead," she says. "Forest Royale, right? I forgot

something at the store. I forgot I'm completely out of facial tissues. Just give me the apartment number." She looks at the truck in the corner of the parking lot.

"One twelve," you say, reading the numbers from a license plate.

"Fine. I'll see you shortly." She reaches for your hand, squeezes it, and smiles. Then she heads for the store, diagonally, through the brittle rain.

It's cold, and the sky has turned inky blue. You stand under the overhang for a minute, watching Sarah Garner walk stiffly away. At the door to the Safeway she turns, sees that you are still watching, and waves. You wave, too, in a quick, jerky movement, then step out into the parking lot, whistling, looking over the tops of the sparkling cars for your black Mazda.

# Feeders

IRIS SHARES a two-bedroom town house in Meadowdale with Polly, a nursing student. Iris hates it way out there, so when I mention on the telephone that Mrs. Jaymar has moved out of my duplex, Iris says she wants it. It's the second floor of my house, and since we used to live together, I say I'm not sure this is a great idea. She says maybe we could meet at Coleman's, a restaurant we used to go to, and discuss it.

"Her son got a condominium in Lakeland," I say. "The last day, she asked if she could leave her plastic bird feeders, which are all over the trees like party lights, and I said O.K., so she gave me a bag of seed."

"She's wonderful," Iris says. "I remember. So how about six-thirty?" When I don't answer, she says, "I know, I know. You aren't promising anything."

Coleman's is a storefront in a thirty-year-old strip shopping center not far from my house. When the neighborhood was re-vitalized, Coleman's was revitalized too—now it's all palm trees and captain's chairs and Varathaned tabletops. At first I don't recognize Iris, who's sitting off in the corner of the porchlike front of the restaurant with her back to me. Then she waves, and I squint and wave back. It's the first time I've met Polly, and it's a little awkward; she doesn't say anything, just looks at me and gives me a short nod. At the next table there's an almost bald man in a short-sleeved shirt, who's bent backward over his chair, telling her what to do about ordering. "This steak-and-seafood

218

might be good. But it depends what kind of steak it is. If it's some junk cut, round or even porterhouse, you shouldn't get it."

"Right," Polly says. "O.K."

"We know him," Iris whispers.

Except for the hair—Iris's is black, Polly's red—the women look surprisingly alike. Both have dark circles under the eyes, chiselled faces, pale hands. Iris is older and more delicate, but her eyes are hard, like colored rocks. Polly is wearing a scoop-neck black pullover and worn khakis, Iris a pin-stripe dress shirt I think I remember, and a thin silver tie knotted off the neck.

The guy at the next table is staring at Polly's back. "But if it's a petite filet, then it might be good."

"A what?" Polly says, craning to look at him.

"Petite filet. Like this up here, only smaller." He reaches over and bops on her menu with his knuckle. "Sometimes they try to nick you on the platters."

"Oh. Thanks," Polly says.

Iris leans close to me. "We don't want any trouble, Eddie."

"Who is this guy?" I say.

"Never mind," she says. "Don't worry about it." She gives Polly a stern look, and Polly shrugs helplessly.

I make a joke about inviting the guy to join us, and Iris smiles dryly and says, "It's a little late for that, don't you think?" She writes a check for the rent.

"Shouldn't we discuss this?" I say.

"Don't be silly, Eddie," Iris says. "That's all over. It's O.K. I mean, unless you feel funny about it." She presses the kinky hair back off her forehead and then tears the check out of a red checkbook. "Polly's at the university, and I'm still with the telephone company. Putting 'em in, I mean." She waves a hand toward Polly, who brightens theatrically as if she's been hit with a spotlight. "She's going to be a nurse, maybe. Or a doctor."

Polly shakes her head, then looks out the large window at the

street in front of Coleman's. There's a Quik Stop drive-in grocery across the street, and in the parking lot two police cars are
parked side by side, nose to tail, the drivers talking to each other
out the windows. "I think you two ought to discuss it," she says.

"We're quiet, no pets, regular hours," Iris says. "Ideal tenants." She pushes her check across the glossy wood tabletop.
"Well, is it a deal or what?"

Iris was always too direct, too demanding. Now it's as if she's
challenging me to take her on as a tenant. But even though I
haven't seen her very often in the last eight months, when I have
seen her we've gotten along all right; the separation was a suc-
cess. "I guess I can stand it if you can," I say. "When do you
want to move?"

"Soon," Polly says, glancing over her shoulder at the guy at
the next table. She turns to Iris. "Are we going to eat?"

"No. We're going to finish and go. Take it easy."

"It's four seventy-five—can you afford that? I pay water."

"I remember. See? It's here." She picks up the check and
waves it casually. I take it and she stands up. "That's a deal.
We'll be coming tomorrow. I'll knock for the key, all right?"

"I don't want to be squeamish, Iris, but you're sure this is
what you want to do?"

She smiles and says, "You look good, Eddie." She pats my
cheek in an unpleasant way—three short, light slaps—and then
she and Polly leave. The guy at the next table waves and watches
them go. When they're out the door, he turns to look at me. I
nod and glance over my shoulder, as if to be sure he's not looking at something behind me, but the only thing there is a wall
covered with snowy paper and pink flocked birds—cranes or flamingos. When I turn back, he's pushing his chair out. He almost knocks over his tea glass. He comes straight to my table
and points to Iris's chair. "Do you mind?"

"Excuse me?"

He sits, pulling up close to the table. "I didn't want to barge in like this. My name's Putnam. Cecil Putnam. I'm over here waiting for my daughter." He jerks his head toward his table. "She didn't show yet, so I thought I'd come over a minute." He reaches across the table to shake my hand.

"How are you?" His hand is small and covered with soft black hair.

He frowns, then bends closer and whispers, "You know these women?" He points at the chairs. "I don't want to pry. You can tell me to go to hell."

"They're renting an apartment from me. Why?"

"Oh." He nods gravely. "Tenants. I thought you might know them more personally."

"No."

"See, I know the one with the red hair, that's all. She's a body builder, right? She has arms, you know what I'm saying? This one does." He points at Polly's chair again. "I mean is she Portuguese or something? The arms are real good."

"Student. That's what she told me. She didn't say anything about weight lifting."

"It's not weight lifting."

"She told me student."

"She'd look swell with that oil they slop on, you know? Glistening, wearing one of those tiny pouch bikinis—you know the kind I'm talking about? You ever watch 'em?"

He's hunched over my table, drawing greasy circles with his finger on the tabletop. I'm staring at the top of his head, where the hair is brushed forward in queer spikes that stand out from his scalp. He looks as if he might be fifty years old. "I think you've got the wrong girl," I say.

He seems displeased, but he doesn't want to leave. He glances over his shoulder at his table, then back to me. "My girl's a body builder, that's how come I know about this stuff. I watch 'em on television. This girl here is a pal of my girl's, I think. I wanted to check it out. They kill me," he says. "The oily business kills me every time. I'm a sucker for it."

The waiter has come up and is giving me signals with his pad and pencil, asking if I'm ready to order.

"Excuse me," I say, pointing over Putnam's shoulder to the waiter.

"Oh, hell yes," he says. "Lemme get out of your way here." He pushes his chair back and stands, then steps around the waiter. "Sorry to bust in. Listen, you try that combo platter, hear? But check the meat."

Iris and Polly show up on bicycles at nine the next morning. I answer the door in my checked robe. Iris is in jeans and a plaid flannel shirt; she has a tool holster slung low off a leather belt around her hips. She keeps pushing the holster back as she shifts from foot to foot on the front step. "Welcome home," I say.

"We'll go around to the upstairs entrance," Iris says. "O.K.? You bring the key?"

I show them the apartment, and Polly thinks it's perfect except for the ochre carpet.

"I hate it too," I say.

"It's good and thick," Polly says. "Anyway, we won't see it when we get the pads down." She drops cross-legged to the floor and rocks back and forth a few times.

"Pads?" I say.

Iris pats my shoulder. "Don't get worried. No furniture, so we put quilts on the floor. Kind of Japanese, you know?"

"Yeah," Polly says. "We've got different colors for each room. And plants, of course. How many rooms are there, anyway?"

I try to imagine the apartment with wall-to-wall quilts. "What about the kitchen? What do you do in there?"

"She makes a Key lime pie that'll rip skin off your tongue," Polly says, getting off the floor and going to the window. "But you probably know that." She bends to look at the control panel of the air-conditioning unit. "This old or something?"

"Of course it is," Iris says. She tugs on Polly's work shirt.

I point out the windows at the trees in the front yard. "The feeders disappear when the leaves come."

"We like it," Iris says. "You give me the seed and I'll take care of the birds."

"It's a deal," Polly says.

That afternoon they bring clothes and some boxes in the back of a dark-blue Volvo station wagon. I prop open the screen door of the upstairs entrance with half of a concrete block and then offer to help with the boxes, but Iris says it isn't necessary, so I go back to my apartment and put on a Bob Marley record. Then I remember it's a record Iris sometimes put on when we made love, so I take it off the turntable and put on something else, a New Wave band that I don't like at all. I stay up late, sitting in my dark living room listening to Iris and Polly walk around upstairs.

Putnam knocks on my door at six in the morning. He hasn't shaved, and he looks as if he's been beaten up. There are small abrasions all over his face and hands. "Remember me?" he says. "I met you at Coleman's. I asked about the girls."

It's barely light outside; the grass is shining. I'm cold. "It's early, isn't it?" I rub my eyes and squint at him in what I hope is a discouraging way.

He sticks a boot in the door. "Let me talk to you a minute, Ed."

I look at him and he looks back, and that tells me he's not going to leave, so I lead him into the kitchen.

"Ed," he says when we're sitting at the table, "I'm an educator. Been an educator twenty years and I never did anything like this before. But there's a good reason, and it's not what you think. Bear with me a minute here, will you?"

"I don't think a thing. You want coffee?"

"I'll do it. You look tired."

"Up late."

He's a small man with a too large upper body; when he goes across the kitchen, he moves in fits and starts, like a gorilla going around a cage. "Me too. All night in the van." He points at the ceiling. "I'm in radio, TV, and film," he says, opening and closing a couple of my cabinets. He's wearing an olive-green cardigan sweater, khaki pants, big work shoes with rawhide laces. "Where's the coffee, anyway?" He picks up a can of Final Net from the counter and points the nozzle at me. "What's this about?"

"Roaches. The coffee's there with the red top."

He puts the Final Net back where he found it. "I guess that slows 'em down pretty good, huh?" He spoons coffee into the percolator and plugs it in. "I know you got a clean place, Ed, but just let me help you out here." He wets a paper towel and comes across the room to wipe the table. When he finishes one pass, he leans on the table with his elbows, looks straight at me, and says, "That's my baby girl you got upstairs, Ed. I know it's peculiar, me coming in here like this and everything, but I'm checking to be sure you're O.K., you see what I mean? That's the way I have to do things."

He stands alongside the table and pours me a shallow cup of coffee. I look at his free hand, which is opening and closing very fast. Then it straightens out and the fingers wiggle jerkily.

When both coffees are poured, he takes the chair opposite me, pulls the thick-lipped mug to his mouth, blows on his coffee.

There's a yellow fleck that looks like a pencil shaving floating on the surface of my coffee, so I stick the tip of my finger into the mug.

He watches me for a minute, then relaxes and surveys the kitchen. "How long you had this place, Ed? You got a pretty good mortgage on her?"

We chat for half an hour, and at quarter of seven he abruptly has to go. "Let me rinse these first." He sweeps our mugs off the table and takes them to the sink. "I hope you understand, Ed. I'm an educator and I know what I have to do—you follow me? It's not my first choice. I got to look after these women, see what I mean?"

"Sure," I say. "Gotcha."

Then I follow him to the front door and watch through the mini-blinds as he cuts across the front lawn toward a bronze van with a couple of bubble sunroofs, parked next door.


Iris comes out about two that afternoon, wearing an aqua leotard, leg warmers, a down-filled flight vest, and French canvas hiking shoes. I'm on the porch painting the doorframe blue. She walks like a clown, rubbing the small of her back with both hands. "Good morning," she says vaguely. She crosses the small yard to the Japanese rain tree and studies the bark on the trunk.

"Your friend Putnam came for breakfast," I say, balancing the brush on the lip of the paint can. Her back is to me, about ten feet away. I wipe my hands, then jump the two steps off the porch and come up behind her.

"I'm sorry," she says, picking at the tree trunk with her nails.

I look up and down the street. No van. There are birds on the telephone wires but none in the trees. There's a dull, even light everywhere—it reminds me of the "cloudy-bright" on Kodak film directions. "What's the story on the guy, anyway? I mean, Jesus, Iris."

She turns to face me. Her hair is pulled straight away from her face and there's a washed-out red in her cheeks from the cold. Her eyes are a little bit blue. "I can't stop him." She shuts her eyes, then opens them and looks past me at the house. "I don't know why he can't just leave us alone."

She looks beaten and pretty, so I smile and say, "None of us can," reaching to brush a bit of hair away from her forehead.

She ducks and jerks her hand to her face, knocking my fingers aside. "That's not what it's about, Eddie." She looks down at her hands and rubs the fleshy part of one thumb over the other's nail. "I can't take care of everything. Polly works for him, and he's around. If you can't handle it, we can go somewhere else."

She's thin—thinner than I remember, in spite of the thick jacket and the leg wraps, or because of them—and she looks frail.

I pull some blackened berries off a branch. "What about the college? He said he was at the college."

"He says whatever he wants to say. I thought since you're a man, he'd back off."

I follow her to the Volvo parked at the curb and watch as she writes her name in the dirt on the fender. "I don't want to deal with him, Iris. It's your business, not mine. But what is it? He going to be around all the time or what?"

"I don't know. Probably. He won't hurt you or anything."

"That's terrific."

"He's not a terrible guy, Eddie. He's friendly."

"So I see. But he's your friend, Iris. I mean, I'm just renting an apartment here, right?"

She starts to write something else on the fender, then quits and faces me. "So what—you'd rather I was alone?" She pushes past me and walks off, following the line down the middle of the street.

\*       \*       \*

Two nights later Iris calls. "We're ready for the dinner," she says. "Can you come tonight?" I haven't talked to her or Polly since the day Putnam came, although I've seen them carrying things up the drive, and I've heard them at night, arranging things, padding around on my ceiling.

"Sure. Want me to bring the wine?"

"Wine? Nobody up here likes wine. Just bring yourself. Eight o'clock."

She hangs up without saying goodbye. I look across the kitchen at the clock on the stove, but I can't read it from where I'm sitting, so I have to get up and go across the room. It's five-fifteen. I wrap the rest of my sandwich in aluminum foil and put it on the top shelf in the refrigerator. Then I see some brown stains on the wall of the refrigerator, so I get the sponge from the sink and wipe them off. While I'm doing that, I notice a hair stuck to the bottom of the milk carton. The refrigerator is a mess. I start to clean it, taking everything off one shelf at a time, then removing the shelves and washing down the inside walls. I throw away a sack of carrots I find in the crisper, but the three apples look O.K., so I save those. The lettuce is bad, so I toss it, and I toss the mushrooms, celery, and peppers, and the soft black banana. By the time I get everything back together, the refrigerator looks clean and empty. It's almost seven. I take the bag of old food out to the cans by the garage.

At eight Iris calls and tells me Polly needs a lemon, so I get one I saved, rinse it in cold water, and go around the house to their entrance.

The apartment doesn't have any furniture in it, just the way they said. There's a square white Formica coffee table in the center of the living room. The ochre carpet has been covered with bright solid-red quilts. In the corners and along the wall where the windows are, they have plants, and a large Monet garden poster is pushpinned to one wall. The coffee table is set for four.

"This is the only room we've finished," Iris says. She points to a pile of cardboard boxes covered with a clear plastic dropcloth in the next room. "We like to do one at a time. That's all our stuff there."

I follow her through the apartment. There's a mattress on the floor in one of the bedrooms, but otherwise the place looks the way it did after Mrs. Jaymar left. Polly is in the kitchen staring into the glass plate in the oven door.

"Oh, hi. You bring my lemon?" When I give it to her, she says, "I don't know how I could have forgotten this."

Iris takes me back into the living room and points to the coffee table. "You want a Coke?"

"Fine." I sit clumsily on the floor, facing one of the place mats. In the center of the table there are two square red plastic flashlights and a small box wrapped in burlap, made to look like a cotton bale. "What's this?" I ask, pointing at the box.

"Music." Iris slides to her knees and tips open the top of the cotton bale, and a soft tinkling version of "Dixie" comes out.

The dinner is chicken wings and rice. The wings are served with a brown sauce, and the rice is full of vegetables and nuts. Polly tells a story about finding the wing recipe in the *New York Times*. "I always liked wings, but nobody would believe me. So it was great finding this recipe."

"They're very good," I say.

"Try the sauce on the rice," she says, passing a coffee creamer with about an inch of sauce in it. "Not too much."

My back starts hurting after I've been on the floor twenty minutes. Both women are careful not to disturb the fourth place at the table, and when the setting gets cleared with the rest of the dinner dishes, Iris says, "We were expecting somebody else."

"We invited Cecil," Polly says. "Iris saw him at the Spa." Polly pours two-thirds of a cup of coffee for me, then offers a creamer just like the one used at dinner; I wonder if they have two or if she quickly washed it after the meal. "She's trying to get herself back into shape."

"You don't seem out of shape to me. Maybe thin."

Polly looks at Iris. "You think she's too thin?"

"I've got small bones. Take a look at these wrists." Iris pulls up her sweatshirt sleeves and thrusts both arms out over the table. "Didn't you like the sauce? It's Cecil's. He copied it from somewhere."

"According to Iris," Polly says, "everything is copied from somewhere. Do you believe that? I think it takes something away."

"I guess he made part of it up," Iris says.

"Cecil's a caution," Polly says, folding her napkin into a flower shape and pressing it down on the table.

"So, Polly, how's the nursing business?" I say.

"I'm looking for something else in my field."

"Gore," Iris says. "She's in gore, primarily. The stuff she knows about would curl your hair. Tell him about that printer at the hospital."

Polly looks at me out of the corners of her eyes. "It wasn't anything. They put these hands on the wrong guys one night. Sewed 'em on."

"One was a printer's hand," Iris says. "This guy had an accident."

"A mix-up," Polly says. "They had to act fast. So they switched these hands. The printer got another guy's hand, one the surgeon had to take off. The other guy got the printer's hand, because when the surgeon found the printer's hand it looked O.K. and he thought he'd made a mistake. Neither hand worked. Cosmetically it worked, though."

"Cosmetically it was great," Iris says. "The printer was Italian and very dark, and the other guy was a poet or something."

"After a while they looked O.K.," Polly says. "The hospital did follow-up—color photographs and stuff. After a while you could hardly tell. Iris went out with the poet."

"Just twice, and he wasn't a poet. He was something else. But he could type real fast one-handed."

"Cecil was going to do this documentary about it," Polly says. "That's how we met him. But he was so messed up he couldn't carry it off. Then he got in on this Spa deal with some AA guys."

"He didn't want to do it anyway," Iris says. "That was just an excuse."

Polly rolls her eyes. "After the poet, it was Cecil. She's hittin' 'em hard, this one, since you guys quit."

"That's crap and you know it," Iris says. "Besides, we never really saw each other, not that way."

"Picking 'em up and putting 'em down." Polly grins at me. "He's like a father to her."

"Oh, Polly." Iris takes her coffee into the kitchen, leaving me and Polly staring at each other.

After a couple of minutes I point at the flashlights. "What's with these?" I say, taking one of them off the table.

"Lanterns," Polly says. "They were great when Hurricane Monica came through last year—or was that the year before?"

"Seventy-nine, I think."

"They float. I took one of them—that one, not the one you've got—to the bathtub to test it. They really do."

I snap on the light and shine it around the room, making twisty shadows out of the plants.

"Sometimes we have wars," Polly says. "In the dark. It's pretty much fun." She takes the second lantern and clicks it on and off several times, hitting me in the face with its beam. "I shouldn't tease her, should I?" She holds the lantern with both hands and shines the light up into her face. She looks very sexy and mysterious with the light on her that way. "I really shouldn't nag her," Polly says. "But it's so easy." She turns off the light and puts it back in the middle of the table, then struggles to her feet and goes into the kitchen.

I hear her talking to Iris, whispering, but I can't make out what's being said. I wonder if I should just go ahead and leave without saying goodbye, but I decide that would be worse than staying, so I sit and drink my coffee. I shoot the lantern beam around the room, then out the window, where it hits one of Mrs. Jaymar's feeders. I play the light out there for a few minutes, thinking about Iris and me, how we used to roughhouse together and how we used to do certain things—like wear heavy coats inside in the winter. That's when I spot Cecil, wrapped up in a lime-green parka, hugging the trunk of the willow.

# Rain Check

HOPING FOR QUICK intimacy, I start telling Lucille things I'm afraid of. It's a late dinner, our first meeting, a date arranged by a friend of hers who works in my office, and we go to the restaurant Lucille chooses, a place called Red Legs, where all the waiters work in dresses. "It's antebellum drag," she says. "Isn't it crazy?" Red Legs doesn't look very antebellum to me. It has a low ceiling and, along the wall, a thirty-sheet Coppertone billboard of a very tan girl. There's tropical flavor, too—a couple of dozen giant dead banana plants. Lucille says she's not afraid of anything, so I shut up about loneliness.

Our waiter, a stumpy guy wearing a satin hoop skirt, stands about two feet from our table, dangling a menu in each hand as if he were holding freshly dressed chickens by their feet. He has a diseased-looking black beard floating over his chest. "Do we want to see a menu?" he asks.

Lucille tries to swipe one from his hand, but he jerks back out of reach. "Great," she says. "Let's see the menu." She looks at me as if I've already failed to perform.

I hold out my hand for the menu. "Send the cocktail waitress, will you?" I'm careful not to look at the waiter.

When he's gone, Lucille says, "I've been seeing this Oriental guy—he's only twenty. How old are you?"

"Forty in December."

"Damn," she says. "Forty." Then she ducks her head behind the menu. "I guess that's not so bad. My dad's about forty, maybe forty-five, and he's all right."

I smile at her menu. "It's not as bad as it's said to be. Where's your friend tonight?"

"Who? Oh, Wang? He's out of the country. He had to go to New Guinea or someplace. Did I tell you he's from Oklahoma? I don't know how they got all these Orientals in Oklahoma, but they're there. I think it must be the oil—they're good with oil is what Wang says."

There's a red bug with two black dots on its back near the edge of the table, crawling toward me. I try to flick it casually in the direction of the nearest banana plant, but my hands are cold and I mush the bug into the tablecloth.

Lucille comes out from behind her menu. "What's that?" she asks, pointing at the small stain by my hand.

"Nothing." I pull my napkin out of my lap and wipe at the mess, which makes it a little better.

"Oh," she says.

After some more difficulty with the waiter, we get the dinner. Lucille gives me a play-by-play of her off-again, on-again romance with the Oklahoma playboy Wang. She keeps apologizing for boring me with his exploits and opinions, but she doesn't stop. By midnight I feel like Wang's mother.

I'm trying to finish the lemon-yellow dessert soup the waiter recommended when Lucille starts showing me the bruises on her shoulders. "He's real good," she says. "But very Oriental, if you know what I mean."

"Uh-huh," I say, looking around for the waiter. I finally have to stand up to get his attention.

"How was the duck?" he says when he arrives.

I point at the check, but he doesn't want to give it to me; he keeps writing on it and looking off toward the kitchen, then writing some more. It's late and there isn't anything going on in the kitchen as far as I can see; they've turned off most of the lights in there.

"What duck?" I say. We didn't have any duck; he must have us mixed up with somebody else.

"The duck. You know," Lucille says. She nods at the waiter and fingers the skirt he's wearing, pulling him closer to her. "The duck was excellent; we loved it. You got meringues tonight?"

He puts away the check. "So you want the meringues? You want the soup and you want the meringues too."

Lucille smiles and says, "Wavy ones. O.K.?"

When the waiter turns to me, I nod and say, "O.K. on the meringues."

We wait in silence for him to bring them, and when he does, Lucille asks me how I like them and I say, "They're wavy."

The waiter returns and drops the check into my hand. I give him Visa, then ask for it back and give him American Express, because I don't usually use Visa; then it dawns on me that Lucille might think I've got some problem with Visa, like I'm over limit or something, so when the waiter leaves I say, "I really hate Visa, don't you?"

"Hate Visa? Why?"

Before I can reply, the waiter is back. "Listen, we're out of American Express charge slips. Would you mind going ahead with the Visa?"

I shrug and bend forward to pull my wallet out of my pocket, and while I'm doing this he says, to Lucille, "I'm really glad you enjoyed the duck."

"The duck was superb," I say, handing him the Visa. He's not getting me twice on the duck.


Outside it's raining and everything is glittery—the lights, the glass slabs in the storefronts, the car tops. Even the street is glowing like some street in the movies.

Lucille says, "Let's take a walk, O.K.?"

"Sure," I say. "Why not?" I can walk. I know how to go for a walk.

So I start off, and Lucille, who's two or three yards ahead of me already, stops and pivots on her heel and says, "What in the name of Jesus are you doing?"

I flip my arms out to one side and say, "Dancing. I'm dancing. What are you, the only woman in America who doesn't know shine about going for a walk?"

"I've done all right in the past," she says. "Besides, Wang and I spend a lot of time in the Lagonda."

So we walk a couple of blocks, and the rain starts coming harder. We stop for a minute in the doorway of a place that sells kitchen appliances and watch a few cars go by. Finally I say, "Maybe we ought to get back to the car?"

"It'd be drier."

"You want me to go get it? Pick you up here?"

"Would you?"

Lucille is very pretty when she's pleased, so I splash back toward the restaurant and the car, thinking maybe I should take a harder line with her, maybe that's the problem. But when I get the Pontiac and pull it up to the curb by the appliance store, she's not there. I get back into the car and drive up and down the street a couple of times, a couple of blocks each way, but I don't see her. About the third time I pass Red Legs, there she is under the awning, waving at me, so I turn the car around and pull up.

"I had to make a call," she shouts when I roll down the window. "Have you been looking long?"

I motion her to the car, and she comes over and leans in the passenger-side window and says, "I want to ride in back, O.K.?"

"You what?" I laugh when I say it, but by the time she figures out I'm not pleased, she's already in back and making chauffeur jokes.

"Sometimes," she says from the back seat, "when Wang is

reading the sports section in the morning, you know? We'll be sitting there at the table and he'll have the sports flattened over his cereal bowl and I'll watch him until I can tell he's interested in some article, and then, real quick, I'll turn the page, you know? It's funny."

"It is funny. Where do you want to go?"

"Across the river. I want to go to the zoo."

"Zoo's closed, Lucille."

"So what's the big deal? Open it up, why don't you? Ram the gates."

"No, Lucille. I don't want to drive across the river, so maybe we just go home, huh?"

"I always go home. Wang takes me home all the time. I want to stay out and do stuff."

"Blow up the zoo?"

"Yeah. What's wrong with the zoo? What, you hate animals or something?"

She must be down on the seat; I can't see her silhouette in the rearview mirror anymore—just the back window plastered with thousands of tiny colored water bubbles. She's quiet for a bit, so I drive around the neighborhood where we ate, past the City Hall and the Federal Building, alongside Tornado Park, with its neon scale replica of the 1947 tornado, dedicated to the victims, through the Peter J. Lamilar Memorial Tunnel, which bypasses the Fourth Ward and brings us out in an old residential district on the South Side. I'm a little nervous, because she's so quiet.

"You O.K.?" I ask. I turn around and see her balled up on the back seat. "Hey, Lucille?"

"This is our first date," she says softly. "And already you hurt me."

We're on a brightly lit tree-lined street, going slow. "What do you mean, hurt you?"

"Hurt me—you know." She's crying now, and I can barely

hear her through the sniffling. "I don't know why you couldn't just do what I wanted. It wasn't that big a thing. Just because you're old, you don't have to take it out on me."

I turn the car around and head back toward downtown. "What're you talking about?"

"Zoo," she says. "What's this rag back here for? Can I use it?"

"Help yourself."

"And that's not all," she says. Then she blows her nose on the hand towel I keep under the seat of the Pontiac so I'll have something to wipe my hands on if I have to change a tire. I make a mental note to stop at the K Mart tomorrow and get another towel.

That's what I'm thinking about when we come out of the tunnel and the car starts skidding across the street. I can't get control of it. We go through the red light, and a truck slams into the front fender of the Pontiac, sliding us up over the curb into a room-size blue plywood Salvation Army drop.

"Kowabunga!" Lucille says.

"You hurt?" I switch off the ignition and lean over the seat back; she's on her knees in the foot well, her shoulders wedged in between the rear cushion and the back of the front seat.

"I'm doing great," she says. "I'm having the time of my life."

The guy from the truck is out in the road hammering on our window with his ring. "She hurt?" he says. He's a kid about twenty-five; he's got long hair in a ponytail down past his shoulder blades. I get Lucille loose and sitting up in the back seat, and then get out of the car to see how bad the wreck is.

"Skylar," the kid says, sticking out his hand. "Baby Skylar. Listen, it's going to be all right."

His truck is still running, sitting sideways in the intersection, the wipers clacking back and forth, a cone of gray-white smoke pumping out of the exhaust. It's an ASPCA truck.

"The city'll pay for everything," he says. "All we gotta do is tell the cop you had the light."

"Right."

Lucille joins us in the intersection, walking a little unsteadily. She wraps her arm around my waist for support. The kid explains the deal to her just the way he explained it to me, and she says, "That's not what happened. This one went through the damn light sideways is what happened."

"He knows that," I say.

A big dog presses his snout through the open wing window in the passenger door of the truck and barks twice, then stares at the three of us standing in the middle of the empty intersection.

"That's Collingsworth," Skylar says.

Lucille waves at the dog.

There's a four-story apartment building backed up to the edge of the block where the tunnel ends, and now there are people opening windows and shouting to see if anybody's hurt.

"It's O.K.," Skylar shouts back. "Call the police, will you?"

"Call 'em yourself, Motormouth," somebody says. Then somebody else says, "Oh, shut up, Ralph. I'll call them."

On another corner, above the all-night blinking sign on a cut-rate camera shop, a woman who looks as if she's covered in sequins pulls up a window and thrusts the top half of her body outside. "What in the hell you kids doing out here?" she yells. "It's four in the morning and people are trying to sleep."

Lucille shoots the woman the bird and shouts, "It ain't much past two, Fatso, and if you were trying to sleep I'll feed you for a month, even if I have to get a bank loan to do it."

The woman screams something obscene and slams her window so hard the glass breaks and tinkles into the street like a Taiwanese wind chime.

The three of us sit down on the curb beside my car to wait for the cop. The rain has let up, but there's still a mist, and while

Lucille and Skylar talk about rock bands, I remember that rain like this is supposed to be a great pleasure.

It takes three-quarters of an hour for the cop, who looks as if he's about thirteen, to get to the scene, and another hour to do the paper work with his stubby yellow pencil, so it's almost four when we finish with the accident report. Lucille gets in the front seat of the Pontiac, and with the help of the two guys outside we get the car loose from the Salvation Army box and into the street.

"That was fun," she says as we drive away. "The car's not bad, is it?"

"Could've been worse."

She takes something from her purse and holds it out toward me—not right in front of me but over to the side and low, so that at first I just see her hand coming at me and I flinch. "Silly," she says. "It's only a mint. Don't you want it?"

I take the mint.

"Don't you like the way everything looks in the rain?" she says. "So mysterious and Latin American?"

"It's fine. It's really fine."

"So what's eating you? You don't have to jump all over me because you had one tiny little wreck. Jesus."

I watch the road. "I pay my way. Some women even like me."

"I like you," Lucille says. "I do. I'm not slumming, if that's what you think."

We have to go slow because the right front wheel feels as if it's about to fall off. There's a terrible scraping noise whenever I turn a corner, so I try to calculate the straightest route to Lucille's house from where we are. She helps by describing a short-cut that sounds like the Lime Rock racing circuit.

We get to her building, and I get out to walk her to the door just the way I've been walking women to their doors for better than twenty years. In the arched recess in front of her building she says, "Do you want some breakfast?"

The invitation sounds tired but sincere, so I say, "Not now. Maybe I'll take a rain check."

"A what?"

"Another time."

Then, with the garbage men going up and down the street singing some kind of lilting reggae tune, and the cans clanking around and rolling in the gutter when they're thrown from the truck back toward where they were picked up, Lucille says haltingly, "So. What about a shower?" I give her a long look, letting the silence mount up. I stand there with her for a good two minutes, without saying a word, trying to outwait her, trying to see what's what. It's nearly five o'clock and the light out is delicate and pink. The garbage song dies off up the block, and half a dozen fatigued-looking kids in matching jackets pull up in a green Dodge and pile into the street, making catcalls and whistling and pointing at us. She smiles at me as if she really does like me. Maybe we've been there longer than two minutes, but when the smile comes, I see her lips a little bit apart and her slightly hooded eyes, and she traces her fingers down my arm from the elbow to the wrist and stops there, loosely hooking her fingertips inside my shirt cuff, pinching my skin with her nails.